Ms. LEAD

Drive Me Wild #3

AMY BOOKER

eBook ISBN: 979-8-9859875-8-4

Print ISBN: 979-8-9865651-3-2

Published by Renaissan Publishing Limited, Cuyahoga Falls, Ohio

www.amybookerauthor.com

Author's Note

If you've read my previous books, you'll know that the chapter names are all song titles. Music has been an integral part of my life, and it always sets the mood. Whether it's the overall energy of a song, the lyrics, or even just the title, that tone carries through into my written words on the page. The playlist and a link can be found at the back of each book, or you can find them on my website: www.amybookerauthor.com.

Chapter 1

Life's Gonna Kill You (If You Let It)

Oliver

Staring at the tiled ceiling of this hospital room, counting the little bubbles in the paint, is really getting old. Especially since the painkiller I was given a little while ago hasn't started to kick in yet. Activities like counting objects or focusing on one item are supposed to help with this sort of thing. At least, that's what all the professionals keep telling me. I've yet to find a reliable way to distract myself from pain. It's rather becoming a way of life for me now.

"You know, if you ever want to see me, you could just phone. This whole 'spraining your ankle' thing is taking it too far. Even for you." My literary agent and friend, Darcie, appears in the doorway and fills the frame, hands on her hips. She thinks she's being funny.

I'm not amused in the slightest.

"They won't let me leave without a ride. It wasn't my choice to call you here, believe me." The disdain in my voice is for the doctors, not her. But she knows that. We've been friends since university, and things like this are becoming par for the course lately. "I'm sure I'll be fine once the drugs start working. Besides, it's barely even a sprain."

I try to be as nonchalant about the situation as possible, but she knows me too well and sees through it instantly. Nothing gets past Darcie.

"Seriously, Oli. What happened this time?" Her brows draw together, and her tone softens.

With that one look, my worst fears flash before me. *The concern.* An expression I never wanted to appear on my friend's face. Not towards me, anyway. I need to look back up at the ceiling to avoid it. I can't stand it. I knew it would be coming eventually, but now that it has, it makes my stomach churn.

"It's nothing, really. I just missed a step in the stairwell of my building. I've done that a million times. This time I just landed awkwardly. It's not a big deal. Some decent drugs, ice, rest, and I'll be good as new." My words ring hollow in my ears as they're spoken, but I force myself to smile for her sake.

"Well, you really need to find a flat with no stairs. We can't keep doing this. And, that thing you're doing with your face? That's a grimace, just FYI." She swirls a well-manicured finger in a circle in front of my nose. "Not the confident smile you think it is."

"Well, unsolicited advice regarding my living arrangements is exactly that, *unsolicited*. And as I said, the painkillers have yet to present themselves to my pain. I'll be grinning from ear to ear just for you once they do. Better?"

That gets a corner of her mouth to twitch, at least, and her scowl relaxes.

"Are you able to take regular painkillers with your new prescriptions?"

It's an innocent enough question, but the barbs on the subject matter snag on my vulnerability. Darcie is a great friend, and I can count on her for anything I could possibly need, but sometimes she's *too* involved in my life. I don't know what I'd do without her, but I do like to let myself wonder about that very scenario in times like this.

"Darcie..." I warn.

She leans away and holds her hands up defensively. "Okay, okay. I just want to make sure your A&E doctors know what else is happening with you. That's all."

My intense answering glare is enough to let her know it's time to drop the subject of my care.

Clearing her throat nervously, she asks, "What does this mean for your trip to the states? Are you going to be able to go as you planned?"

For my next book, I've arranged to spend one month in Las Vegas to research the connections between the Mamana and Calnetta organized crime families and the city. Darcie has scheduled interviews with some key local players for me. Spraining my ankle like this was not on the agenda for my travel preparations, but it's still a couple of weeks away, so I'll have time to heal.

"Nothing should be upset by this little mishap. Don't worry." I shrug a shoulder. "You know I can't... *don't* drive anyway, and that's all been prearranged with your contact at that car service, Mischief, whatever."

I cringe internally at having to be carted around the city and not free to wander as a whim might take me. But, like it or not, this is the reality I face now. While I've always preferred rail over the road, having the road option removed is frustrating on a deeper level than I bargained for. It's strange to miss something that isn't even a *thing* but an essential activity in daily life for most people.

"Mischief Motors," she mumbles, now distracted. "Maybe I should go with you to help—"

"No. Absolutely not," I say, my voice flat and emotionless, the words clipped. "I don't need your help."

I impulsively drag my hands through my hair and sit up. Being treated like an invalid chafes against my pride and will not work for me or our friendship. She should know this. I don't know what's changed in our relationship for her to think she should even offer, but I don't like it.

I don't fucking like it at all.

The surprise and hurt in her eyes at my outburst makes me shift my gaze away again. I don't want to see that; the pain I cause others. Because I do a lot of that lately, and she's just the latest innocent bystander to be added to my tally of collateral damage.

It would be easier if I could just cut everyone out of my life, which I've attempted to do and have been largely successful. Darcie, however, won't let me quit, making my lashing out at her even more heinous and deepening my guilt. It's a vicious cycle that I can't seem to escape.

"I'll see when they're going to let you go." Her back is to me, and she's out the door before I can even think of a response or apology if I was going to give one. I don't think I have one to offer. Because I'm not sorry for lashing out. I happen to think I've earned the right to strike out at the entire world.

What I *am* sorry for is hurting Darcie because she doesn't deserve to be the victim of my rage. She's been nothing but tolerant of me, which is much more than *I* deserve from her.

She's back within minutes carrying a set of crutches, with a nurse following behind, pushing an empty wheelchair. The sight of both disability aids causes a sinking feeling in my gut to spread as I glimpse my bleak future unfolding in front of me. Perhaps a distant future, but ultimately mine just the same.

"I told her you'd refuse the wheelchair and opt for the crutches if given a choice, but she insisted on presenting both to you." Darcie lifts her shoulders in a shrug. "So, what'll it be? Limp along on crutches to the car? Or make me your slave and force me to push you in the chair? At your own peril, I might add."

"The chair is only to get you to the car. You don't get to keep it," the nurse chimes in, her voice stern. She's clearly not happy with Darcie's interference.

I'm not happy at the suggestion that I'd be excited to keep a wheelchair to use. That's the last thing I'd be excited about.

"Crutches are fine." The scowl on my face must be harsh since both women blanch at my response. I'm not in the mood to deal with niceties or be polite now, and I just want to go home. "Let's go."

Filching the crutches from Darcie, I hobble my way awkwardly toward the exit without looking back or saying another word. I'm too busy trying to hide the fact that I'm clenching my jaw in extreme pain. I've had my fill of doctors and hospitals to last a lifetime, so if I don't need to be here, you can bet I'll haul my ass out of here at the first opportunity, crutches or not.

I just want to go home where I can get away from that look of concern from my friend, who doesn't even know she's doing it, or what it's doing to me. Where I can prep for my trip to the states alone and in peace.

I'm looking forward to being around people who don't know me or my condition and will treat me like a normal human being, not the ticking time bomb everyone here thinks I am. To be fair, they're not entirely wrong. Time is something I'm now keenly aware of, and how precious it is.

Tick. Tick. Tick.

Chapter 2

Crash

Bianca

This is so typical. Something happens with Normandy or Chelsie, the half-sisters and co-owners of Mischief Motors, and I automatically get nominated to take over whatever project they suddenly can't handle.

This time, Chelsie has gone into labor early with her second baby, and now I've been assigned to cart around some pretentious British writer for an entire month. And I need to babysit on top of it. I don't know when I signed up for all of this.

While on the outside, and to Normandy and Chelsie, I make it out to be a huge inconvenience to watch the kids, in reality, I absolutely love it. Normandy's daughter Ava and Chelsie's son Jett are usually a breeze to watch, and I like spending time with them. They can be more fun to be around than adults since they speak their minds so freely and don't care about social niceties.

While I tend to voice my opinion on things, there's always that tiny honest bit that is held back or filtered for fear of retribution. Young children can completely be themselves and say what they think when they think it. I envy that freedom.

"His flight arrives at 1:30. He'll be staying at Bliss casino, and I've already emailed you his complete itinerary," Normandy says as she rushes toward the door. "There's supposed to be a barbeque at our house on Sunday, but that might have to get moved to next weekend. Thanks again for doing this. I'll call you as soon as there's news." She halts in her tracks, then returns to give Ava a quick peck on the cheek and tousles Jett's dark hair before hurrying out the door.

Normandy and I were friends before she became my boss, and while sometimes the lines blur between our friendship and our jobs, it's usually not a problem. She's the high-strung overthinker, and I'm usually the laid-back, go-with-the-flow one. It works, especially during emergencies like this.

Once the door shuts and quiet settles over the

three of us, we look at each other expectantly. Jett is the first to react.

"I'm hungry." He gives me a pitifully starving expression while rubbing his allegedly empty stomach.

"Don't believe him," Ava argues with a heavy sigh, placing her fists on her hips in disappointment. "He just ate lunch at my house."

"But that was a long time ago," Jett whines.

"Was not."

Before I need to start a full-blown mediation, I suggest a plan.

"How about we pick up Mr. Bellamy from the airport and deliver him to his hotel, and then we'll all grab a snack together?"

The two toddlers eye each other warily, gauging who will be first to cave in to my suggestion. This is a new dynamic I wasn't expecting. In the past, it's been a race to see who can go along with me first. I'm not sure how I feel about this new approach. I sense a power struggle approaching on the horizon; of course, it would be at the worst possible time.

"You two think about it while I get the car ready."

As I install their car seats, I can hear them bickering between themselves about what they ate for lunch, whether it was good or not, who is a better cook between their mothers, Normandy wins that one, who is hungrier, what the best snack in the world is, turns out it's french fries, and who could eat the most fries in one sitting.

My money's on Jett, who is turning into a bottomless pit when it comes to food. He's been named appropriately and is so active anything he eats gets burned off almost instantly. How Chelsie and Noah keep their refrigerator stocked is a modern miracle.

"Alright, *cugini*, hop on in your seats. We'll be late picking up Mr. Bellamy, and you don't want Aunt B to get in trouble, do you?"

I herd them into the back of the car and their respective seats, ensuring they're buckled in securely.

"You wouldn't get in trouble," Ava says matter-of-factly. "I'd protect you."

"Me too," Jett nods in agreement, not wanting to be left out.

These kids. I swear to God. If I didn't have a job to do right now, I'd be a melted puddle on the floor. For an almost four- and three-year-old, the things they randomly say are so thoughtful it blindsides me sometimes. I can only hope that my own kids, whenever that happens, are as kind and sweet as these two. Normandy and Chelsie are doing something *very* right with them.

"Well, thank you. I appreciate that," I'm finally able to say as I get behind the wheel. "It's good to know I have you two on my side." I glance at them in the rearview mirror. "Ready to go to the airport?"

They rambunctiously reply in the affirmative in unison at a decibel level I don't think is appropriate for the interior of a car. *Oh no.* Mr. Bellamy is in for one hell of a crazy welcome to America.

Mischief Motors is extremely close to the airport, so I'm not really worried about being late picking up Mr. Bellamy. Being a car service, having a location nearby is kind of imperative for business.

We arrive with some time to spare, so I park and take the kids inside to meet Mr. Bellamy at baggage claim instead of the regular pick-up and drop-off spot.

We have a sign that reads "BELLAMY" that the kids argue over who will get to hold. They eventually agree to my compromise, and each takes a side of the sign. It keeps them together and, in my sight, at least.

Normandy didn't give me a description of what this Mr. Bellamy is supposed to look like, but considering the kinds of books he writes, I'm assuming he's an older gentleman. He's probably a tweed jacket-with-patches-on-the-elbows kind of guy. Maybe he even smokes a pipe. *Do people smoke pipes anymore?*

My mind wanders as I search through the crowd of newcomers circling like vultures around the baggage carousel, anxious to get their bags first like it's some kind of achievement. I don't see any older gentlemen with patched elbows in the group.

What my eyes do catch on is a tall man in his early to mid-thirties, with blondish hair that's well cut but still longish on the top, well-tamed scruff on his square jawline, and in very well-fitting jeans, with a button-down shirt and dark suit jacket. A perfect example of traveling business casual.

Our eyes meet and lock, and something happens in my chest that I've never felt before. I swear a million butterflies are fighting to fly free from my rib cage, and all tension leaves my body. Every nerve on my skin comes to attention, and my brain seems to stutter as we gaze at each other.

I think time passes, but maybe it stands still. I can't tell, and I don't care, either. I can't restrain my smile, and he responds with his own, and it's gorgeous. It lights up his entire handsome face. I have no clue what we're smiling about, but we are, thirty yards apart in the middle of a busy airport and smiling like idiots at each other. *What the hell are we doing?*

"Maybe he didn't come." Ava's voice reaches me from far away, and I reluctantly drag my eyes away from the man to glance down at her.

"What's that?" Her words still aren't registering

in my brain. I look up quickly, trying to find the man I was just supernaturally connected to. I don't know how else to put it.

That wasn't just a moment we shared; it was an experience. I need to find that man again.

Immediately.

Ava says something else, maybe repeating what she just said, but it's drowned out by my pounding heart, needing to find that person I just saw. I can't believe I can't locate him. It's as if he magically disappeared as soon as I looked away. *Great.*

Maybe I imagined the whole thing. Maybe he was smiling at someone behind me, not directly at me like I thought he was. I turn around quickly to see if there's someone there, and there isn't.

Am I going crazy?

Then I find him. Or he finds me. I don't care which. We both must have been searching out the other because our smiles are back once we reconnect. He starts to walk toward me, and I do another quick check behind me to make sure it's me he's smiling at, and I still don't see anyone there.

It's me. He's smiling at me. *Holy cow.* I need to know who this guy is and why I'm reacting this way to him from out of nowhere.

As he gets closer, he notices Ava and Jett. He tilts his head to the side, rubbing his chin, and a frown erases the smile he just wore so beautifully. I don't understand the sudden shift in moods. I also don't appreciate the scowl he gives the kids.

Who the hell is this guy?

"I take it you're Normandy," he snaps, his tone edged with disdain. He doesn't ask if I am. He just announces it.

"No, that's Aunt B," Ava explains in a rush, correcting him. "My mom had to go to the hospital to help Aunt C have a baby, so we came to get you. And we're gonna have french fries. Aunt B promised."

"I said a snack. I didn't say which kind." I can feel my ears turning red with embarrassment, but I will not be pressured into french fries. It's only now that the situation dawns on me. He thought I was Normandy.

This is Oliver Bellamy. My recent out-of-body experience was with the stuffy British author I've been enlisted to escort around the city.

I don't understand his attitude. I guess a long flight like the one he just took can make anyone grumpy. I give him the benefit of the doubt and extend my hand to him.

"I'm Bianca Torino." He begrudgingly takes my hand, and our eyes meet again, but this time his are guarded, and he quickly looks away. I cannot get a read on him at all. The sensation of his skin against mine, however, is another story. Once again, every single one of my nerves is aware of his presence. "These two are cousins Ava and Jett. As Ava was kind enough to inform you, Normandy's sister went into labor early, and she's unable to escort you as originally planned. So, I've been recruited to take her place." I try to smile, but it falters, and I don't know why.

An odd sense of losing control or falling settles over me. It makes no sense. None of what's happened in the last five minutes makes any sense.

He doesn't seem impressed in the slightest, and his scowl deepens as he absently tugs on an ear.

"Is it normal in America to bring children to work with you? Especially other people's children?"

"No. Of course not." *Wow. What is happening?* I can't believe he's being so rude. This can't be the same man from a minute ago. "This is a special circumstance, obviously. And these two are great kids."

As if on cue, Ava and Jett start to chase each other around Oliver's legs, grabbing at him and screeching as they go. He rubs the back of his neck, which is turning red, and glares at them first, then turns it on me. He is not happy with this situation. I need to fix this fast.

I reach out and grab Jett mid-run, swooping him up and resting him on a hip while extending my free hand to Ava to take, which she does without protest, thank God.

"Well, the sooner we get you to your hotel, the sooner you can get started on your book." My tight smile hopefully lets him know I'm now annoyed with him. Two can play that game. If he can't be friendly around two perfectly innocent kids for a few minutes, perhaps he shouldn't be around people at all.

It's not as though Chelsie went into labor early just to upset his arrival. I'm half-tempted to leave him here to get an Uber or something to his hotel. Unfortunately, even Ava and Jett couldn't protect me from the trouble that would get me into.

"Right. Let's go then." He doesn't even look at me. Going from shared smiles to glares and no connection at all is jarring. It's taking me a minute to process it all.

When we finally get to the car, I buckle the kids into their seats only to find that Oliver has left his suitcase for me to load into the trunk. And it's not a light suitcase. It's an entire month's worth of stuff in one bag. Putting his suitcase into the trunk isn't a problem; it is my job, after all.

It makes no sense, but after the experience we shared minutes ago...being treated like just his driver...hurts.

Chapter 3

Santa Cruz Tomorrow

Oliver

I'm exhausted. An eleven-hour overnight flight without sleep has left my brain foggy and my eyes blurry. Being met by toddlers doesn't help my mood any, either. It's not that I don't like children, but I don't like surprises, and Bianca and company are a definite surprise.

When I first saw Bianca, something happened. I don't know what exactly, but there was a connection there that I'd never felt before. It was almost as if I'd known her forever and was seeing her again after a long time apart. An odd sense of relief came over me that makes absolutely no sense. As if she was the one thing I'd been waiting for my whole life, and something in my chest loosened that had been wound too tight for too long.

What the hell am I thinking?

A connection like that with a total stranger? It's absurd. It's insanity even to consider. I can't start letting myself believe something like that is in my future anyway because I know damn well that it's not.

This is more of my brain fog imagining things that aren't there. There's no way any of these feelings are real. I desperately need sleep. A *lot* of sleep.

Bianca gets in behind the wheel, and I can't look at her. I know leaving my suitcase for her to care for was a knobhead thing to do, but it's too late to fix it now. In my gut, I knew I couldn't trust myself not to drop the bag while lifting it, which would have made everything even worse.

Maybe after a good night's sleep and some time to recuperate from the jet lag, I'll be able to function like a polite and normal human being. That is always the goal, after all.

"So, London to Las Vegas must be a long flight, huh?" Bianca eyes me warily in my peripheral vision. I deserve that.

"Yes." Pathetic. I don't even possess the mental fortitude to withstand small talk.

Her hands grip the steering wheel tighter, and her

knuckles pale with the pressure. At least, I think they do. The blurriness is kicking in now, and my eyes are starting to hurt. A headache is on its way too. *Lovely.*

A sudden screech from the back seat pierces my skull and nearly makes me jump out of my skin. It's followed by hilarious laughter, which is unexpected. I turn to see the cause of the ruckus and find the children having some sort of hand-smacking contest. I can't make out exactly what they're doing, but it's apparently amusing.

"You guys, keep it down back there, okay?" Bianca calls, staring them down in the mirror. "Mr. Bellamy had a long flight and needs some quiet."

This gets muffled giggles, but they've listened, and the volume lowers.

I take this opportunity to study Bianca briefly. Well, as much as my blurred vision can. Her dark hair is nearly black and is pulled up in a loose knot, exposing her long inviting neck. Her red lips and olive skin are equally enticing, but her eyes slay me. They are intense and passionate, throwing me back to our shared smile at the airport. Meeting her eyes exposed something in me I didn't know was there. Something I can't allow.

Hope.

"Mr. Bellamy? Are you okay?" Forcing myself to focus, I see Bianca with a concerned look leaning toward me. *Oh no.* Concern from her too. "We're at your hotel. This is the Bliss Casino where you'll be staying."

That was a lot quicker than I expected. Or maybe it took forever. I've been in my own head the entire time. Days could have gone by.

I shake off the mental cobwebs and nod.

"Right. Thanks."

"Bye, Mr. Belly," the little girl chirps in a sing-song melody.

That makes me laugh. I've never been called "Mr. Belly" before.

"You can call me Oli if you want."

Now that I'm so close to being able to sleep, my mood is lifting. Plus, I have to admit these kids are pretty decent for toddlers.

"I like Mr. Belly."

"I kind of do, too," I whisper. "Right. Mr. Belly it is."

I give her a wink as I open my door, making her giggle again. If I've done nothing else positive today, I've made a child giggle.

My bag is already on the scorching hot sidewalk when I get out of the car, and Bianca stands next to it, arm resting casually on the handle. She looks so comfortable in this oppressive heat, her tanned skin glowing in the blazing sun. I get the sense she wants to say something about our initial connection, but that is not something I want to get into now or ever. I need to pretend it never happened if I have any chance of getting through this month unscathed. Spending time with Bianca could throw all of that into a tailspin. I have to deny my attraction to her.

"So, are you going to be my chauffeur this entire month? Or was today a one-off?" I try to keep the hope out of my voice and think I come off arrogant enough to pass.

Her pained expression lets me know I succeeded. *I'm going straight to hell.*

"I'm not sure, actually..." she hesitates. "Did I do something to upset you, Mr. Bellamy? I am sorry about the children coming along to meet you."

"What? No. Not at all. The children were fine." I can't believe she came right out and asked that. I wasn't expecting to be called out or confronted about my attitude. Especially not from a stranger. But then, Bianca doesn't feel like a stranger. "I'm just fatigued. I'm sorry if I came across—"

"Oh, thank God," she rests a hand on my arm, and something inside me ignites. It might be the smallest of pilot lights, but it's a fire, nonetheless. And precisely what I didn't want to happen.

What *can't* happen.

I physically force myself to step back and out of her reach, trying not to be too obvious about it, but I can tell by the frown on her lips that it's hurt her.

God damn it. I can't win. I can't fucking win.

My vision starts to blur again, and this time it's welcome, because now I can't see the results of my being a total jerk to this beautiful woman that doesn't deserve it.

I need to get away from her. I can't do this right now.

"Have someone email me with the arrangements. Thanks."

Turning away from her quickly and heading to the entrance, I can feel her gaze on my back as I go. I also feel her disappointment in me press on my shoulders. I'm surprised there's room with all of my own discontent with myself taking up so much space.

Once I check in, I have a porter bring my bags up with me. Not because I'm that full of myself, but because my eyes are so bad right now, I can't see the floor buttons on the lift, let alone room numbers. When we get to the room, I tip him, knowing at least what I'm giving him. I've learned to keep my money in a specific order in my wallet for situations like this. I'm generous anyway. He didn't try to make small talk, and that's worth a lot in my book.

I'll be back to normal once I get some sleep. I keep telling myself that. Maybe if I say it enough, it will be true. Maybe.

Chapter 4

I Knew I Loved You

Bianca

As I watch Oliver Bellamy turn and walk away from me to enter the hotel, I can't help but wonder what the hell I did to deserve him acting like that toward me. For the life of me, I can't think of anything. I barely said two words to him, and he's been nothing but rude.

Sure, he apologized briefly just now, saying he was tired, but it didn't feel like he meant it. Add to that his initial response to the kids coming along, and it doesn't add up to him being a nice guy. Quite the opposite, actually.

Whatever happened between us at baggage

claim is starting to feel like a figment of my wild imagination. I wonder if I didn't make the entire thing up in my head.

There was a connection there. I know it. What happened to it? Where did it go? I have no idea. But now I'm left with this version of him that is rude and self-important, and it feels wrong somehow. Like it's not real. He's putting on an act to come off as an asshole.

But why? Why would someone do that? Who *wants* to be thought of as rude? Did he only like me when he didn't know who I was? Is my being a driver not good enough for him? That doesn't feel right, either. He doesn't seem like the type that would judge people that way. But I can't say that with any certainty, either. All of this is intuition. And my instincts are almost never wrong.

Well, I can't say that either, considering I was jilted right before walking down the aisle five years ago. My instincts were way off on that one. My former fiancé, Colin, ran off with our wedding planner three days before we were to be married. I even ignored my brother, who told me that Colin wasn't the type of person I thought he was. I should have listened or at least considered what he was saying. At the time, it was just a "feeling" he had, nothing concrete, so I dismissed it. Since then, saying I've got trust issues is an understatement. So, why am I letting this stranger bother me so much?

"Can Mr. Belly come over sometime?" Ava asks, interrupting my thoughts, her voice tired. Maybe they'll both take a nap when we get to Normandy's house. I'd love a nap too. *I wish.*

"Um...I don't know. That's going to be up to your mom and dad." I'm surprised she's asking. From what I saw, she didn't get any attention from Oliver. Maybe they talked in the car when I was getting his suitcase out of the trunk. "Did you like him?" Kids are known for their good instincts about most adults.

"Yeah, he made a face at me that was funny."

I glance at the mirror and see her scrunching her nose up and shutting her eyes tightly. I think it might be an attempt at winking. Jett starts to copy her at once.

"You like people making faces at you?"

"No!" she laughs. "Just when he did it. It was funny."

"Oh, okay then." I nod my understanding. Because, of course, that's entirely logical. I like kid logic.

Once at Normandy and Brandon's house, there's still no news about the imminent baby, so the kids and I have some popcorn for a snack and sprawl on the huge couches with super soft blankets in the media room to watch a movie.

They're asleep within ten minutes of the movie starting, and I'm almost right behind them, but my phone buzzes. When I check the screen, I see my older brother Lorenzo calling, so I slip out of the room to answer.

"Hey, Enzo. How are you?" It's odd for him to call in the middle of a weekday like this, so his call worries me.

"I'm fine and dandy. How are *you*?" His emphasis on *"you"* has me curious.

"I'm fine too. Why? Should I not be fine?"

Maybe something happened to someone else in the family, and he thinks I should be upset.

"No. I don't know...."

"What's going on? Why are you calling me at two in the afternoon on a Thursday? Did you get arrested or something? Are you calling for bail?"

"What? No." That at least gets a laugh. "I just had a weird feeling to call you, that's all. So, I wanted to check."

"Check what?" This isn't the first time he's done this, calling me after getting a weird feeling. It always scares the shit out of me when he does it. Our grandmother always said he could see and talk to spirits and stuff like that, but he's always denied any supernatural gifts. When he gets like this, though, I tend to believe my grandmother.

"Just that you're okay, *sorellina*. I'm your big brother. I'm allowed to check on you once in a while."

"Alright. You're allowed. And I'm...fine."

"Uh-huh. Right there. You hesitated. What happened?"

"Enzo..."

"Don't "*Enzo*" me. Talk."

He can be more stubborn than me, which is saying something. Because I can be downright unmovable.

"It's nothing."

"Bianca Maria Carmen Torino. Don't make me call on our ancestors."

"There was a guy that I met today...." I start, unsure where to begin or what to say about any of it.

My brother and I are close and talk to each other about almost everything. *Almost.* He's used to this kind of thing from me.

"Oh boy." He starts laughing. "If I'm getting these vibes from this guy all the way in L.A., you better marry him. Like yesterday."

"What?" He's crazy. "Who said anything about vibes or getting married? Slow down, Enzo. We just met today, and we're not even getting along anymore, so marriage is probably off the table. You can kick that idea right out of your head."

"Ouch. I don't know what to tell you, sis. You know how I am. Wait, you said "*anymore,*" does that mean you were getting along earlier? What happened to change that?"

Damn. He's too observant for his own good. How

do I explain our intense look earlier without sounding completely stupid?

"Promise you won't laugh, Lorenzo. I mean it."

"I promise," he chuckles. I'm glad he finds this funny because I certainly don't.

"He's a writer from Great Britain who is in town for research, and I had to pick him up from the airport since Chelsie went into labor early, and Normandy had to go to be with her. So, I had the kids with me too. But before we even met officially, we saw each other across baggage claim, and I don't know...we just stared and smiled at each other, and it was the most amazing thing."

"But..."

"But then he saw the kids were with me, and he completely changed into an asshole. He said he was tired from his long trip, but I don't know. I can't figure out what exactly happened either way."

"To be fair, that is a pretty long flight. What, eleven hours? At least?"

"I know. It was just such a change. And then he left his suitcase behind the car for me to load into the trunk for him."

"Whoa. Not cool." There's a protective edge to his voice now. My big brother, ready to beat up the world for me.

"It's my job, Enzo. It's not that big of a deal. But still, it felt weird."

"Well, I don't like it on your behalf. Want me to

come rough him up a little bit? Let him know who's boss?"

I can tell he's joking, but I know deep down that if I wanted him to come all the way to Vegas from L.A. to protect my honor, he would do it in a heartbeat. And I would do the same for him.

"No, but thanks for the offer."

"I don't know, sis. Something about this guy. Sure, he sounds like a first-class dipshit, but I don't get these weird feelings so strong that I have to call you very often, if ever. Just keep your mind open. There might be something there."

I want to roll my eyes and scoff at how ridiculous he's being about this mystical stuff, but I know he believes in it. And he's right. I do need to keep my mind open. I'm relying on a first impression, which I know from experience doesn't always go smoothly. Maybe I should give him a chance to prove he's not a jerk.

"Fine. I'll keep an open mind. But just for you."

Before we hang up, he promises to call again in a few days to check our progress. It's silly and utterly ridiculous to think anything will come of this, but I play along to appease my brother.

It's not like his "vibes" are real, anyway. Right?

Chapter 5

End of Sequence

Oliver

The sound of my phone incessantly ringing from across the room is the only thing that can pull me out of bed. As I make my way toward the desk where my phone is, I see that it's still light outside, but I can't tell what time it is. Maybe it's already tomorrow, and I slept straight through the night. It's hard to tell.

It's Darcie calling. *Shit*. I forgot to let her know I arrived safely.

"Sorry I forgot to text," I say, putting the phone on speaker as I try to orient myself again to the room. It's always strange to wake up in a different place for the first time. Though I do notice that my vision is no longer blurred. The nap definitely helped.

"Gee, thanks for that. Now I can go on about my life." She sounds annoyed. It can't be because I forgot to text her. She'd let that roll off her back. Something else must be the matter.

"Isn't it the middle of the night?" I try to do time travel math, but I'm not awake enough yet.

"It is, but you know how I get when I can't sleep. And you're finally in a time zone where I can bug you with my insomnia."

"This sounds like a job for your wife. Not me."

"Oh, Pamela normally would be up with me, the darling, but I needed to check on you anyway."

I sigh inwardly and start doing stretches. I have a feeling this is going to be a conversation.

"So, why did you really call me? Something's up."

She's quiet for a long moment, and the silence bothers me more the longer it goes. This is so unlike her. Darcie is never at a loss for words.

"I think I might come out to Las Vegas." She speaks so softly that I almost don't hear what she says.

When it does finally register, I'm confused.

"Come to Vegas? Why would you do that?"

She hesitates again briefly. "This is your first trip since your...." Her voice trails off momentarily.

"Well, I think it would be good for me to be nearby in case."

"In case of what?" I do not like where this is going.

"In case you needed anything."

Stopping mid-stretch, I drag my hands down my face in frustration. We've gone from her overt concern a few weeks ago when she picked me up from hospital to now wanting to stick to me like glue. I thought Darcie knew me better than this.

Our friendship has lasted this long because we stay out of each other's personal business. Sure, we talk about and listen to everything going on in our lives, but we never interfere. At least we hadn't until now.

"Not the entire month. Just until you're settled."

As if that makes it better.

"No."

"Oli. Be reasonable. It couldn't hurt to have me there for support."

"Couldn't it?"

It already does. That she even suggested it hurts more profoundly than she'll ever know.

"You wouldn't even have to see me. I'll stay completely out of your way. I could just be around if something happened."

My body starts to vibrate with anger, and I have to step away from the desk where my phone lies before I grab it and hurl it across the room. I'm not even mad at Darcie, necessarily. I'm angry that this situation even exists that puts us in these positions.

Gritting my teeth, I walk back toward the phone. "Darcie. I'm going to hang up now. I'd suggest you rethink your travel plans. Regardless of your intentions, if you step one foot in this city, I will no longer call you my agent or my friend."

"Oli—"

I disconnect the call.

After showering, I order room service for dinner since I'm not up to eating alone in public this evening. I usually don't mind, but tonight the thought puts me off. I don't think too hard about it, and actually, since my call with Darcie, I purposely try to avoid deep thoughts altogether.

I even turn on reality television to scrub my brain of anything worthwhile. But it doesn't work. My mind keeps replaying the entire day.

I'm confident Darcie and I will be fine. Eventually. Our friendship has withstood a lot over the years. It will survive this. She needs to know my boundaries, though. More importantly, she needs to understand that even if she is my friend, it doesn't give her permission to cross those lines for any reason. No matter how altruistic her intentions may be, she needs to leave it alone. Maybe this time away will give us some clarity on issues like that.

And I'm thinking deep thoughts. *Damn it.* I need to shift gears.

My mind instantly goes to Bianca. *Fuck.* I was hoping our initial interaction at the airport was just a product of my jet lag and not real, but she's been on my mind since I woke up. Not always the forefront, but constantly lurking in the shadows in the corners of my mind.

I've been trying to put a name to what happened between us, and somehow me, a wordsmith, can't think of one. Not a single adjective comes close to describing it. It's entirely cliché and like something out of a bad romance novel. *'Two lovers' eyes meet across a crowded room, and they knew instantly they were destined to be together.'* I'd also scoff at it if I didn't experience it.

Destined. Destiny. Is that even a thing I believe in? Love at first sight? Soulmates?

I can't think of anything to logically explain why I was so impacted by just seeing Bianca. I'm not religious and don't buy into the whole 'everything happens for a reason.' Theoretically, there's always a cause and effect to everything anyway, so the phrase, while accurate, is just science.

Maybe that's my problem. I'm trying to solve something illogical with logic. But feelings like this aren't rational. From my experience, love is the most irrational emotion in the world.

Love.

I am getting ahead of myself, completely overthinking one small interaction with a stranger. I must focus on my work here and not get swept up in silly romantic fantasies.

A mail notification from my phone snaps me out of my mental downward spiral. Checking my inbox, I see a new message from none other than Bianca. A shiver runs through me when I see her name.

It's just a coincidence you were thinking about her. Nothing more.

From: <u>bianca.torino@mischiefmotors.com</u>

   To: <u>OliverBellamyAuthor@email.com</u>

   Subject: Scheduling

   Mr. Bellamy,

   I hope you are settling into your hotel and aren't too jet-lagged from your trip. I'm reaching out to confirm your itinerary for the next few days. Unfortunately, Normandy cannot assist you as planned, so I will be stepping in to escort you to your appointments. We hope this change isn't a problem for you.

   Your schedule lists tomorrow as a day off, which I assume is to help you acclimate to the time change. However, should you need anything before your first scheduled appointment, I am at your disposal. My number is listed below.

Sincerely,

Bianca Torino

Lead Driver

Mischief Motors

Well, damn. She's at my disposal? I've always found that phrase curious, and right this second, it's giving me ideas. Ideas I shouldn't be having.

Pulling up my calendar, I see that she's right. I don't have anything scheduled for tomorrow. Darcie must have arranged for the day off after traveling. A pang of guilt hits me at the thought of her arranging time for me to get over the jet lag, but I push it aside. I can thank her later.

Right now, I'm wondering if I want to wait until Saturday to see Bianca again. It seems like an eternity from now. Another wave of guilt washes over me as I picture the hurt look on her face when I backed away from her earlier. Not only that, I was rude to her. Considering that I'm going to be spending a lot of time with her over the next month, I should probably make amends. I also need to figure out how to be in her presence without losing myself. That will be the tricky part.

Baby steps. I need to take this in baby steps.

From: OliverBellamyAuthor@email.com

To: Bianca.Torino@MischiefMotors.com

Subject: Disposal

Bianca,

Please call me Oliver. And thank you for stepping in to help with my project. Your time is appreciated, as I'm sure it will pull you away from your regular duties.

I realise I did not make the best impression when I first landed, and I would like to request a second attempt at a first impression. I am open for lunch or dinner tomorrow if you can meet. We can discuss my book project in more detail and go over the itinerary to ensure I have everything covered. Since you stated that you were at my disposal, I will assume this is acceptable.

Please advise which meal you prefer to share.

Yours,

Oliver

The Rude Author

Right. That's not too cheeky and rather friendly if I do say so. Fingers crossed that I'm at least on the right track to mend my earlier blunders.

Chapter 6

Save Yourself

Bianca

An invitation? For a meal of my choice? I did not see this plot twist coming. I'm not sure how to feel about the one-eighty in his personality yet again. Is it going to switch back tomorrow? I don't know which version of Oliver is real. I keep telling myself to give him the benefit of the doubt, he was probably jet-lagged earlier, but part of me thinks he showed his true colors.

I don't want to say no. I want to get to know him better and see if he felt the same thing when we first saw each other. That feeling keeps sticking with me and won't let go. I want to experience that again with the original Oliver. I want to bottle that emotion so I can enjoy it at will. It's like a drug that I instantly became addicted to. It's also insane. To even imagine that he felt the same thing is beyond ludicrous. But I still need to know for sure.

Here goes nothing.

From: bianca.torino@mischiefmotors.com
To: OliverBellamyAuthor@email.com
Subject: Meals
Oliver,

Your request is granted. Dinner would be lovely. Since we are assuming things, I suppose we will be dining at your hotel, so I will meet you in the lobby at seven.

I look forward to hearing more about your book.

Sincerely,
Bianca
The Forgiving Driver

There. Dinner should be neutral territory. Lunch would seem too casual, and drinks would be too forward. Of course, now I'm second-guessing everything. Maybe I should have said lunch. Dinner now feels like a date. Is that a bad thing? Maybe not. Am I overthinking this? Absolutely. Well, I've got 24 hours to overthink it some more.

As I pull up to the Bliss Hotel and Casino the following evening, the valet on duty, Connor, gives me a once over and a smirk. I know almost every valet attendant in Las Vegas since I often see them with work. Connor has been with Bliss for a long time, and I expected to get a reaction like this from him. We tend to poke fun at each other if given a chance. He's an older gentleman, but he always comes off as a player with smooth moves, though he's been happily married for years.

"Well, look at you, cleaning up all nice," he purrs, taking my keys from me. "Hot date tonight?"

"Was that actually a compliment, Connor?" A blush is spreading on my cheeks, so I need to deflect. "And, no. A business dinner. But was that jealousy I heard?"

It's his turn to blush. "I'm just thinking I need to switch to whatever your business is to get me one of those dinners."

I give him a wave as I turn to head into the hotel. As soon as I do, I can see Oliver watching me through the glass windows of the lobby. Our eyes meet, and it's like being hit by lightning again.

I trip and have to stop myself from walking for fear of falling on my face. I might have caught one of my heels in the indoor/outdoor carpet on the entrance sidewalk. I look down to check my shoes, and when I glance back up, he's no longer in the lobby window.

"Are you alright?" A worried voice asks.

It's Oliver at my side and putting a hand under my elbow to guide me through the doors. He must have moved at the speed of light to get to me so quickly.

I'm so stunned that I almost don't register his hand on my bare skin, but another shock goes through me when I do. And this time, I think it goes through him, too, since his hand seems to shake for a second.

We both stop and look at each other. He appears as unsettled as I feel.

"Did you just—" He starts.

"I must have shuffled my feet on the carpet out there, causing a static shock." His gaze is too intense. I don't know what to do with everything he's expressing. I have to look away. "Sorry about that." I try to laugh it off and start walking again toward the restaurant. He hesitates but catches up quickly.

Whatever is going on between us, I need to be careful. Whenever look into his eyes, I see something deeper, personal, and private that no one else has seen. But I also don't know what it is I'm seeing. It's so confusing. Maybe I should avoid looking him straight in the eyes just to get through this dinner.

"No problem," he says as if he believes my lie. He's much better at recovering from crazy than I am.

We move on, and this time he puts a hand on my lower back to usher me into the restaurant. Nobody is shocked or hit by lightning this time. Small mercies.

We're seated at a private table, and it hits me that this dinner will probably be more than I was planning on spending. I must have gone pale because Oliver quickly reads my mind and eases it.

"I get to expense everything on this trip, so get whatever your heart desires. My publisher will hate me, but that's nothing new."

A shy grin that is so damned attractive spreads on his face, and it's all I can do not to lean over and kiss his cheek. He holds my chair for me, then takes his seat. *Manners. He has manners. That's it. I'm in love.*

"Why would your publisher hate you?" While I've seen his rude side, I don't think it's enough to warrant hate.

His smile falters slightly. "They have this thing about deadlines. I was supposed to start this book last year, but...." His voice drifts off, and he looks away quickly. He was about to reveal something.

"But?" Curiosity for everything about him and his life is taking me over. I want to know all there is to know about Oliver Bellamy.

"But it didn't work out that way." He busies

himself with unfolding his napkin and spreading it on his lap, careful not to look directly at me. We're both avoiding looking right at each other again. Probably for fear of another lightning strike. It's kind of crazy at this point. "Timing and schedules never matched up to make it work."

"I see." It's nagging at me that it was a vague answer, but I don't want to press him too much on our first meeting. I'm sure he had good reasons for not meeting the deadlines and not telling me the exact truth about it. "Well, you're here now, so they'll get their book soon enough."

"Exactly. How about you? How did you come to work for Mischief Motors? It's not a typical profession for a woman." He arches a brow at me as though he's impressed, but still, our eyes don't meet.

"Oh. Yeah. It's not." I have to think for a minute. I haven't done the whole 'Once upon a time, Bianca did this or that...' spiel in a long time. "Long story short, my older brother Enzo used to work there, and once I graduated high school, he brought me on and showed me the ropes. When he left for L.A., I took over as Lead Driver."

"Enzo is an interesting name."

"It's short for Lorenzo, but I rarely call him that." I laugh to myself, thinking about his phone call yesterday.

"Are the two of you close? Do you have other siblings?"

I dare to glance up and into his eyes, and something clicks in my brain. He's genuinely curious about my family and my job. But for some reason I can't explain, I feel like I'm repeating myself to him. Like he knows all of this already. The déjà vu with him is off the charts.

"We are extremely close, and no. He's it." I shrug. "How about you? Any siblings?"

"No. My parents were stuck with me alone." He smirks as if that would have been a bad thing. I can't imagine anyone not wanting to spend time with him. Family included.

I can't take this anymore. My mother always said my mouth would get me into trouble, and, well, she's not wrong.

"Oliver, can I ask you something?"

"Of course."

"It's kind of crazy." Doubt is starting to creep up, but I've already started down this road. I need to stay on it.

He gives me a questioning look that turns suspicious.

"What sort of crazy?"

"The kind of crazy that feels like everything about you is familiar to me somehow. I can't explain it." That's not what I wanted to say. I shake my head. "*Damn it.* This isn't coming out right."

"Well, in all of that, you didn't ask a question. Is there one?" His eyes are kind, not judgmental of my insane babbling. Points to him for that, at least.

"Yeah." I hesitate for only a second but lean in closer. Making sure I catch his reaction to the question. "Do you feel it? The feeling of déjà vu? Or that you already know me? I kind of got the impression that you might."

I'm glad I focused on his response because his face suddenly becomes expressionless. As though he never knew what a single emotion ever was, let alone felt one. I don't think I've seen someone shift straight into neutral like that. Completely devoid of emotion. A chill skitters across my heart at the sight of it.

I briefly hide my face, which I'm sure is bright red behind my menu, and laugh it off.

"You know what? That was crazy. Forget I said anything." I wave the whole thing away as the crazy thought it is. He still hasn't even flinched. It's like he completely unplugged. His lively gray eyes now seem vacant. I, on the other hand, have to make a concerted effort not to cringe so hard that I fold in on myself. "Anyway, you were going to tell me about your book? I haven't looked at the itinerary that closely yet, so I'm not sure how much I can add to it."

The more I talk, the further away he seems, so I shut up. I don't think he was even listening.

There is a painful lump in the back of my throat from constantly resisting the urge to get choked up. I want to go home, crawl under my blankets, and not come out for a month. Or at least until Oliver leaves to go home. My embarrassment is now complete.

Chapter 7

The Loneliest

Oliver

Shit. I knew this dinner was a bad idea, but I had to go and invite Bianca anyway. Why did I do this? Just to torture myself?

Well, top marks, you've achieved your goal, idiot.

She's looking at me expectantly, her face flushed from what I can only guess is embarrassment at her earlier question, and I swear there is hope behind it too. I *want* to be honest. I *want* to yell to the whole restaurant, *'Yes! Since the moment I met this woman, I've felt a connection!'* But, of course, I can't bloody do that. I can't allow myself to give in to these feelings she is stirring in me.

I also don't want to lie to her. How the hell do I get out of this? Do I ignore the question since she's moved on from it? I've got to say something. I've stalled enough.

"Okay, well, the book is an in-depth look into the Calnetta and Mamana families, their ties to each other, and organized crime here in Las Vegas. I understand that the families' illegal activity goes back decades to the city's beginnings."

There. Subject changed. Crisis averted.

The disappointed look she gives hits me straight in the heart and tells me exactly how big of an asshole I am. She covers it up quickly, but it's unmistakable.

That's right. I'm an asshole. You'll be better off with someone else.

I hope the change in subject is enough to warn her off. God, this is difficult.

"Oh, wow. I didn't realize those families were here that long." She seems interested but also distracted.

I, too, am distracted, watching her lips move as she speaks, wondering if they're as delicious as they appear. I take in her bare shoulders, imagining my hands caressing all of her curves, getting her out of that dress, or maybe leaving it on while I—

"Oliver? Are you okay?"

I eventually realize she's calling my name and force myself back to reality.

"Yeah. So sorry. I'm still fighting jet lag." And I'll be using that excuse for everything for the next four weeks. Or, at least as long as jet lag can reasonably last, I can get away with it. "You were saying?"

Leaning her head to the side, she eyes me curiously, trying to read me before continuing. I have the scary feeling that she can see through the walls I'm putting up between us. This is only the second time I've been in her presence, and each time I have felt entirely vulnerable but utterly comfortable at the same time.

"I asked if you would interview Normandy and Brandon at the barbeque on Sunday. Is that the plan?"

The disappointment is back, and I hate it. I hate that I have to make her feel that way.

"Yes. That is the plan. I know most of their stories from news reports, but I like to get firsthand accounts as much as possible."

"And Max Calnetta? Will you talk to him too?"

Max's father and brother kidnapped Normandy before she and Brandon were married and tried to ransom her for $10 million. The plan went to hell, and Normandy got shot but luckily survived. Max turned his entire family into the authorities and testified against them for immunity. His input would be helpful for my book.

"I hope to, yes. He's been a little difficult to locate and communicate with. Darcie's been able to get hold of him a few times, but she can't get a confirmation for dates or times from him. He's flying way under the radar now."

"Darcie?"

I sense a bit of jealousy in her questioning tone, and my chest clenches. I like it, even though I have no right to.

"My agent." I debate telling her the rest but give in. "And friend. I've known her since university."

"Oh, nice." She nods, and her clipped words make it obvious she's jealous.

I suppress a smile I shouldn't even feel. I'm hiding a lot at the moment.

"Her partner Pamela is a writer as well. She used to represent her before they tied the knot a few years ago."

Bianca's shoulders drop in relief, and I can't help but laugh out loud, but I'm able to turn it into a brief fake coughing fit. She is just too adorable for words and such an open book with her emotions. I wish she could see the look on her own face because I know she would laugh too.

"Are you okay?" She pours water from the carafe on the table into a glass and slides it toward me. "Here, drink this."

Her sincerity and concern only add to the pile of guilt I'm constantly wading through when it comes to her. I hate this. My head is starting to hurt again, and now my right foot is tingling from out of nowhere. *Not good.*

"Thank you. I'm fine now." I compose myself as best I can.

Our waiter comes by and takes our orders, and once he leaves, silence falls over us. I notice that our hands are close together on top of the tablecloth, and I am so tempted to reach those few inches to take her hand into mine. I also see that she's staring at our hands, and I get the feeling she's contemplating the same thing.

Neither of us moves a muscle.

It's unsettling how easily I can read her mind or sense what she's feeling without her telling me. I feel so attuned to her when she's near, as though we are connected somehow. Like right now, I bet we could power the entire Vegas strip with the energy sparking between us. It's not even entirely sexual energy, either.

And this is now utterly ludicrous. I've seriously lost it. I imagine a connection that isn't even there. But she did ask about it, so that's not true either.

I lift my hand from the table and away from Bianca's. This breaks the spell we're both under for the time being.

We continue our conversation through the meal, with Bianca asking all the questions and me giving short answers. Of course, we have almost everything in common, from our love of auto racing to our confusion at Australian Rules Football. We enjoy the same fiction authors and hate the same movies. Our taste in food varies, but I like that we have that cultural difference to learn from each other. The same musicians are in our respective playlists, and neither of us has an artsy bone in our bodies. We even share the same guilty pleasure of watching trivia game shows.

The desire to let loose and foster this relationship grows stronger whenever we have a similarity. At the same time, I'm forced to dig deeper into myself to keep up my mental and emotional armor. It's getting harder and harder to maintain these defenses the more I get to know Bianca.

It's clear. No, it's *been* clear that she is absolutely the woman of my dreams. There's no way around it. I knew it when I first saw her, and even more now that I've gotten to know her better.

But I. Can't. Do. This.

As soon as we finish eating, I get up, ready to see her to her car. She's surprised at my abruptness but goes along with it. I beg off with more jet lag bullshit even I wouldn't believe. She's gracious as usual and follows me back to the valet.

"Thank you for dinner," she mutters, awkwardly looking anywhere but at me. "It was nice of you to offer."

"It was my pleasure. Thank you for coming."

I'm equally awkward and also avoid direct eye

contact. If our eyes meet, I swear I will pull her into the most passionate kiss we have ever experienced. I need to be careful not to let that happen in these last few minutes.

We're silent again for a long minute before Bianca says, "I'll be back to pick you up in the morning around 9:30 if that works for you. I can meet you right here if you like."

I nod, looking around anxiously for her car, which is taking forever.

"That will be fine. Thanks."

She's got her head down and is looking at her shoes. My heart craters, knowing that this should be going so differently. This *could* go differently if I let it. If I let her in. But that would be entirely selfish of me to do to her. Any relationship with Bianca outside of professional would be mind-blowing, soul-filling, and life-altering. But it would also be highly disappointing, heartbreaking, and burdensome for her.

I couldn't do that. I won't do that.

Her car arrives, and we give each other small waves and smiles. It suits because right now, I feel small. Minute. Insignificant. Nothing.

Chapter 8
Can't Break What's Broken

Bianca

Driving home, I can't help but replay the entire evening in my mind, minute by minute, trying to figure out what actually happened. A huge part of me wants to believe that I saw something in Oliver, proving he does feel the same way about me. He gets the same weird déjà vu that I do. But why would he lie about it? Because it sounds absolutely crazy? I have to agree with that much. I believe in it, though, because I feel it, and I just know he does too.

How strange that when I was with Colin, he could hide his feelings for someone else *from* me, and with Oliver, he's hiding his feelings *for* me. The difference now is that I didn't know Colin was hiding something. I *do* know that Oliver is. At least, I think I know that. I want to.

One thing that's bothered me all evening is the look he would get when we were quiet. They weren't awkward silences and were actually very comfortable, but his eyes would change slightly. *Regret*. I'd swear he felt remorse for something but couldn't for the life of me say what.

If I could break through the barriers he keeps putting up, I think something special could happen between us. He just needs to let me in.

This is crazy. I've known him officially for two whole days, and I'm already jumping into the deep end. I need to figure out how to live with this.

Tomorrow is our first day working together, and I'm curious how we'll be with each other. Or, more specifically, how *he* will be with *me*. Will I just be his driver? Or something more? I need to prepare for either direction and not get my hopes up. As my grandmother used to say, *'If you don't expect anything, you can't be disappointed.'* I also need to consider how I'm going to treat him. He obviously doesn't want to admit his feelings for me, so there's got to be a reason for that. I need to respect whatever it is, and let it go.

But I don't like to let things go. Especially if I know something is there.

I'm early to pick him up today. Like, really early. It's not even 9:00, but when I get out of the car to stretch and prepare for a long wait, Oliver pushes through the doors and walks toward me.

He's wearing a light gray summer suit with an open-collar shirt that looks so damned good on him that I can't tear my gaze away. The blonde highlights in his hair are bright in the Vegas sun, and the scruff on his jawline is perfection. Add on top of all that handsomeness the vintage aviator sunglasses that make him look like something out of a Hollywood movie, and the butterflies in my stomach are going berserk again.

The smile he directs at me is wide and honest and melts me even more than the summer heat, which is saying something because it is *hot*. I flash him a quick smile back but restrain myself. After last night, I know better than to try for anything more with him than a professional relationship. I don't need to be hit over the head with how much he doesn't think or care about me. It was silly even to consider.

"Good morning," I say stiffly, keeping my tone professional. I round the back of the car and open the passenger door for him as he approaches.

He stops on the sidewalk a few feet away and tilts his head curiously at me.

"What's this?"

"What's what?" I look around, trying to figure out what he's talking about.

"Why are you opening my door for me?" His words come out accusatory, like I've offended him somehow.

"Excuse me?" I'm still confused. "This is my job." I'm matter-of-fact about it because it's true. I do this all day, every day. I shrug at him. "It's kind of what I do? And what you're paying me to do."

His head snaps back as though he's been struck. "You open doors for men? And they let you?" He really does sound offended. And to be honest, more than a little sexist.

"Yes. I do..." I repeat, so he gets it. "As I said, *it's my job*. I understand that you're trying to be chivalrous or whatever, but it's really not a big deal for me to open your door for you."

He studies me closer, probably trying to see if I'm joking, which I'm not. His brow is furrowed, and a frown pulls his beautiful smile down. I don't know why he's so upset about something so small.

"Well, can I ask that you not do that for me? I'd like to open my own doors if you don't mind." He really didn't like me doing that for him. Interesting. He didn't have a problem with me hefting his suitcase yesterday, but okay.

"Sure thing." I shrug. I walk around the front of the car and get into the driver's seat, turning the air conditioning on full blast since the doors have been open for so long. It doesn't take much time for the heat to turn the inside of a car into a sauna.

We drive silently for a few minutes, and today everything is awkward. Especially silences. Something has shifted in the vibe between us. I don't know what's changed, but it's now uncomfortable.

I don't like it. It doesn't feel right.

"Did you have a pleasant evening?" He asks, breaking the silence. I almost jump at the sound of his voice as I was beginning to expect him to not talk at all the entire trip.

I grip the steering wheel tightly, my adrenaline pumping and my heart racing after being startled.

I guess we're talking now.

"Yes. I turned in not long after getting home from dinner, so it was a short evening." I leave it at that and don't return the question.

I can feel him next to me, expecting a question of him in turn. It's a nervous energy I wasn't expecting. Well, he's not getting one. It might be impolite, but I'm not in the mood to play games today.

One thing the Vegas heat does is make me cranky. You'd think I'd be used to it by now, but it never fails to assault my senses.

He shifts in his seat as though resigned to my silence and settles in for a long ride. The drive should take about ten minutes this early in the day. This could be the longest ten minutes of my life at this rate.

"Have you been to the mob museum?" he asks. His voice is overly friendly and polite. Even I can hear how forced it is. He doesn't want to make small talk, so I don't know why he's trying. "I know locals sometimes avoid tourist traps like this and never see them."

Sticking to my guns, I just nod. "Yes, I've been there." I keep my attention on the road ahead and the traffic around us. This is a job, just like every other person I've driven around. Other than him sitting up front with me, this is no different. It's becoming a mantra I need to keep repeating.

"And how did you find it?" He's not dropping it. A for effort, I guess, though I don't understand what's changed from yesterday.

"You mean, how was it?" I ask, and he nods. "I don't know. It's a typical museum. Since you're writing about it, I'm sure you'll find it more interesting than I did."

"It was boring, huh?" he chuckles, and the sound twists something in me, making me want to make him laugh again. It sounds like music to my ears.

Okay, he wants to banter. I can banter.

I shrug, relaxing a little. "There's now a speakeasy in the basement where I'll be waiting for you. That part is interesting." My lips twitch into a smirk, and his laughter does continue, forcing me to smile.

"Does this mean I'm going to need to drive *you* home?" He tries to sound stern, but his smile is devilishly wicked, as if he's having inappropriate thoughts. No. I'm sure I imagine that part.

He's an entirely different person when he's like this. Charming, engaging, irresistible, and sexy as hell. I can feel the ice around my emotions melting, but I'm cautious. I know how quickly he can switch his mood.

"No. I don't drink on the clock, so no worries there."

He lets out a long breath as if relieved. "Oh, good. We wouldn't want me behind the wheel. Even sober." His laughter trails off.

That sounds interesting. "Oh? Are you a bad driver?"

He suddenly grows serious, and there it is. The switch I was predicting. I knew it would show up eventually. He doesn't answer but instead kind of nods to himself and turns to look out the side window, so I can't see his face. I'd swear he's purposely hiding.

"Oliver?" I get the sense we touched on something sensitive with him, but I can't figure out what for the life of me. All we talked about was driving, not anything earth-shattering. "Are you okay?"

It takes a second, but he eventually realizes I've been talking to him.

"What's that? Oh. Yes, I'm fine. Thank you." The dismissive way he says this clues me in that our conversation is over, and I shouldn't ask him any more questions. That's fine. I don't need to talk to him at all. I was just responding to him in the first place.

We pull into the parking lot of the mob museum, which used to be an old courthouse, and find a spot easily since it's still early. When I turn the car off, we both hesitate, as if something needs to be said, but neither of us says anything. After another long moment, I open the door and get out.

I've heard of the term 'emotional whiplash' and can now say I'm experiencing it in real-time. I could really have done without this life experience.

Chapter 9

Ghost

Oliver

My leg has gone numb. My fucking leg has pins and needles shooting down my right calf. My initial instinct is still to massage it or pound my leg to wake it up, but I know damn well that won't do a thing. What I *don't* know is what will happen if I try to step out of this car and walk to the entrance, but I can't stay in this increasingly hot car, either.

Bianca is staring at me curiously from the sidewalk, probably wondering what the hell I'm doing just sitting here. My fists are clenching and unclenching automatically, and panic is winding its way up from my heart to my brain. I'm starting to break out in a sweat, and I need to do something before I overheat.

God damn it.

This is precisely what I was afraid of. This helplessness. This soon-to-be felt humiliation. Maybe I can play this off as the typical falling asleep pins and needles that ordinary people get. Who cares if we've only been in the car a few minutes. It could happen.

Sure. Lie to yourself some more.

Taking a deep breath, I pull on the handle and swing the door wide so I can turn in the seat and use my left leg to stand. Bianca's gaze is piercing through me, straight into my embarrassment. I can feel it. The sun beats down on me relentlessly, making everything feel even worse.

After I shut the door, I lean my hand on the car while I navigate walking with a leg that feels like it's wrapped in cement. It'll take a few steps, but I should get used to it.

"Everything okay?" There it is again. That bloody concern. I can't even look at her, not just because I don't want to see her expression; I have to concentrate on walking.

"Yeah, just a bit of a dead leg. I must have sat awkwardly. I'll be fine in a minute. Just need to walk it off. Nothing to worry over." I overexplained that, but to hell with it. I don't stop walking and pass her to limp up the stairs and enter the building. This time I'm able to hold the door open for her. She bestows me with a nod and a smile, accompanied by a blush on her cheeks.

Once in the lobby, I glance around, looking for the Chair of the Advisory Council for the museum, who is also the former agent in charge of the FBI's Las Vegas division, whom I will be interviewing today. I don't see her yet. We are very early.

"I'll see you in a few hours?" Bianca asks, heading towards the stairs to the basement. She seems to be in a hurry to get away from me. I can't blame her. I'm not exactly easy to deal with. Especially lately.

"Yes. I'll come to find you when I'm done."

She doesn't even nod or acknowledge my response, practically running down the stairs to the speakeasy. I'd run away too. If I could run.

The private tour and in-depth conversation with the Chair of the Advisory Council take several hours, and I almost take the lift down to the basement to find Bianca when we finish. However, my leg has not improved, and it's actually getting worse as the numbness spreads to my foot.

It's getting more and more difficult to walk

normally, so I decide to make my way to the car and text her to meet me. It's a shitty thing to do since we agreed to meet in the speakeasy, but I don't trust myself. More specifically, I don't trust my legs.

One thing I didn't account for is the incessant heat. Hot weather only worsens my problems, so I hope Bianca is quick. Leaning against the car, I use it for what tiny bit of shade it offers while I wait. It's not enough.

Luckily, I don't have to wait long, and she comes out soon after I text her. Her brows are set in a slight scowl. She's not happy, and there isn't much I can do about it.

Heading to my side of the car, she stops herself and must remember my request to not open my door, and she pivots to the driver's side. After she opens her door, she waits for a few seconds to let the trapped heat from within escape. Once I can get in, I clumsily take my seat quickly since I'm starting to feel vertigo set in.

I can't believe how quickly I'm being taken down by these symptoms. It's never hit this hard and fast before. Stress and heat, and probably jet lag, are making everything worse. Plus, I haven't eaten today, which doesn't help.

Bianca pulls out of the parking lot and doesn't even attempt conversation, which is fine with me. I'm not in the mood for small talk anyway. I need to get to my room and my medication.

Needing to increase my doses of anything during this trip isn't something I anticipated. This could become a problem later on. Some of my drugs may not be available here. I'll need to look into that.

As the car cools down, I start to feel a little better. The lightheadedness is going away, but the vertigo is still kind of there at the edges of my brain. This is a right fine mess.

Spending the entire ride back to my hotel trying to appear calm, cool, and collected on the outside for Bianca's sake is torturous when inside, my adrenaline is pumping in complete panic mode. The fear of humiliation is one of the hardest things to get over. Being seen as 'less than' is a thoroughly narcissistic and egotistical dread, but it's there, nonetheless. I can't change the emotions that pop up. I can only react and deal with them. So far today, I think I'm doing okay. So far.

Bianca stops when we pull up to the hotel but doesn't even put the car in park. She pauses only for the time it will take me to get out of her hair for the day.

Perfect. As much as I hate it and all of this, I don't want her to like me. I don't want her wrapped up in this chaos that has become my life this year. Usually, saying somebody doesn't know what they're missing is a derogatory statement, but in this case, it's only a good thing.

I try to psych myself up to get out and walk into

the hotel as normally as possible. Maybe I'll even wait at the curb while she pulls away and out of sight for good measure to ensure she doesn't see how bad I've gotten at walking. I'm sure it's a sight with it feeling like an entire bag of sand is wrapped around my lower leg and foot.

"Thank you for the ride and for waiting for me,' I say, stalling for time as I work myself up to exit the car.

"Of course." Her voice sounds small and far away, as though she's thinking of something else entirely. We're both staring out the windscreen, not daring to glance in the other's direction.

"I'll see you tomorrow then, for the barbeque at the Carmichael's?"

I hope to God this all passes overnight somehow, and I recover completely before seeing her again. It never works like that, though.

"Yeah. As far as I know, it's still on for tomorrow, but it might change with the new baby in the family and everything. I'll confirm and get back to you." She's all business. No emotion. *Good.*

"Right. Till tomorrow then." I offer a brief smile, but she's not even looking my way to see it.

Taking a deep breath, I open the door, pushing it while I turn in my seat to stand. Then I use the door to lift myself to my feet and step gingerly aside to close it. I tap the top of the roof like I've seen in TV shows to let Bianca know that she can pull away now, and she does.

I guess that really works, then.

Watching as the car circles the drive and turns onto the main road, a wave of dizziness overtakes me, and I stagger slightly. The heat again is beating down, making me feel like an ant under a magnifying glass being burned alive.

Turning towards the front doors, my body suddenly doesn't respond to what I'm telling it to do. The leg that has gone numb drags on the pavement, and my other leg hasn't accounted for that, so I stumble but can catch myself. Sweat is breaking out on my forehead, and the world seems to have become a solid wave of heat. I try again to walk to the doors, but my right foot scrapes the sidewalk, and I falter, unable to catch myself this time.

As I fall, and the cement rises to meet my face, the only things I can think of are that I'm glad that Bianca isn't here to see how pathetic I am, and I hope that I haven't scuffed my shoes.

There's a loud cracking sound as my head hits the pavement and everything goes black.

Chapter 10

I Can't Breathe

Bianca

Almost as soon as I pull out of the casino driveway, my brother calls.

"Hey, Enzo, what's up?" I cringe inwardly, knowing he will want to talk about Oliver. I am not in the mood for this right now.

"Hey yourself, I just wanted to check in on my baby sister. Any...news?" He doesn't need to say it. I know what, or more specifically, who he's referring to.

"Nope. No news. I think your wires are crossed, bro."

He chuckles. "Bro? Since when am I your "*bro?*"

That means something bad happened. Want to talk about it?"

"Not really." The last thing I want to do right now is talk about how wrong he is about Oliver and how disappointed and hurt I am by it all. Dwelling on all of that isn't going to be productive or help me get over it.

"Okay, if you change your mind, you know where to find me." That's what I love about my brother. He knows when to push and when to let things go with me. He's so intuitive about this stuff. It makes me jealous. I wish I was so insightful. Then maybe I could figure out what's going on with Oliver. But I'm not so lucky.

We hang up, and when I'm almost back to the depot, my phone rings again, and I see that it's Connor, the valet at Bliss Casino. I answer with the hands-free.

"Hey Connor, what's up?"

"Hey Bianca, this is Connor at Bliss." He sounds distracted.

I shake my head and laugh to myself. "I know, Connor. What's up? Does your wife know you have my number?"

"Your boyfriend just got carted off to the hospital."

It takes me a minute to realize who he's talking about, and when it hits me, my breath catches. "Oliver? What happened?"

"I don't know his name, but it was the guy you had dinner with last night. I think he was still out when they took him, too, but I can't be sure." Connor sounds upset, which isn't like him. He's usually a cool cucumber about everything, so it makes my anxiety amplify. But he still hasn't told me what happened.

"Connor, why was he out? You haven't told me what happened." My imagination runs wild with crazy ideas of what could have gone wrong.

"Right after you left, he fell on the sidewalk and hit his head. There was a lot of blood...."

I'm stunned and have to pull to the side of the road. Oh my god, what the hell would make him fall like that? Did he just trip? I need to go to him.

"What hospital?"

"I think St. Rose. It's closest."

Disconnecting the call, I make an illegal U-turn in front of several cars. Horns are blaring at me, but I don't care. I have to see if Oliver is okay. I have to be there for him. It feels like my chest has been ripped open and my heart was stolen. I've never felt like this before, so worried about someone else's well-being. I've been concerned for people, sure, but not like this. This is on another level entirely.

The hospital isn't far, and I get there in a matter of minutes, thanks to a bit of stretching of the speed limit. I park and sprint to the Emergency Room.

I do not like hospitals. And not just a normal,

'*eww, hospitals are gross,*' I mean, it's almost to the point of a phobia how much I dislike them. Besides babies, nothing good ever happens at a hospital. It's an irrational loathing that I fully recognize, but I've never claimed to be rational.

When I approach the front desk, I have to wait a full five minutes before one of the intake nurses is free. During that time, my anxiety skyrockets to an all-time high. Knowing that Oliver is in this building somewhere strange to him and in an unknown condition that might be life or death, I have to wait to see him. I am not handling this well, on top of my original anxiety about hospitals.

"I'm here to see about Oliver Bellamy. He was brought here by ambulance not long ago?" I don't see the point in covering my emotions to this nurse. I'm sure she's seen it all. My hysteria is nothing new.

"Let me check, hon. One sec." She's so casual. Like the end of the world isn't happening right now. "Are you Normandy Carmichael?"

The name surprises me, and I jerk back reflexively when I hear it. Why would she think I'm Normandy?

"No. I'm Bianca Torino. I was just with Oliver this morning before this happened."

She studies me briefly with a look of complete disinterest.

"His international contact listed on his

paperwork is Normandy Carmichael, so I can't tell you anything, unfortunately. Sorry, hon."

If she calls me *'hon'* one more time, I will lose my shit in this lobby. I bite down hard on the inside of my cheek to stop myself from saying something mean.

Taking a deep breath, I say, "Have you been able to reach Normandy?" I whip out my phone and pull up her contact information immediately.

She rereads the computer monitor. "All it says is she was notified. Whether that was a conversation or a message, I couldn't say."

Shit. Normandy needs to be here. *Now.*

"Thanks," I mutter, and step away to dial Normandy. It goes to voicemail, so I hang up and dial again. This time she answers.

"Hey, Bianca, what's up?" She sounds completely normal and oblivious to what's happening.

"I'm at the hospital. Oliver was just brought here, but they won't tell me anything. Connor told me he fell and hit his head pretty badly. You're listed as his contact here. They said they notified you. Didn't you get it?" I take a deep breath since I just rushed all of that out. I shouldn't be this upset, but I can't help it.

"I've been outside swimming with Ava. I just heard my phone now. What do you need me to do?"

"I don't know. I don't know how any of this

works. I just need to know that he's okay." The urgency in my voice has to come through because Normandy snaps into action.

"I'll call them and get what information I can, and then I'll call you back. In the meantime, I'll pull Ava and me together to head to the hospital. Is it St. Rose's?"

"Yes. And, thank you, Normandy."

"No problem. Sit tight. I'll call you back in a little bit."

I sit in the waiting room to bide my time until she calls back. It's pretty crowded, I think, for an early Saturday afternoon. It seems like a lot of groups of families, and they're all captivated by the talk show on the room's TV, showing someone getting the results of a paternity test or something. I don't know. My attention is elsewhere right now. I don't think I could pay attention to anything at the moment if I had to.

A few minutes later, Normandy calls back. "So, they didn't tell me much. He tripped and fell, and since he hit his head, there was a lot of blood, but it's not serious, and they're just watching for a concussion."

The air rushes out of my lungs again as I sigh in relief. I thought the worst when Connor said there was a lot of blood and a head injury.

"Are they going to let me see him?"

"I didn't ask that. I'm sorry I didn't even think

about it. Ava and I will be there soon. Just sit tight."
That is so much easier said than done.

After the longest thirty minutes I've ever waited through, I hear, "Aunt B!" and see little Ava running straight toward me with her arms out wide. I grin when she practically slams into me for a big bear hug. Normandy isn't too far behind.

"Hey, sorry it took so long to get here." She sounds out of breath as though they ran. "Little Miss Ava was anxious to see her Aunt B and check on how Mr. '*Belly*?' Is doing?" She scrunches her face at the name, but Ava and I laugh. We know what's up with that name. "I assume that's Oliver?"

I nod and smile at Ava. "It is." Something in me snags at the thought of him and Ava having that little connection.

"I'm going to see if they'll let me back for a visit and see if we can't get you in to see him, too. Can Ava stay with you for a few minutes?"

"Of course. Thanks, Normandy."

Eyeing me carefully, she asks, "Is something happening between you and Mr. Belly? I mean, Bellamy, that I should know about?"

"Happening?" I'm so surprised I barely get the words out, but I can't hide the blush I can feel spreading on my face. Normandy is known for her keen ability to read people; I guess I'm no exception.

She sighs with a small laugh. "It's not a big deal if there is. I've given up trying to stop employees from getting involved with one another or with clients. Mischief has apparently become a matchmaking company on the side."

I lower my head, now trying to hide my disappointment in the *lack* of something happening between us.

"Well..." Words escape me.

Ruffling Ava's hair, she nods and says, "Say no more. I got you," and leaves. I pull a few books out of Ava's backpack and settle in to read while we wait. I'm grateful for the distraction, though I read to her with one eye on the door to the main hospital for any sight of Normandy returning with good news. News that I can see Oliver and confirm that he's really okay. I need to see that for myself, or I'll go crazy.

Thinking of things that are crazy, I'm reminded of my brother's phone call out of the blue again right before Connor called me to tell me about Oliver's accident. Did Enzo get another one of his weird 'feelings' that something was wrong? He's been doing stuff like that a lot lately, and while I didn't use to believe in it, I might now be a convert-in-the-making.

Chapter 11

Dull Knives

Oliver

After waking up in an ambulance and being told what happened, it's as if my worst nightmare has come to life in vivid technicolor. Now in the hospital A&E, that nightmare is continuing unfettered.

It being a Saturday, plus the time difference between the U.S. and the U.K., of course, my neurologist can't be reached to discuss my treatment with the doctors here.

While I have a medicine passport listing everything I take, one of the prescriptions is experimental, and I had to declare it when I entered the country, as well as show a letter from my doctors. It's bullshit bureaucracy at its finest. The question now for the doctors here is about that experimental medicine. Is it not working? What can and can't I take with it?

Everything is up in the air until the doctor in charge of my care gets the bright idea to directly call the institution running the clinical trial I'm in. Once that is done, my treatment plan is finalized, and I can breathe a little easier. A heavy dose of IV steroids should tide me over until I return home in a few weeks.

What none of my medicines or doctors can do is cure my rage. Fury at myself for being in this pitiful position. Anger at the rest of the world that doesn't have to go through this. Annoyance at the hospital staff, who are overly pleasant and cheerful, when they should be as outraged as I am at this situation.

And if they're not kind and smiling, they have that look; the look I abhor and the word I'm tired of thinking about. *Concern*. I'd be more than happy to tell them what they can do with their fucking concern.

"Oliver? How are you feeling?"

I open my eyes and discover a grown-up version of that little girl, Ava, whom I met the other day, standing in the doorway. Blonde hair, blue eyes, and a tan. Emitting a paradoxical beach vibe in the middle of the desert.

"You must be Ava's mother," I say, coldness in my tone. It only now dawns on me that the hospital must have called her since she's listed as my emergency contact here in the states. At least it's not Bianca.

"And you must be Mr. Belly," she chuckles as she steps into the room, and I can't help but smile at the name Ava gave me.

"I am indeed. I think it's officially become my new nom de plume."

"Well, I'm sure Ava would be ecstatic if that were true."

"After today, I may need to permanently change my name, so I'll keep that one in the running." I instantly regret saying that because I know it opens the door to discussing what happened. I'd really rather not talk about it, especially with Normandy Carmichael. I need to maintain professional neutrality with her and not get into personal issues before interviewing her.

"I'm sorry I couldn't meet you when you arrived. I hope it wasn't a problem having Bianca take over for me as your guide." She sits in the one chair in the room, making herself comfortable. I hope this doesn't mean she's staying for any length of time. I don't do visitors. "My sister going into labor so early wasn't on anyone's agenda, so we've all been scrambling."

That, of course, hits me directly in the heart. Not only for the trouble their family is enduring but the guilt overtaking me for how I have treated Bianca. It's for the best, though. I must keep reminding myself of that, and each time I do, my self-loathing grows.

"Hopefully, both mother and baby are doing well?"

Her face lights up at the question. "Yes, I'm an aunt for the second time. This time to a little girl, Grace." She shrugs a little. "You'll get to meet her at our barbeque whenever we get to do that. With you in here and Chelsie and Noah still coping with a newborn, I think tomorrow is out of the question. Maybe next weekend or the one after."

I wave at her dismissively. "I think my weekends are free the rest of my time here, so whatever works for you will work for me."

My in-person interviews can be done over the phone or via video call if it comes to that. I just prefer to conduct them live so I can see the emotions that aren't expressed in people's words. Quite often, the two are very different from each other.

"So, is it terminal?" she asks with a chuckle, and my stomach sinks. She must notice because she's quick to follow up. "I'm so sorry. I didn't mean it that way if it's...."

"No. No. It's okay. I just tripped and fell. It's not a big deal." I force my face into a neutral mask. One I'm getting used to wearing.

"Bianca's in the waiting room. She's quite upset

they won't let her back here to see you. I should probably change your emergency contact to her—"

"No." My voice is loud, clear, and sharper than I want it to be. Every muscle in my body seems to tighten at the sound of her name. Normandy flinches, and I'm forced to devise a reason to be so emphatic. "I don't want to burden anyone else."

"But Bianca will be with you almost every day. It makes sense to—"

"No," I repeat. The ice in my words cracks into pointed shards. I probably sound completely mad, but I can't have Bianca wrapped up in my mess of a life in any way, or at least no more than she already is. "Please, Normandy. Let's keep Bianca out of all this and leave things as they are."

She studies me for a long minute, her eyes tightening but changing to something softer as she stares at me. Then she moves to examine the IV needle in my arm and the machines monitoring my vital signs. Her eyes finally land on the IV bag itself, and I hope to God she either can't read it or doesn't understand what it is.

After a while, she nods. "Okay. We can keep it as is for now. But if something else happens, I *will* change it."

I nod. "That's fair." I suppose I can't ask for more. Not without telling every secret I hold.

"Good." She stands to leave. "How long are they keeping you? Do you know yet?"

"Overnight, in case of a concussion, they don't want me alone tonight."

My mind instantly switches to thoughts of Bianca and better ways to kill time at night. I shake the idea away. Maybe I do have a concussion.

"Well, I'll have Bianca fetch you in the morning then." She turns as if to leave, but I stop her.

"No, wait." I can hear the heart monitor next to me beeping frantically as anxiety takes me over at the thought of Bianca seeing me like this. "Is there someone else that can pick me up tomorrow?"

Turning back to me, there's now shock in her eyes. "Did something happen between you and Bianca that I should know about?" I sense her getting defensive, ready to do battle for her friend and employee. It's honorable of her.

"No, of course not." I can't think of anything to say to rationally explain why I want to keep Bianca away. My brain can't function at any speed quick enough to help me. "Nevermind. It's fine. Forget I said anything."

She stares at me again, and I grow uneasy. I don't like being examined like this, and she keeps doing it. An actor, I am not, so trying to hide anything is nearly impossible for me. It's why I cut most everyone out of my life, so I don't have to deal with moments like this. My problems shouldn't be anyone else's. It's not fair.

"Take care, Oliver," she says, her eyes narrowing

slightly as she backs out the door. "I hope you feel better soon."

"Goodbye, Normandy. Thank you for stopping by."

I flash a weak smile and give a wave as she goes. As she goes to tell Bianca to leave. As I sink deeper into the mire of my own creation that I've expertly developed in my short time here in America. As I stew in remorse and regret for how I've treated Bianca.

I need to seriously rethink my life. I can't keep this up.

Chapter 12

Save Me (I'm Not Crazy)

Bianca

I can't believe what I'm hearing. "What do you mean he doesn't want to see me?" I need to keep my voice down, but it's so damn hard. "What did he say?"

Normandy smooths Ava's hair as she hugs her leg nervously. She doesn't like it when people are upset for any reason. My heart craters as I see her reaction to my outburst.

"He just said he doesn't want to get anyone else involved." She shrugs as if this is no big deal. Well, it is a big deal to me. "He didn't give his reasoning, and I didn't push it. I didn't feel comfortable pressing him

91

for details on anything. I just met the guy. It's not like I can just ask him anything I feel like."

"So, he didn't say anything?" I find it hard to believe that nothing was said about me. "Did you tell him I'm out here and want to see him?" I hold my breath because if he knows that I'm here and purposely denied my visit, I'll know where I stand with him once and for all. It will kill me, but I'll finally know that my feelings and intuition are wrong.

She looks away, not meeting my gaze, and my stomach clenches. There's my answer. He said no. *He said no.* I swallow hard and straighten my spine. Fine. If he doesn't want to see me, he doesn't want to see me. I don't want to be where I'm not wanted, either.

"You'll still need to pick him up tomorrow morning. They're only keeping him overnight, I guess." Her tone is laced with sympathy and something like it, which irks me, too, for some reason.

I might just be overly sensitive about anything Oliver-related. Actually, I know I am, but I can't help it. Just the thought of him hurt and bleeding tears at my soul as though I can feel his pain too.

"Are you sure he wants *me* to pick him up?" I have to ask. If he's not letting me see him, I can't imagine he wants me to pick him up tomorrow. It sounds more and more like he wants nothing to do with me, and I have to straighten to compose myself and not start crying in the middle of the waiting room. I'm getting severe jilted-bride vibes from this situation, and my stomach starts churning at this familiar feeling.

Normandy shrugs slightly and grabs Ava's hand to lead her out. "You're his driver. So, you'll pick him up." She announces this like it's a foregone conclusion, but it's anything but. I can't argue with her. Even though we're good friends, she is still my boss, and I still need to do my job.

"Can I come tomorrow with Aunt B to pick up Mr. Belly?" Ava asks, squirming out of Normandy's grip and running to me, wrapping her arms around my leg tightly and slowing my progress.

I stop and look down at this tiny human barnacle now attached to me and back up to Normandy. I wouldn't mind if she came along, actually. She could be a buffer of sorts between Oliver and me. A good distraction, at least for me, and probably Oliver too. We both look up hopefully at Normandy, standing with her arms crossed, shaking her head at us.

"No, ma'am. Mr. Bellamy will need quiet and rest once he's released tomorrow. He doesn't need little girls peppering him with questions the whole time."

Ava hides her face behind my leg, frowning and disappointed. "I can be quiet...." My heart breaks, and I look at Normandy to find she is not impressed in the least by this show. I guess I'm a pushover because I would have given in at that point.

I gently run my fingers through Ava's hair, trying to soothe her. I know she's uncomfortable in the strangeness of the waiting room, so her emotions are a little raw.

"I'll tell Mr. Belly that you wanted to come to see him, okay? I'm sure that will cheer him up." I force a smile I don't really feel, and she sniffles and nods at me.

"Okay."

I know the fine line you need to walk with Ava when she gets overemotional like this. I pry her off my leg and transfer her hand back to her mother's. I think we've avoided a complete meltdown so far. We just need to make it to the car.

On my way home, I consider the last few days' events. All of the days I've known Oliver and every interaction we've had. I look at every positive indication that he's given me that he feels something for me. I know I'm not crazy. I *have* seen it with my own eyes. But I've also seen him cover those feelings up and try to hide them. He's not very good at that.

He's been hot and cold and everything in between, with nothing consistent. I don't know what to believe anymore. He says one thing, but I feel another. And I don't just feel it. It's as if it's etched in writing on my bones. It goes that deep.

But sending me away from the hospital without being able to see him? Even for him, that's cold-hearted. He could at least have let me see him and sent me away himself, not have Normandy do it. And then, on top of everything, I still need to pick him up tomorrow morning. So, I'm back to being just his driver. I can live with that. Right? Can't I? No. I don't think I can.

I will not be able to go an entire month this way. If he doesn't or can't admit his feelings, I'll need to step aside from being his driver. It's absolute insanity to even be thinking about these things after only knowing him for a few days.

I blame Enzo. He got all of this started in my mind, and I'm now making it into something it's not. If he hadn't planted the seed about the universe wanting Oliver and me together, maybe I wouldn't be here now. Perhaps I'd be able to take Oliver at his word when he says no, he doesn't feel anything for me.

I need to develop a way to be around Oliver without going through this every time. Somehow, I have to shut off my feelings for him. I've never had to do that before, and I'm not sure I'll be able to. How does somebody do that? How do I stop my heart from aching for him? My mind from worrying about him? My body from yearning for his touch? Where do I even start?

I start by stopping. Stop thinking about him constantly. Stop worrying about him. Stop imagining and hoping for something that will never happen. Just fucking stop. You'd think that would be easy with the short time I've known Oliver, but you'd be wrong. This is the hardest thing I'll ever have to do.

Chapter 13

How Did You Love

Oliver

Overnight I'm moved to another room and continue to be pumped full of steroids, and by morning I feel almost human again. I'm given a prescription for more to take when I leave hospital, and then I'm released back into the wilds of Las Vegas.

I'm notified that my ride is here, and I make my way out to the waiting room, steeling myself to see Bianca for the first time since this happened. I don't know what kind of reception I'll get from her after denying her visit yesterday. I presume it will be a chilly meeting.

The numbness in my leg is subsiding little by little, and all dizziness is gone, so I can walk normally for the most part. When I reach the waiting room, I notice Bianca before she sees me, and I stop to watch her for a minute. She's scrolling through her phone, but she looks anxious. A knee is bouncing, and she's biting her bottom lip. Her near-black hair is down for the first time I've seen, and she seems to be trying to hide behind it as it curtains her face. She's breathtaking, especially when she doesn't know she's being watched.

As I take her in, I can feel that supernatural pull toward her again that I've had since the first time I saw her at the airport. It's like I'm tethered to her, and whenever I'm in her presence, it yanks at me to get closer. And when we're not together, it reminds me that we're still connected, so she's never far from my thoughts. I've never felt anything like it, and I'm still unsure how I feel about it.

To be honest, it scares the shit out of me, but at the same time, it also feels like the most natural thing in the world.

She finally looks around and discovers me watching her. Our eyes meet for only a second, and it's not long enough for me to gauge her mood. She stands quickly, and I see that she's actually wearing what looks like a uniform. A typical chauffeur's outfit, but sans the hat and gloves. Black dress trousers, a white blouse, and a short black jacket.

While it's sexy as hell on her, it isn't what I expected at all. It makes me think she's trying to send some sort of message. Hell, if I know what it is, but I can guess.

"Are you ready to go?" she asks, looking everywhere but directly at me. Her eyes initially caught on my forehead and cheekbone wounds but quickly shifted away. "Do you have everything?"

"Yes. We can go." I fall in next to her as she moves to leave. "Thank you for coming to get me. I do appreciate it."

A shoulder rises dismissively. "Just doing my job."

There it is. The truth I knew would surface eventually. I guess I just wasn't expecting to have to face it right off the bat. Of course, I should have known that Bianca says what she means and means what she says. The problem between us is that I don't. No, I shut down, shut off, and push away.

The difference now is that Bianca shows me what that does to someone. With everyone else I've pushed away, I wasn't forced to spend any time with them afterward, so I got away with it reasonably unharmed. Not this time. This time I'm going down in flames as I witness the carnage I create.

Bianca walks ahead of me, and I can't tell if she's sped up her pace to purposely not walk with me or I'm just that slow, and she has no patience. Either way, she turns to me when we get to the exit doors.

"Wait here, and I'll pull the car around for you."

"Bianca. I can walk to the car."

Her eyes narrow as she studies me. Probably trying to tell if I'm fit enough for the exertion needed to cover the distance to the car. I try my best to seem unphased by the visual test, but inside I can almost taste my vulnerability, and it's bitter on my tongue.

Meeting her eyes finally, I can't read them. She's completely shut off from me now, and it hurts more than I anticipated.

"Fine," she mutters before turning and pushing through the exit and straight into the wall of heat outside.

As I follow her out, the heat seems to steal my breath from me, and by the time I reach the car, well after Bianca does, a sheen of sweat covers my face. She didn't even park that far from the building, but I'm really not used to the high temperatures here, so I need to be more careful. Heat and I don't mix, as was proved beyond a shadow of a doubt yesterday. At least she's started the car already, so the aircon is blasting when I get in.

"How can you tolerate living here in the summer? This heat is a killer." If anything can break the ice between us, a discussion about the hot weather will surely do it.

She pulls the car out of the lot and heads toward my hotel.

"You get used to it." Her tone is flat. Zero

emotion. This is not going to be easy, but I didn't think it would be.

We go for a few minutes in complete silence; not even the car radio is on, which only makes things worse. I didn't think that was even possible. How low can this go? Do I really want to see? Or, do I say something now to get things on the right side of friendly, at least? One of us will need to set aside our stubbornness and bend. It may as well be me.

"I'm sorry, Bianca, that I didn't want any visitors yesterday. I was a bit of a mess." She stiffens next to me, probably surprised I'm talking about this. "It was just your typical male ego at work, not wanting to be seen like that. Nothing more. I hope you understand." Maybe making light of it will ease things.

My stomach is in knots about all of this. Everything that could go wrong so far on this trip *is* going wrong. And everything I didn't expect to happen *is* happening. It's hard to negotiate the different emotions going through me at any one time. There are far too many to count, let alone organize.

Thinking for a while, considering my words, she seems to relax and finally says, "I understand." And, nodding, she continues, her voice getting stronger as she goes. "But you need to understand that I was very worried about you. Nobody could or would tell me anything, so I didn't know what was going on for an extremely long time. And when I finally did, it had to come from Normandy. I didn't like being shut out when I was with you right before it happened."

The truth and honesty of what she's saying hurts. Even though I knew it would, it hits me hard. I deserve every ounce of disdain she's giving me, if not more.

"I know. It was rude of me. I'm sorry you felt that way."

She glares at me sideways and scoffs. "So, you're sorry for how I felt but not for *why* I felt that way. Got it."

I cringe. *Fuck.* This is why I don't deal with people anymore, or their *feelings*. I don't know how to talk to anyone without screwing everything up. Like now.

"That's not what I meant –"

"No, I get it. Loud and clear, Mr. Bellamy. You don't need to explain any further. Thanks."

"No, you very much *don't* get it, but I'm not going to argue with you anymore, Bianca. You obviously have your mind made up about me and what my intentions are, so it would be pointless for me to try."

This is sliding down a slippery slope I didn't anticipate and going way out of control. I'm having a hard time keeping up with what's happening. I can hear my blood pumping in my ears as my temper rises.

This is not how I wanted this to go. Not at all.

I glance over at Bianca, and her lips are pressed into a hard line, a muscle in her jaw twitching as I'm sure she's grinding her teeth, just as angry as I am.

This is ludicrous.

I take a deep breath. I need to fix this. I can't stand us being at each other's throats over something so stupid.

"Actually, I will argue this because it's a dumb misunderstanding." She shoots another glare, and I raise my hands defensively. "I *meant* to say I'm sorry I *made* you feel that way. I would never intentionally cause you any distress. I wasn't thinking about anyone else except myself in the moment. I'm sorry."

The muscle in her jaw relaxes, and she looks over at me briefly, probably double-checking that I'm not trying to pull one over on her, and I hope she sees my sincerity. I am sorry for worrying her. No matter my reasons, I didn't want her upset by it. Honestly, I didn't think she would be affected after our rough morning.

"Okay," she replies, nodding again. "Thank you for the apology."

On the outside, I'm stoically staring out the window, unphased by the whole thing. Inside, I'm letting out the deepest sigh of relief. I hope we're now past this bullshit and can move forward. Wherever that leads. It's got to be better than where we're currently at, that's for sure.

I've got an entire month ahead of me, dancing

along this strange line between us. A line I barely even know what it's dividing anymore, but the thought of crossing it feels like the worst thing that could possibly happen to either of us. So, I don't know if I'm protecting myself or her. Maybe it's both.

Or, maybe it's neither of us, and I'm just an idiot.

Chapter 14

Everything Is Embarrassing

Bianca

I got an apology. I'm kind of surprised I got one, too. Oliver doesn't seem like the outwardly remorseful type for some reason. Not that I think he's purposely unkind, but maybe more that he keeps things like that to himself. He'd rather cut someone off entirely than deal with an argument, which, to be honest, is no way to go through life. Everything in life is not that cut and dry. There are always gray areas.

"So, I'll need to be at the coffee shop listed on the agenda by 2:00 since I've rescheduled that meeting. Do you mind coming back for me around 1:30? I'd like to get there early to find a private table." He looks at me expectantly.

Shit, is he serious? "You're going ahead with your interview this afternoon? I thought it would be canceled today, with everything going on...." I shoot a panicked glance at him, and he shrugs and shakes his head. "I've promised to babysit Ava this afternoon. Since I assumed you'd cancel all your meetings today, I thought I'd be free...."

"Oh...I see." But his tone is clear that he doesn't.

"I can call Normandy and tell her that I can't—"

"No. No. Don't do that." He rubs his chin thoughtfully, and I can't help but steal quick looks at him. He is damned attractive when he's lost in thought. "Bring her along."

"What? No. I couldn't." I can't keep bringing children with me on business routes. It's completely unprofessional.

"Sure, you could. That is if Ava doesn't mind hanging out at a coffee shop for a while or somewhere else nearby." His following smile is so charming. I want him to smile at me like that all the time. "Also, if you don't mind, too. I should have included you in that. I don't want to upset your plans if you made any."

"No. We haven't made any concrete plans yet." We're at a red light, so I can turn to him fully and study him to make sure this is really okay, and he's not just saying it is. "You're sure you don't mind? I think she'd really like to see you. She asked about you yesterday at the hospital. She was worried about you."

His reaction starts as surprised, turns happy, but then morphs into an expressionless mask that I'm beginning to get used to. It seems practiced, and it feels as though it's some kind of defense mechanism for him. "Well, that was very kind of her, but there was nothing to worry about."

That doesn't help in reading him at all. I wish we could stop doing this. It feels as though we're dancing around a bonfire full of our real emotions, letting everything go up in flames instead of talking about anything substantial. If we could just get past this, we'd be so better off.

I try to catch his eye, but he avoids my gaze completely. Maybe I should give up. Abandon all the crazy thoughts in my head and heart and just let him be. It kills me, though, the idea of not pursuing this fully. I'll have so much regret if I don't say something, but maybe now, when he's just been released from the hospital with a head injury, isn't the best time.

A car horn sounds from behind us, snapping me back into the present, and I start driving again. Maybe that was the sign I needed to let it go for now.

"Okay, so I'll drop you off and grab Ava and come back for you. Does that sound alright?"

"Perfect." It's hard to gauge a mood from one

word, especially when it's said with no emotion. So, I have to take it at face value. *Everything is perfect.*

After dropping Oliver off at his hotel, I pick up Ava from Normandy's house. She is beside herself with excitement to hear that she'll be able to see 'Mr. Belly' this afternoon and proceeds to tell me all about the stories she wants to tell him. This makes me question whether or not this is a good idea after all. He's got an important interview for his book lined up this afternoon. He doesn't need a toddler peppering him with questions.

"Just remember that Mr. Belly...*Bellamy* has work to do, okay? So, we need to leave him alone to do that, right?"

"I know." The innocence on this child's face when she lies is astounding. I can see the wheels turning behind her eyes, already planning how she will spend her time with Oliver, regardless of what work he needs to do.

When we pull up to the hotel, I instinctively open my door as if to get out to open his and shut it right away, almost catching my foot in the door. Hopefully, nobody saw that.

"What are you doing, Aunt B?" Ava asks. Of

course, she saw and has to comment. Nothing gets past her.

"I was just checking something," I lie, buckling my seat belt again. I can see through the passenger window that Oliver is almost to the car. I whisper to Ava, "Remember, best behavior." She nods her understanding, but I'm still nervous about it. Kids can be so unpredictable.

Oliver gets in the car quickly, probably to get out of the heat, and as soon as he does, his cologne, aftershave, soap, or God knows what it is that smells so good, so *Oliver,* hits me, and the scent transports me somewhere else. *Somewhen* else. Pretty sure that's a word. It's as if I can see my future in my mind, and it smells like him. It's not arousing or sexual, necessarily, but comforting and exhilarating at the same time.

"Mr. Belly!" Ava's voice cuts through and snaps me back to the here and now. I'm able to catch Oliver's initial reaction, which is a smile so heartwarming, it takes over his entire being. And he doesn't do anything to hide it like I thought for sure he would.

He turns in his seat to face Ava, giving her the widest and brightest smile I've seen from him to date. "Why, good afternoon, Miss Carmichael. Lovely to see you again."

She blushes and starts chewing on a knuckle absently as she smiles back at him. But then, she must notice the wounds on his forehead and cheek, and her smile disappears. Taking its place is the saddest frown I've ever seen on her, and my heart breaks.

Putting her hand up to her own cheek, she says shyly, "You have an ouch."

Oliver turns sad briefly, too, but then recovers quickly with a wide grin. "I do, but a very kind nurse named Neil gave me these stickers since I was a good patient and said I could give them to you." He reaches into his suit jacket, pulls out a small roll of stickers, and hands them to Ava.

Her eyes widen, and her frown is now completely gone as she looks over her surprise. I can't help but smile too. That was very thoughtful of him.

She glances up at him, back to her old self. "You didn't say hi to Aunt B."

He scowls at her, brows furrowed. "Well, I must remedy that right away." Turning to me, the frown transforms into a warm smile, and his eyes sparkle as if he's highly amused. "Hello, Aunt B." He adds a smirk for flavor, and our eyes meet for the first time in what seems like weeks.

And there it is again, that pull, that certainty, that unexplainable connection between us. It makes me return his smile, but mine is tentative. I've been here before, thinking something was happening between us but being horrifically wrong. I don't want to go through that again. I lost days trying to work out what happened, and I still don't have a good answer.

"Hello, Oliver." I nod to him briefly and then focus on putting the car in gear and driving. That's my job, after all.

He doesn't react initially, but I think I see him deflate slightly at my short greeting. Wouldn't that be nice, if he really cared that much?

"That's not Oliwer. That's Mr. Belly, silly." Ava is quick to correct me.

Oliver recovers. "I'll just be Mr. Belly for you. How's that?"

Watching her in the rearview mirror, she considers his question carefully. Once she decides, she nods. "Okay. But you need a name for me."

He rubs his chin thoughtfully. "How about Miss Avocado?" Turning, he sees her scrunch her face and shake her head in distaste at the nickname. "No? Well, then, I'm going to need some time to come up with something as amazing as Mr. Belly. Is that alright with you?"

She sighs heavily, the weight of the world on her little shoulders. "I guess so."

Somehow, I keep a straight face during the entire interaction. I sense Oliver next to me, smiling. When I glance over, our eyes meet again, and lightning flashes through me, making the hair on my arms stand on end. *God damn it.* I rub my arms to get rid of the goosebumps, and Oliver is still watching me.

It's unnerving now since he is apparently immune to anything having to do with me. It's not fair.

My phone rings in the car's Bluetooth over the speakers. Looking at the dashboard screen, I see it's my brother. He really has horrible timing. I touch the screen to send the call to voicemail.

"Isn't that your brother?" Oliver asks, and I'm surprised he remembered my brother's name for some reason, though I don't know why. I have no basis for thinking that.

I nod. "Yeah, I'll call him back later."

As soon as I say that, the phone rings again. Enzo never does this unless it's an emergency.

"You should probably get that, no? It might be important." The concern in his voice scratches at me. He doesn't have the right to be concerned about my family or me.

I sigh heavily. He is right, though. I need to answer. I touch the dashboard again to accept the call. "Lorenzo? What's the emergency?"

"Hey, sis, the emergency is your sorry excuse for a love life. I'm calling to check on things with you and your British book boyfriend. Any progress?"

Oh. My. God. I'm going to kill Enzo with my bare hands the next time I see him. The heat that rises in my cheeks from embarrassment could leave sunburn. I'm stunned and speechless, which is rare for me. I can't believe what's happening right now. Even my ears feel like they could burn off.

I instinctively disconnect the call yet again with a fast swipe at the dashboard. If I wasn't aware of Oliver next to me before, I sure as hell am now. It's not helping that Ava is giggling in the back seat at the whole situation. Maybe I can find a convenient black hole to jump into nearby.

To his credit, Oliver doesn't say anything, but he does chuckle softly to himself. I suppose I'm glad that he finds it amusing. But then, what exactly is he laughing at? The idea that we would be together? Or that I would want that? Maybe it's all of the above. It's all a joke. *Me* especially. I'm the biggest joke of all.

Chapter 15

Black Butterflies and Déjà Vu

Oliver

British boyfriend? Unless I'm completely daft, I know that was a reference to me. Has Bianca been talking to her brother about me? What has she said to him that would make him refer to me as her boyfriend? I'm intrigued, but I can't ask her about it with Ava around. I know Bianca had feelings for me when we first met, but that seems to have cooled off since then. And rightly so. Denying her visit yesterday didn't help to warm her to me again.

Is that what I want? Do I want Bianca to have feelings for me or not? She'd be wise not to. And I shouldn't pursue it if she's already past it. It would be selfish and cruel to revive those emotions in her if nothing can come of it.

So, if I were smart, I'd let it go. But when it comes to her, I'm completely dead from the neck up.

However, I don't think I can go an entire month feeling this intense attraction to her and not acting on it in some way. Despite all of my issues, or maybe because of them, I don't have much inner strength left to focus my attention on resisting her. Perhaps there is a chance that she still feels something for me if her brother's words are any indication. The idea ignites my imagination with possibilities.

We arrive at the café, the bright sun streams through the large windows, and the smell of coffee hangs heavy in the air. For a mid-afternoon, it's pretty empty of patrons.

After retrieving drinks for all of us, I settle in at a table to wait for Theo Thompson to arrive for our interview, and I'm able to watch Bianca and Ava interact with each other. She is so good with her, keeping things fun but orderly. It's easy to see that Ava not only likes Bianca, or 'Aunt B,' but also admires her. It's an entirely different type of sentiment. I can tell the little girl looks up to her, and something like that is earned, not just bandied about on a whim, even for a small child such as Ava.

My heart tugs toward Bianca again, and I find myself yearning for things I can't have, as I seem to be doing a lot lately. Seeing the two of them together pulls emotions out of me that I not only didn't expect but didn't think I was capable of anymore. The past year, I have shut down everything in me that had any sort of hope for a future, but Bianca Torino is somehow sparking life into those dreams. Dreams I have no business having, let alone the right to pull someone else into the nightmare those dreams will inevitably become.

The pins and needles shooting pain in my foot and leg that still remains is a reminder of the nightmare I still need to face. I can't expect anyone else to want to face that with me. It would be pure hubris to even ask.

Their melodic chorus of laughter reaches me and melts something inside. Something that is trying to convince me to try to have a relationship with Bianca, that she'll be understanding, and that it would be worth the effort in the long run.

It's *hope*.

Something inside me still wants to hope, and it's the scariest thing I've ever felt. It twists my stomach into knots, but not entirely in a bad way. Now that I'm allowing them to surface, I'm unsure what to do with all these new emotions.

Fortunately, I don't have time to dwell on it anymore as a man a few years younger than me, probably in his late twenties, enters the café. This must be Theo.

"Uncle Theo!" Ava exclaims, sliding off her chair and running to hug him.

I'd forgotten that Theo's brother Noah is married to Normandy Carmichael's sister Chelsie. It's not a direct relation, but I know titles like *'aunt'* or *'uncle'* are used frequently for extended family. Just like Bianca is *'Aunt B.'*

He swoops her into his arms, and she gives him a sloppy kiss on his cheek, but he doesn't seem to mind.

"Are you here to talk to Mr. Belly?" she asks, and I can't help the blush climbing up my neck at the nickname. It's one thing to use it around Bianca. It's another thing entirely to use it around one of my interview subjects.

"I think I am." His brow furrows in confusion, but Bianca secretly nods her head in my direction with a smile.

"He's over there." Ava points at me as he lowers her back to the floor, and she climbs back into her chair.

"Mr. Bellamy?" he asks, stepping over to me and tentatively holding out a hand to shake.

I stand and return the gesture, shaking his hand. "Please, call me Oliver. Thank you so much for meeting with me today and rearranging the time." I wave at the chair across from me for him to take, and we sit. I nod at Ava and give her a wink in appreciation for the hand off.

"Not a problem. I'm happy to see you've recovered quickly." He indicates the obvious wounds on my face.

I shrug it off and dive into the interview. Theo has inside information into the Mamana crime family that previously owned the Bliss casino where he works and is now owned by the Carmichaels. He witnessed money skimming and other nefarious activities that have led to their ultimate arrests and convictions, though at the time, he was unaware of their illegality or significance.

Over the course of our conversation, I'm able to glean some valuable insight into their dealings with other crime families and city officials, which are now under suspicion. A lot of his story hasn't been in the press or official reports that I've been able to study thus far, so this fresh insider information is invaluable for my book.

About an hour into our discussion, little Ava comes up and takes our order for refills as though she were a server working for the coffee shop. Bianca stands behind her, shrugging and mouthing the word '*sorry*' repeatedly. We give her our requests, and she pretends to write them down on an invisible note pad and proceeds to approach the counter to place the order. I get the sense this was a compromise between the two for some sort of interaction with us.

Once she's gone, Theo studies me briefly and asks, "Do you have any children?"

It's an innocent enough question and not entirely out of the ordinary considering our recent interactions with Ava, but something about it hits me wrong. It's the worst possible question he could have asked at that moment.

That hope I was feeling not long ago has begun to wane. I've spent the past hour trying not to watch Bianca and Ava talk and play with each other, but it's increasingly difficult.

Realizing that I've not given an answer, I attempt to shake off the shroud of negativity. "No. No children." I try to keep my voice neutral but can tell by Theo's quick frown that I've failed. I can feel my hope poking through my words.

He nods knowingly as if he can know anything about me. "Well, maybe someday we'll both be blessed."

I swallow the scoff starting to rise at his statement, and quickly change the subject back to local organized crime. Oddly enough, that's a much safer topic of discussion for me right now.

My interview with Theo takes much longer than expected, so after long goodbyes and surprising hugs from Ava for both Theo and me, Bianca takes her home. We are just wrapping up when she returns, passing Theo as she enters the café.

As she walks toward my table at the back of the room, I'm again struck by her natural beauty. Her long black hair accentuates her olive skin and red lips. Even without much makeup, she's a stunner. Her dark brown eyes are kind, but she carries herself with pure inner strength. Obviously, she doesn't suffer fools easily, and I am a god-damned fool.

"How did your interview go?" she asks, sliding gracefully into the seat across from me. Her genuine interest in my work only adds to her attraction.

I smile. "It went rather well, actually. Thank you."

She nods in response, and I notice she's again avoiding my gaze. I understand why she is since every time our eyes meet, it's like an electrical storm erupts between us.

Watching her become increasingly uncomfortable with me, I take a minute to reevaluate things. This is ridiculous. I'm only here for a month. What would be the harm in a brief romance? No secrets would need to be divulged, and it would be understood that I'll be off back to England in a month's time.

Maybe she would be interested in a temporary arrangement of some kind. We're adults. Surely a no-string relationship is possible. Especially since we'll spend so much time together over the next few weeks. It would solve the desire problem and make the month ahead of us bearable.

"Are you ready to go?" She pushes on the table to stand, but I reach over and grab her wrist, making her freeze in place.

"Have dinner with me tonight." It's not a request, and my blood starts to pump faster in my veins as possibilities start running through my mind. I'm getting ahead of myself, but I don't care. If I don't act on these feelings that have been scorching through me since I first saw her, I will incinerate to ashes right here in this coffee shop.

Now that I've had the thought, I can't unthink it. My body is just following instructions at this point.

She's startled but recovers quickly and studies me for a long minute. She must be satisfied with what she sees because she nods slowly.

"Okay...but I'd like to change out of this uniform if that's alright with you."

"While I think you're beautiful no matter what you wear, that's perfectly alright with me."

Her eyes widen, and her face flushes at the compliment. I admit, I'm laying it on pretty thick, but I'm enjoying how much this is flustering her. She's damned cute when she's thrown off her game.

"Oh," is all she can say as her forehead creases in confusion.

Letting go and leaning into these feelings and emotions will be fun. I take her hand, brush my lips across her knuckles briefly, and lead her out of the coffee shop. I can't help but smile at the shock on her face.

Allowing myself a temporary tryst while I'm here could go a long way to sustaining me once I leave. *If* I can get Bianca to agree. I think our physical attraction for each other is mutual. I'm pretty sure I'm reading the signals from her accurately. It's a risk, but I need to take this chance.

The early evening dusk casts a purple haze over everything, and the afternoon heat has only slightly dissipated. The palms of our hands grow warm from the friction as we walk across the lot to the car. This feels so natural between us, as though we're a well-established couple, and we do this all the time.

At the front of the car, we stop, and I turn to her, sweeping the hair out of her bright eyes as she stares at me with wonder and confusion. The wind has picked up and is swirling around us, cocooning us in warmth.

"Can I do something?" I ask. Suddenly unsure what the hell I'm doing. I was all confidence and bravado inside the café, but now self-doubt is starting to creep in. What if she says no?

Narrowing her eyes at me, she tilts her head, curious. "Do what exactly?"

I swallow hard. My nerves are all over the place. "May I kiss you?"

I'm surprised to see fear and uncertainty in her,

and she averts her gaze once again, not answering my question, but I'm undeterred.

"Bianca, I have wanted to kiss you since I first saw you at the airport. I've restrained myself till now, wanting to keep our relationship professional, but I'm finding it bloody impossible."

She takes a minute but seems to resolve something within herself and straightens her shoulders.

"Then don't."

"Don't?" I'm not sure what that means. Do I not kiss her? I'm confused.

"Don't restrain yourself."

She doesn't have to tell me twice. I step closer, place a hand under her chin, and tilt her face to mine. Her lips part, and her eyes flutter closed as I lean in, barely grazing her lips at first. Cupping her face with my hands gently, I kiss her again. This time, our tongues slide against each other, and the taste and feel of her are beyond what I ever imagined. Again, a sense of déjà vu overtakes me, and I already know how to kiss her and touch her in a way that makes her respond to my every move.

The kiss deepens, and my hands instinctively glide through the silky strands of her hair to the back of her neck, pulling her even closer to me. She doesn't resist and melts into me, pressing her chest against me. Her fingers slide over my shoulders and up into my hair. Every connection between us, our lips, our hands, our bodies, buzzes with energy and sends thrills vibrating through me.

For a moment, we both forget where we are, and who we are, for that matter. We're no longer relative strangers who just met a few days ago. We're long-time lovers reuniting after centuries apart. For a split second, I'm not a broken man with a doomed future; instead, I'm a strong protector, showing the woman I care about exactly how much I do.

Wait.

I pull away and try to catch my breath. I need to be extremely careful here. I can't *care* about Bianca. Not really. Not if either of us is going to get out of this unscathed. But as we stare at each other, and she smiles at me so sweetly, I could fall to my knees right here and now and confess everything dreadful about myself to her.

I know instantly that I've already fucked this up. There's no way we're getting out of this without a great deal of pain. Not now. It's too late now.

Chapter 16
World Stops Turning

Bianca

My head won't stop spinning. I have never been so thoroughly kissed in my life. Where did this change in him come from? How do I ask something like that? Reading his thoughts or feelings is nearly impossible when I look into his eyes. I swear I see regret or sadness. Maybe it's both. I don't understand either one after that fantastic kiss. But then he smiles, and it chases those doubts in my mind back to the shadows where they can wait to pop up later.

"Wow." He presses his forehead to mine, being

careful of his injuries, and pulls me closer to him. "That was...something."

My gaze falls onto his lips, where the edges still curve, and I yearn for his mouth on mine again, but my mind is stuck on his initial expression. I can't get that picture of regret out of my head. It completely contradicts how he's acting now, but that's the question - is he acting?

I can't help but compare his actions to my ex, Colin. He did the same thing, acting like everything was wonderful between us when in reality, he was banging the wedding planner behind my back. I don't compare everyone to Colin. I hardly ever think about him anymore, but I can't help it in this case. The stakes are similar in my mind for some reason.

"Let's get going," I say, pulling away.

I extricate myself from his hold and round the car. He stares after me for a minute, then gets in.

He breaks the silence at a red light about halfway to my apartment. "Did I do something wrong?" His head tilts to the side, and his voice softens. "Should I not have kissed you? I think I'm getting mixed messages."

This irony strikes me as extremely funny, and I can't help but laugh out loud. All of my emotions are running high at the moment.

"Me? *I'm* giving mixed messages?"

He stares at me in response while my laughter dies a slow death, not flinching, not reacting at all. I switch my gaze between him and the traffic light, waiting for it to change while I figure out what to do or say. He was apparently serious, and I just laughed in his face. The flush in my cheeks must be burning as I feel it spread like wildfire on my skin.

"You are serious. Holy crow." Shifting in my seat uncomfortably, I face the road again. I can't believe he's surprised by my reaction. I also can't keep my reasoning to myself. One thing he'll learn about me very quickly is that when I feel something, it is tough for me to keep it inside or quiet. That's just not in my nature. "Were you not at the same dinner I was the other night where I basically bared my soul to you? Or at the airport when you first arrived when we couldn't stop smiling at each other? I think my messages have been more than clear. I honestly don't know how I could have been more obvious."

I see him redden from the corner of my eye, and he clears his throat. "Of course, I was there. That's exactly why I took the chance—"

"Well, if you were there, you remember putting me off every time. So, excuse me if I'm a little surprised now at the change of heart you're suddenly having."

"Fair." He nods, agreeing with my assessment. "That's completely fair. I've wanted to kiss you since I first saw you, but there's a reason I've not acted until now. Bianca, I'm only here for a brief time. If anything is going to happen with us, it will be short-lived." A shadow briefly crosses his face as he says this. "I'm okay with that if you are. There's no reason two adults such as ourselves can't have some fun while I'm here, right?"

Fun? He thinks this is all just for some fun? Is that all I'm worth to him? I keep my focus on the road and my expression blank as I consider his words. My first reaction is to lash out at him for being so insensitive. Then I imagine a "short-lived" relationship with Oliver and what that might entail. Would I be satisfied with that kind of arrangement? Would it be any different than the long line of boyfriends I've had since Colin that were meaningless and forgettable?

I don't honestly know if I can shut off my emotions like Oliver seems to be able to. It should be easy, we've only known each other for a few days. The thought of even trying to deny how I feel doesn't sit right with me, but what choice do I have? The only thing being offered to me is a no-strings-attached setup. Is it better than nothing at all? I think it might be. If that's all I can get, that's what I'll take. I'll just need to figure out how to deal with everything when it ends and he returns to England. No problem. I've dealt with worse pain, right? Colin taught me that I can live through just about anything.

Swallowing hard, I throw caution out the window of this car and make up my mind. "Sure.

Fun is great." The forced cheer sounds saccharine and insincere, which is precisely how it feels.

The weight of Oliver's gaze on me is oppressive as I feel him scrutinizing me. It's as though he can see through every barrier I put up or expression I try to fake. If it were anyone else, I think I'd get away with it, but not with him. It's as though superpowers are developing between us, and we're able to read each other's minds, and at this moment, it's incredibly inconvenient.

I try harder and flash a smile at him next to me, and I think it works since he smiles back. When he smiles, it completely transforms his face and does something to my heart every time. It's a straight shot to my soul and feels like it's just for me, and it's our secret to share between us.

How will I give that up at the end of the month as though it's meaningless? Pushing the thought of this ending before it even begins out of my mind, I finish driving to my apartment to get ready for our dinner. The butterflies fluttering around in my stomach might make eating food a bit tricky now that I know things between Oliver and me are changing. And after that kiss in the parking lot, they are heading in a very hot direction.

When we get to my apartment, Oliver looks around curiously, taking in the décor, or, well, lack of it.

"Did you just move in recently?" he asks.

"No...?"

"Oh. So, you're in the process of moving elsewhere, then?" He perches on the arm of the living room couch, the only furniture in the room.

"No," I laugh. "Why are you asking this stuff?"

His eyes widen in surprise. "Do you not see how it looks as though you're in the process of moving? Either in or out?"

I lean on the couch next to him and look around to see things from his perspective. He's kind of right. It does look like I'm moving. I never really cared what my place looked like, though.

I shrug. "I guess it does. But no, I'm not moving any time soon."

"Well, what's in the boxes then?" He points to a pile in the corner of the empty dining room.

I tilt my head as I try to remember what is in them. It's been so long since I've looked inside that it's hard to picture the contents.

"I think that's my grandmother's china, but I could be wrong. That might be in storage."

He's incredulous. "You think? You don't know?" He leans a shoulder into my arm, pushing me a little. "How long have you lived here?"

It takes me a minute to figure that out too. "I

think around eight? Or ten years? I moved in here when Lorenzo went out to L.A."

Being this close to Oliver, in my own personal space, my home, makes me a little lightheaded. And this new revelation and perspective of my apartment looking so empty gives me added anxiety. I must look like a crazy person with no real furniture.

His jaw drops in shock. I knew he'd react this way when I said it. I really do look like a weirdo now.

"You don't have a single knick-knack or tchotchke. Not even a poster of a kitten dangling from a tree branch saying, 'Hang in there!' It literally looks like nobody lives here."

The kitten poster reference gets me giggling. I can picture it, tape in the corners and everything, right above the fireplace.

"Well, I'm usually only here during the week, and even then, just mostly to shower and sleep."

He lifts a curious eyebrow, always the investigative writer. "Where do you go on weekends?"

"Lake Tahoe. We have a house there, and I spend most of my weekends up there." While it feels a little bit like I'm getting the third degree, at the same time, I'm glad he's interested in my life, as dull as it is.

"We? You mean you and your brother Enzo?" I'd almost swear I sensed a tinge of jealousy in the question.

I glance at him next to me, so close I need to lean back a little to see him clearly. It's not quite jealousy in his eyes but something more like hope. But what is it that he's hoping for? Does he want there to be someone else, so he has an out from this relationship? Or is he hoping there isn't anyone else?

"I mean my family. But it's mostly me that spends any time there. Everyone else is too busy." I watch closely for his reaction, and I was right. It was jealousy. There's now relief and a slight sagging of his shoulders at my response. This makes me grin, which seems to confuse him now. I love that all of this is confounding him.

He smiles back reflexively and brushes my hair off my shoulder. His fingers lightly graze my neck, sending sparks through me. "What is making you smile like that?"

"You. For some reason, the state of my apartment and where I go on weekends seems to have completely confused you. It's highly entertaining." I want to say that I should be the one confused since we're only supposed to be 'having fun,' not learning everything about each other.

"Well, I'm glad I amuse you." He catches my hand in his and then covers it with the other, trapping it. The warmth of his skin is so comforting. It chases away my 'having fun' thoughts and turns them to actually having that fun. From the glint in his eye, I think he's got the same idea.

Leaning in, he presses his lips to the base of my neck and traces a line up to my ear, where he nips lightly on the lobe, just deep enough to send a bolt of electricity through me. The next thing I know, he's pulled me around to lean against him, his hands are in my hair, and his mouth is possessing mine. My palms lay flat against his firm chest, and I slide them up and over his shoulders to remove his suit jacket, letting it fall onto the couch. Then I get to work on the buttons of his crisp white shirt.

If this thing between us is just going to be for fun, well, damn it, I'm going to have some fun. A wave of anger rushes through me at the thought of what I might be settling for instead of getting what I want. Anger at myself for allowing it. That resentment is turning into a frenzied passion the longer we kiss. At least I'll get what I need. Right now, I need him. *All of him.*

He glides his hands down my arms and pulls my blouse up and out of my waistband, his thumbs sweeping along the skin of my stomach, to my rib cage, and then my breasts. Deftly, he moves the bra to take my breast full into his hand, teasing at the nipple until I'm pulsing all over and want to scream his name. I can't help but moan into his kiss and grind against him without thinking. My body is now reacting to him on a level I'm unaware of.

My fingers hurry to explore the newly exposed skin when I finally undo his shirt's buttons. His chest is smooth and defined. For a writer, I'm surprised to see any muscle and am aroused by his lithe physique. It lets me know that he's strong and takes care of himself. I like that.

As I get lost in thought while admiring him, he takes advantage of my distraction and grabs my waist, pulling me with him as he slides back onto the couch, and I land on top of him. A yelp and a giggle escape me at the sudden shift, but I don't mind the new position at all. It's self-evident from his steel length pressing against me that he is enjoying this as much as I am.

His mouth is suddenly on mine again, hungry and possessive, as if this is the last kiss he'll ever have, and he wants to make sure he appreciates it fully. Within moments, he shifts us again, and we're each on our side, facing each other, panting and reaching for breath, our chests heaving with the effort. The gray in his eyes is dark, as if a storm is brewing in his mind, and his eyes are windows.

As we stare at each other, we're back at the airport, seeing each other for the first time across baggage claim, smiles growing, but within those smiles is an understanding. We're having more than fun here. This is much more for both of us. The idea does something to me and amps up my desire for him.

He cups the back of my head and pulls me into a languid kiss, and the whiskers of his stubble rub against my chin in the most delicious way. He tastes of mint and coffee and longing, and it's heady how much it affects me. His fingers smoothly unbutton my pants, and his hand slowly slides down, inching closer to my center.

This is taking too long. I can't wait for him to touch me. I try to push my toes against the arm of the couch to move up so his hand will be right where I need it, but I can't reach it and end up further away. I let out a whine of impatience, which is met by a low and gravelly chuckle.

Adjusting himself, his kisses trail down my neck and across my chest until he takes my breast, his tongue teasing the nipple. Every nerve ending in my body is suddenly concentrated on wherever his mouth or hands are, and each touch is ecstasy.

His hand finally reaches between my legs, where he finds me wet and ready for him. I push eagerly against his hand, wanting more of him.

"I think someone might be eager for some fun," he growls into my ear, his breath hot. I reach out for him, but he's slid off the couch and is kneeling on the floor beside me. "Keep your eyes closed. Focus on my touch."

I do as he orders, but I want that touch even more now. He's driving me wild, but I can't reciprocate. I can only take what he's giving me.

All I can do is run my hands through his hair and give myself over to the sensation of his hands and lips on me, exploring and enticing with every move. He pushes my underwear aside, and his fingers find my center with a brief caress that makes my back arch and breath catch.

Jesus, if that's what one touch can do... Another whine or moan is about to erupt as the ache deep within me is becoming too much to bear, but I keep it to a desperate whisper, *"Oliver, please."*

"Are you ready, Bianca?" His voice is back in my ear, low, demanding, and so fucking hot it's almost enough to push me over the edge. I nod, unable to speak since I can't seem to catch my breath. "Good."

I'm dying to open my eyes, to see his expression as he says these things to me, but I keep them closed. Though, I am curious about what he would do if I opened them. Would I get punished somehow? Is he into that sort of thing? I'm not sure I want to find out right this second.

He slides a finger inside me and then another while his thumb expertly presses circles around my clit, and within seconds I am pulsating around him. Fire ripples through my veins as I throw my head back, again arching into his hand. This is the quickest and most intense orgasm I have ever had, and the aftershocks are still trembling through me.

Working his way up my chest and then my neck, his mouth eventually finds mine again once I've somewhat controlled my ragged breathing. As my fingers rake through his silky hair, the kiss hits differently than earlier ones. This one is gentle and sweet, but not in an innocent or naïve way. It's a kiss that assures things I don't think either of us can say out loud, or want to at this point. But we know. The two of us absolutely know.

Chapter 17

Cowards

Oliver

Fuck. That was the most sensual thing I've ever witnessed, let alone been a part of. The sight of Bianca climaxing under my touch and her whispering my name while in the throes of passion, begging for me, is now seared into my memory bank. I will be making withdrawals from that account regularly once I leave just to relive this moment. I want to remember how good it feels to hold her like I am now, her breathing still uneven from her orgasm, her fingers tracing lazy circles on my arm as she comes down.

"So, how's that for fun then?" I ask, maneuvering

to lie next to her again on the couch. While kneeling gave me a great vantage point and access, it didn't do much for the pins and needles pain in my leg. Sliding an arm around her, I pull her closer to me, the heat of her body a comfort against me.

She turns her face to me, trying to read my eyes, so I keep my expression as close to neutral as possible. I can't let my genuine emotions surface, and they are so close it's scary.

Since we first kissed in the parking lot, my control has been slipping minute by minute. That cannot happen. We're in this now, but I can only let myself go so far.

"Yeah...that was...fun." Tearing herself away, she sits up sharply, rearranging her clothing back to where everything belongs, and then stealthily rolls over me to get off the couch without us touching.

It's quite an acrobatic move, and my mind starts to wonder how that skill might prove useful in the future, but I force myself to focus. There's been a drastic shift in the mood here, and I need to keep up with what's happening.

"Bianca? What is it?" As I sit up, she's already halfway down the hall. "What's wrong?" I know for a fact that she just enjoyed herself, so I don't know where this new mood is coming from. It's like night and day.

"Nothing's wrong," she calls from what I think is her bedroom, though I can tell from her tone she's lying. How is it that I know her so well already that I can tell she's not telling the truth?

I wait to see if she's going to expound on that answer.

Silence.

Apparently not.

"Bianca." I'm not letting this go. Not after what just happened. I refuse to believe that she can switch off like this so easily. It makes everything feel cheap. Tawdry. While I don't want us to get too involved with each other, I also don't want us to be cold or uncaring. Maybe it's a finer line for her than I thought. I get off the couch and head down the hallway toward her bedroom. The door is closed, so I lean against it and talk through the painted wood. "Talk to me, please. It's obvious that something is bothering you. What is it?"

Silence again, though I do hear movement.

This will *not* do.

I reach down and open the door to find an empty room. For a second, my heart stops, thinking she's somehow magically left the apartment. That would be difficult to do from the eighth floor with no fire escape. Then I notice light flooding in from an attached bathroom.

As I approach, I catch Bianca wiping under her eyes with a tissue in the vanity mirror reflection, but I can't tell from where I'm standing if she's been crying or not. She's changed clothes and now wears a deep red sundress that looks magnificent. She's absolutely staggering.

"I'll just be a second." Her tone is subdued, and it's a giveaway that she *was* crying.

Before I can ask about it, a second door is closed on me, and I can't barge in this time. That would be rude.

What the hell has gotten into her? We've been having a great time. She, especially, had a great time. We didn't even address the issue of *my* having a good time or *not*, as the case may be. And I'm more than okay with that, but this makes no sense whatsoever.

I go to the kitchen to wait her out, opening the fridge primarily out of the need to have something to do, but after seeing her apartment, I am curious about what might be in it, if anything. I'm greeted with a bright light that bounces off the empty glass shelves except for a small carton of almond milk. There are two cans of Diet Coke and a half bottle of siracha sauce in the door. Definitely not the makings of a meal of any kind.

Glancing next to me, I note that the stove appears brand new. I would bet good money that it's never been used, regardless of how long Bianca has lived here.

"Are you ready to go?" She asks with a heavy sigh from behind me.

I turn and find an impatient woman, anxious to get something over with. Not a woman who just enjoyed a fantastic orgasm at the hand of the man in front of her who is also about to take her to dinner.

What am I expecting exactly? Applause? Thanks? A pat on the back? Congratulations? Of course not. But I would think some sort of acknowledgment would be forthcoming.

I shut the fridge door, and cross my arms, leaning back against the counter.

"No. I'm not."

Her head shoots up, shocked at my answer, her dark locks swaying with her movement. Eyes narrowing, she mirrors my stance and crosses her own arms, leaning against the door jamb.

Lifting a gorgeous eyebrow, she asks, "Why not?" She's still more perturbed than curious.

"Can't you guess?" I tilt my head, searching for a sign from her as to why she's acting this way. She is stone-cold and impossible to read.

Her arms drop to her sides, hands balled into tight fists. "I don't want to play games, Oliver. I just want to go to dinner."

The tether between us is vibrating. I can feel it rattling around in my chest. It's a mythical object of my own overactive imagination, yet I *literally* feel it pulling me toward her. I go with it, allowing the force of it to guide me to her.

She must feel it too because she stiffens as I approach but wraps her arms around herself as if trying to hold something in. Or maybe it's to keep something out, like me.

"I don't want to argue, Bianca," I say, reaching up to run a finger lightly along her jawline. Trying to see if her skin feels any different after I've kissed it. My mind tells me it's softer, but I know it's a trick. "I just want to know what is going on in that brilliant head of yours." I gently tap her temple, which gets a slight lip twitch from her. "You can talk to me."

Hesitantly, she glances up, only briefly meeting my eyes before stuttering, "I'm...I'm not sure I want to just have fun with you, Oliver." She shrinks away from my hand and takes a small step away.

No. No. No. Don't do this.

"You sure seemed like you were having fun a few minutes ago." She can't deny that much, and I need to salvage this. But I need to know exactly what the issue is, and she's not being clear. "What's changed in the last few minutes?"

"Nothing. Everything. I don't know." She brushes past me and starts pacing the length of the kitchen. Her floral perfume follows her and hypnotizes me.

"That's not helpful." I can't fix this if I don't know what is broken. I've been with my body the entire day and don't remember breaking anything. I would have remembered that much.

She stops short in the middle of the kitchen, hands now on her hips, and an accusatory glare sent in my direction, but behind the bravado is pain. Pain that I recognize because I feel it too. But she's about to put words to it, and I can't stop her, no matter how much I don't want to hear it.

"I can't just have fun with you, Oliver. I thought I could, but I can't." Her hands cover her face, hiding from me, and I'm thankful for it. I don't want to witness this. "It was great. Fantastic, actually. And then it wasn't. It was horrible. And cheap. It made me feel cheap. And very much not like me at all." The tears start, and I completely freeze. This is exactly the situation I wanted desperately to avoid.

I can hear it. I can actually hear my heart break. It starts with a slight cracking sound inside my head, then splinters into a million tiny shards. Each piece rends what's left of my soul into wasted shreds. After cutting almost everyone out of my life over the past year, there wasn't much left to begin with.

How can I do this to her? To myself? I'm about to reach for her but stop, remembering what has gotten us here in the first place. The tears she's crying now are nothing compared to what she would face if she stayed with me.

I need to keep her future in mind and what's best for her in the long run, even though it hurts like hell now. She can't see it, but I can. I need to be stronger, much stronger than I have been. What the fuck was I even thinking?

Oh, let's just have some fun. Nobody will get hurt. Bullshit. I should have known better.

"I'm sorry, Bianca." It's all I can say, and even that is a poor excuse for comfort. It does neither of us any good or make either of us feel better. But it's true. I am sorry that I've let us get to this. That I thought we could handle something only physical. That I hurt her this way.

And now I'm staring down an entire month of being around Bianca and not being able to touch her again or even be close to her. I don't think I can live with that, either. Not now that I've felt how incredible it is to be with her. If I think logically about it, I've really only got a little over three weeks left with her.

Surely, in that time, she'll realize on her own that a relationship with me wouldn't work. After all, I'll be leaving the damn country, and it doesn't sound like either of us is willing to expatriate. I could follow through with this and just let nature take its course. That way, neither of us is to blame, and no one will get hurt.

She's dropped her hands from her face and is looking at me expectantly, wanting me to have all the answers. If only I did. All I can give her honestly is a temporary fix.

"Bianca, this is more than fun for me, too," I say, taking a deep breath. I don't know if this is the right thing to do or not, but it's one I can live with. "Let's just see where this goes, okay? We don't need to have expectations put on each other or call it anything. It can just be what it's going to be."

And if it's nothing when I leave as it should be, then it's nothing.

Studying me warily, but with so much hope in her eyes, I want to scream, she steps over and kisses my cheek. And I instantly feel like the ugliest creature in the universe. I'll be breathing fire, knocking down buildings, and destroying Tokyo any minute now.

Shit. Even my internal jokes don't cheer me anymore, and those were my last line of defense.

I'm doomed. I'm fucking doomed. Actually, no, we *both* are.

Chapter 18

The Last Man on Earth

Bianca

After the rollercoaster of emotions I've been on the last few hours, it's nice to sit down to dinner and have a regular conversation. There's something about talking in public that puts guard rails around what we're talking about to keep us from going out of bounds or taking things too seriously. And while we're technically in public, we are also very private at the moment.

We've come to a Mischief client's restaurant, The Library, which looks like it could be an actual library located inside one of the Strip hotels. It helps to be friends with the chef, too, as we are given a private table hidden behind the bookshelves of the main restaurant. Typically, reservations are impossible to come by, but knowing people has its privileges. As Oliver pales at the prices on the menu, I assure him we won't be paying anything but gratuity. His publisher might truly hate him if we had to pay. That gets a sigh of relief from him and makes me chuckle.

Things between us have loosened up since our tense discussion at my apartment, and the mood has lightened too. He's barraging me with decoration ideas for my living room.

"How about a neon sign?" He smirks. "Isn't there even a neon graveyard or something here in Vegas? I'm sure you could find something there."

"It's called the Neon Boneyard and is an actual museum, I'll have you know." He acts as though I've put him in his place. Good. "It's not a store. Although you're right, there is a lot of neon here. That's a thing now, getting sayings made into a neon sign."

He rubs his chin thoughtfully. "Hmm. What kind of sign should you get? Let's think on it. How about something about your job, like 'Boss Lady,' or something ironically self-evident like 'Neon Sign.' It would go with your décor or the extreme minimalist theme you have going on."

"I think I liked the cat poster idea from earlier," I

laugh. Watching him brainstorm ideas is entertaining in itself.

"I've got it. The perfect neon sign for you, and I think even Ava will approve of it. *'Aunt B.'*" He draws his hand through the air between us, writing it out, then smiles, satisfied with himself and his suggestion. It is a good one.

"It is perfect. I love it. I'll order it first thing tomorrow. In pink, just for Ava."

He rests his elbows on the table and his chin on his folded hands, his smile turning melancholy.

I mirror his pose. "What is it? You look thoughtful." Our conversation has flowed so naturally, I'm surprised to see this downturn in him.

"It's nothing bad. On the contrary, it's great. Fantastic, even."

"Oh? Do tell." I bat my eyelashes demurely at him in encouragement, trying to lift his mood.

His brows knit together for a moment as he chooses his words. I can tell he's being careful, which raises my curiosity even more to find out what he's being so cautious about. He's typically pensive, but this amount of care is strange for him.

"You will be a great mother." He pauses, gauging my reaction, or lack thereof, since I'm so shocked, and hurries to expand on his thought. "If you want to be, that is. I don't know your plans for family or that sort of thing. I'm just saying, should you choose to be a mother, you will indeed be fantastic at it." His cheeks flame red as he talks. He must think he stepped on a conversational landmine because he's trying to dance around it like crazy.

I'm tempted to let him keep talking, just to see where he goes with it, but I decide to throw him a lifeline.

"Thank you," I say, but then I feel the need to go on like he did. "I think I would like children one day. If my circumstances ever reach that point."

"Circumstances?" He's curious but now seems even sadder than before. "What circumstances are those?"

"Oh, you know. The usual. Find the right partner. Feel financially steady enough to handle that sort of thing. Get all my ducks in a row."

"So, you're going to try out ducks first? See if you can handle that, are you?" His mouth twitches into a crooked smirk, but his gray eyes are still dark. The humor he's trying isn't reaching. He's deflecting, but who knows from what.

I cock my head at him, ignoring the attempt at deflection. "How about you? Do you want children?" It might be nice to know these things before I get too crazy about him. Although, I think that ship has already sailed.

The dark eyes go black, and his lopsided smile is gone too. A nerve has been struck, and it's an unexpected one. With how he interacts with Ava, I thought for sure he'd want kids. He's so good with them.

He clears his throat and starts spinning his water glass nervously. "No. I don't think kids are for me." He wrinkles his nose and shakes his head in distaste. "I don't mind other people's children, of course, for short periods. But they go home at the end with their parents, and I get peace and quiet. Just how I like it." The fake smile returns with a flash, and my heart instantly aches for him.

I'm not going to argue with him about something so important and personal. There's a reason why he's responding like this. I don't know what it is or could be, but that's for him to tell me in his own time. Maybe he had a lousy childhood and doesn't want to repeat that with his own children. I've heard of things like that. It hurts my heart for him, though, that he would limit himself like that.

"Well, for the record, after seeing you with Ava, I think you would be a wonderful father." I try to meet his eyes, to show that I mean it, but he's pulled farther into himself now. Maybe I shouldn't have said that. "I'm sorry, I didn't mean—"

"No. No. It's fine," he shakes himself out of it and takes my hand, squeezing it tightly. "Sorry, I just spaced out for a minute. That was kind of you to say. Thank you."

And that's it. That's the end of our discussion of future children. I'm not trying to plan our entire future, but that's a pretty big obstacle for us to overcome. And it's not something that can fix itself down the road. It's a fundamental philosophical difference between us and how we see our individual futures and our combined one, *if* there will be one. From the sound of things now, it doesn't look like there is going to be one for us.

My heart feels like it's in a vice, squeezed from two sides. One side is me wanting a family of my own someday, and the other is Oliver not wanting that. They are so diametrically opposed to each other that there is no overlap. No common ground. No compromise to be had on the subject. It's probably the singular thing that could come between us and a future together. Everything else could be negotiated somehow.

Maybe I need to reconsider my desire to have a family. Could I go without children if it meant I could spend my life with Oliver? I'm not so sure that I could.

Enzo pops into my head, and I think of our childhood together. It was great growing up in a large extended family like we did. I cherish that experience and want to continue that with my own family someday.

I think I would regret it if I turned my back on that potential future. Of course, there are no guarantees in life, and maybe children won't happen for me, but I can't *choose* that path now. Not until I've tried.

I swallow hard, trying to push down my extreme disappointment. "So, how is your book coming along?" I ask, changing the subject entirely. I'm going to need a minute to process this huge revelation. It looks like small talk is on the menu for the rest of the night.

This day has seen the highest of highs and the lowest of lows, all within a few hours. That's Vegas for you. Futures here can change in a heartbeat. And sometimes, that future is the *idea* of a heartbeat. I need to decide if it's something I want to gamble for.

The following week, our days are full of his various meetings and interviews with local law enforcement and city officials. I've taken to listening to audiobooks downloaded from the local library while I wait for him, and I have finished three entire books in five days. One of them was surprisingly spicy, and I had difficulty hiding my blush from the other people in the coffee shop. That got me some intriguing stares from Oliver while he worked.

By the end of each day, he's exhausted from working, and I'm too tired from waiting around and doing nothing to be of any use to anyone.

We have passionate good morning and good night kisses, but that's the extent of our physical interaction all week. However, we continue our connection via phone calls that go late into the night. We talk about anything, everything, and nothing at all, and each conversation solidifies my feelings toward him.

I do notice that he is extremely careful not to bring up any kind of future of our relationship, and there is no further discussion about children. I've not wanted to bring it up, either.

On Saturday, we go to Normandy and Brandon's house for a barbeque that is just a cover for Oliver, interviewing both of them for his book. Chelsie and her husband Noah are also here with their son Jett and new baby daughter Grace.

Little Ava is in heaven, fawning over her new cousin. She is definitely going to be a protective force for her as they grow up. I love watching this family expand and grow right before my eyes.

"She is precious," Oliver agrees wistfully, looking over my shoulder at the baby and letting her grab his pinky with her strong little hands. He brushes his lips against my temple and whispers so only I can hear, "You look good holding a baby. It suits you." I can't see his face, but I swear he sounds hopeful from his tone, and something deep within me ignites.

Is he changing his mind about children? Would he ever consider it?

The idea makes me smile, but I don't say anything in response. I don't want to burst my own bubble as I cling to the small hope that maybe things are changing, and possibilities are presenting themselves to Oliver that he's actually thinking about. I'm okay living with this little dream for a while until it gets burst by Oliver himself.

Between his stealthy meetings with Normandy and Brandon, we find each other and seek a secluded location to make out like teenagers. A bathroom, the kitchen pantry, the laundry room, and at one point, we're almost discovered in a side office as Brandon is searching for Ava. We all do pretty good at acting as though nothing was happening, but it was apparent. We all knew.

The hands-all-over-each-other thing is becoming a problem for both of us, and after we eat, and it looks as though things are winding down, we're quick to make our goodbyes and leave for Oliver's hotel. I play loose with the speed limit on the way because I cannot wait to be alone with him once and for all.

It's been building up all week, and we've only made this hunger worse all day. It's no longer a want. It's a need. A desperate need. One I've never felt for anyone else before, and one I can't deny. I don't want to deny it. I want to give in to it completely.

I pull up to the valet where Connor is working, and he gives me a sly wink as I hand him my keys. Oliver takes my hand and leads me inside, and it takes everything I have to not run to the elevators and smash the button to his floor to get there already. Spending the day like this with him, and seeing him in such a relaxed, family environment, where he fits in so easily, has done something to me.

This entire week and a half with him has done something to me. It's shown me a future I could possibly have. It's shown me how fantastic and wonderful it could be. My fear now is that it's a future only I see. Or, even worse, one that only I *want* to see.

As the elevator slowly takes us up to his floor, that fear deepens. My excitement and adrenaline are amping up my anxiety, which in turn makes my fear become dread. My palms start to sweat, and my heart begins to beat harder against its cage.

I've never wanted something or someone so much in my life, and the dread racing at lightning speed through my veins that I'm going to lose all of it is overtaking me. It's irrational and insane, but it's there.

Somehow, I just know that all of this is only temporary, so I need to either enjoy it while I can and put off the hurt until later, or rip off the bandage now and still hurt just as bad.

It's a no-brainer. I need to enjoy this while I can.

Chapter 19

Like A Drug

Oliver

Today has been a rollercoaster. From being around exuberant children all day, and seeing Bianca holding Grace, which pulled on my heart so hard I almost lost it, to talking with Normandy and Brandon each about their experience with the Calnetta crime family and Normandy's kidnapping and shooting. It's left me wrung out like a used dishrag. And then there's been the stolen moments with Bianca, driving me absolutely bonkers with desire for her. I'm having difficulty staying polite as we enter my hotel room.

I know what's coming. At least, I hope I do.

We've been building up all week to this, and our actions today at the barbeque made it even more apparent that we need to have each other once and for all.

However, there is something that's been stuck in the back of my mind all day since interviewing Brandon. There was about an hour during the kidnapping ordeal when he was all the way across the country in New York that he thought Normandy was dead. He had witnessed her being shot on a video call and assumed the worst. He blamed himself and was inconsolable until he was told she was only wounded and still alive.

The nightmares still haunt him to this day, even though they've not only gotten through it but married and have beautiful Ava together. He remarked that he doesn't take a single day for granted. Even with all his wealth, he couldn't buy her freedom or save her life when he needed to. Every day he gets with her is a gift he doesn't feel worthy of and appreciates with all of his being.

I could see it, too, in how they were with each other. I don't know how else to describe it, but they were *careful* with each other. I've never seen anything like it, and it makes me yearn deep down for something similar. Even though I know it's stupid to wish for things I can't have, I can't help myself.

You can't be around that type of relationship and not come away affected by it somehow. It's impossible. I need to remind myself that love like that isn't going to happen for me. Not in this lifetime. That's been stolen from me.

"What are you thinking about?" Bianca asks, pulling me out of my internal thoughts. She kicks off her sandals and pads over to me by the window, looking over the bright lights of the Vegas Strip. It's a Saturday night, so the heavy traffic adds to the cacophony of colors to take in.

As she wraps her arms around my waist, I debate what to tell her. Do I share Brandon's admissions? Do I even put that part in my book? I don't think so. That was a man-to-man discussion, off the record. I wouldn't ever divulge a confidence given to me.

"I'm just coming down from all the excitement of the day. It was non-stop since we got to the Carmichael's this morning, don't you agree?" I pull her arms tighter around me, enjoying the warmth of her body against my back. I could so easily get used to this with her. I feel like I already have.

It's a dangerous feeling.

"It was. The kids sure got a kick out of the newcomer to the fold."

"Grace? Well, that's to be expected with a new sibling in the mix. I think Ava will be happy to keep her under her wing. Although, Jett didn't seem too keen at the loss of attention."

We start to sway a little, our bodies in tune with each other.

"I meant you, silly," she laughs, giving me a slight squeeze. "You fit right in. Especially with the kids."

My body tenses, and I stop swaying. I can feel my fight or flight response kicking in, and I try my best to push it down, but Bianca feels it. Of course, she does.

She unwraps her arms from my waist and pulls me to turn and look at her.

"What's wrong? Did I say something?" Confusion clouds her face as she backtracks her words.

"No. No. It's nothing." I wave a dismissive hand, wanting to move on from this. Any more talk of children is going to push me over the edge. I'm fatigued from being on the go all day and feel a little out of it.

"I didn't mean anything by it. You're just so good with them. Ava especially adores—"

"Stop it, Bianca."

Her eyes snap to mine at the cold tone in my voice. Her confusion now mixes with hurt, and I hate this so much. I fucking hate this. I know in my gut where this is going, but I can't stop it.

For the life of me, I can't stop it.

"I don't understand." She shakes her head, dark eyes now brimming with unshed tears. "I was just trying to say that the kids—"

My hands fly to my ears, trying to shield them from hearing more about how much the children love me, how much fun we had, and how great I am with them.

Blah. Blah. Blah.

A headrush hits me at full force, and I feel like I'm going to be sick.

"Please. Just. Stop." I turn away from her, not wanting to see her pain or show her mine. I don't want to hurt her like this.

It's too much. This is all too much.

"Oliver, why are you so upset?" She lays a hand gently on my back, and it feels like a branding iron searing through my flesh. Every sensation is overloading; sight, sound, touch, and emotion. *Especially* emotion. I flinch away from her without even thinking, anxious to get out of her reach. "What did I—"

Something inside me breaks under this constant pressure. The stoicism and restraint I have maintained for the past year come apart.

I whirl on her, forcing her to take a step away from me.

"I have MS. Multiple Sclerosis, alright?" I snap. The bitter words pour out of me without thought, and they come out with all the rage and hurt accompanying them. These feelings have been bottled up and fermenting for a year, and their taste is like acid in my mouth as I spat them out. "I will not be having children. Regardless of how *'good I am with them,'* or how much I would ever want them.

That no longer matters." I take a step toward her, and she shrinks from me and my jagged words, her eyes wide, and I hate that too. I hate myself for doing this. For doing this to her. "I will not be having relationships either. But I've already told you that. Regardless of how much I care for someone, I absolutely refuse to be a burden on anyone. I will not drag anybody down with me on this descent into hell that my life has become. Especially someone I love."

"But—" She stands straighter, setting her shoulders and lifting her chin to face me, but I'm not done. She needs to understand how genuinely hopeless this all is.

"Do you see this, Bianca?" I point to the scrapes still marring my forehead, but I don't wait for a response. I see her gaze flash briefly up, then back to my eyes. I at least have her full attention. "This is fucking nothing. This is just from my lower leg and foot growing heavy while walking on a flat god-damned surface. That was days ago, and I *still* can't feel the front of my calf, even after being pumped full of steroids. Did you know that before I even came here, I ended up in hospital with a sprained ankle and was laid up for weeks after missing one step in front of my flat? *One step*. Imagine what would happen if I missed two or three."

"Oliver—"

"I'm not done." Her mouth clamps shut, but she defiantly crosses her arms over her chest. "I already know what you're going to say because I've heard it all. I've heard it from my doctors, agent, and family, but you know what? None of you are me. None of you know what this is like for *me*. You don't have the slightest clue what I'm losing day by day of myself. And what I've already lost because I *choose*, now hear that word clearly, I *choose* to go this alone without burdening a single soul but my own. You can't possibly know what this is like. So would you please, I beg you, *please* stop talking about children?"

I'm shaking. My hands are in my hair, grabbing it in fistfuls, and I tilt slightly with dizziness. Suddenly, I feel weak all over, as if releasing these pent-up emotions has left me physically empty.

Bianca moves quickly to guide me to sit on the edge of the bed, and the next thing I know, my head is on her shoulder, and I'm wrapped in her arms. Her fingers slowly comb through my hair as she kisses my forehead gently.

She doesn't say a word and just holds me until the shaking subsides, and my breathing returns to normal. The sensation of her arms around me is so soothing it makes me feel even worse for the outburst I just displayed.

She didn't deserve any of that rage.

"I'm sorry," I say. I mean it, but I feel completely hollowed out.

Every bit of self-loathing that kept me together has been scattered in my explosion, leaving me bereft. I don't know what to do with myself now that I've exposed my raw nerves to the open air like this.

The pain of what I've just done hasn't even begun, and regret doesn't begin to cover what I'm feeling toward Bianca. She should be running away right now, not holding me together. I don't deserve this kindness. I just exposed to her my darkest side, a side that nobody has seen, not even Darcie, and she's still here.

I sit up and look at her, trying to read what she might feel after all this. Surprisingly, I don't see judgment, anger, or any negative emotion I thought I would find. What I do see is hurt. A *lot* of hurt. Of course, I've hurt her. How could any of that not?

Wasn't that oddly my goal? To hurt and push her away? I've got the inflicting pain part down pat, but why on earth isn't she running away?

Chapter 20

The Way Down

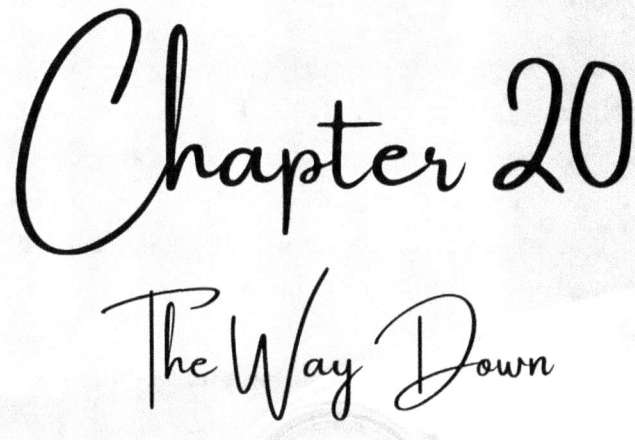

Bianca

There it is. The reason why Oliver has been so hard to read this whole time. Multiple Sclerosis? I don't know a damned thing about it, but I sure as hell am going to learn everything I can. I don't think it's a fatal disease, but I know absolutely nothing about it.

What I do know is that Oliver is in pain, and I will do whatever it takes to help him through it. Yes, his words hurt me, but I will survive. I need to make sure he does too.

My heart is breaking for this man, looking at me as if he is so lost he'll never find his way again. He must be dealing with so much and doing so on his own. It's not fair. Nobody should have to go through something like this alone.

Yes, he says he chose this path, but it's got to be out of some sort of self-punishment, not out of reason. And as I think about it, it's a very self-centered thing to do.

"Well, I think you're being pretty god-damned selfish about the whole thing." I let go of him and stand up, my bare feet moving soundlessly as I start to pace.

His head jerks up at me, shocked.

"Excuse me?" He's incredulous that I would take this sort of stance with him. I admit I'm a little surprised myself.

I stop in front of him, hands on my hips.

"You say you *chose* to face this alone, but do you know what that does?"

He shakes his head, dumbfounded.

"That takes away *my* choice to stay or go. I no longer have any options. Because big, brave, Oliver wants to do everything by himself. Well, gee, thanks for that. Thank God I don't have to make that big, brave decision. I don't think my tiny little brain, or better yet, my tiny little heart, could handle something so fucking important."

My ire is building steam as I talk. It's my turn to let loose.

"Bianca—"

"No. You had your say, and now I get to have mine." His mouth drops open, but I go on. "All this time, and you didn't even give me the courtesy of a 'hey, by the way, I've got this going on,' or, I don't know, maybe educating me about it. You automatically assume I know anything about MS? Whatever gave you that idea? And instead of teaching me about it, you hold it against me that I don't know what you're going through? How could I possibly know if you never told me you were going through anything?"

"I wanted to try to—"

"Uh uh. Nope. My turn, remember?" I shake a finger at him as my angry tears start to flow. I hate that I cry when I'm mad. It makes me feel weak. I wipe my damp face with the back of my hand and sniffle loudly. I don't care. "You are not being fair, Oliver. Not only in taking my choices away from me, but you're holding your choice against me. I don't know the first thing about MS, but I see your anger, and it makes me just as angry. You probably have every right to be pissed off at the world. I see your utter despair about having children, and again, not knowing anything about it, it hurts me *for* you because I know you would be an amazing father."

His head falls into his hands. "Bianca..."

I drop to my knees in front of him and pry his hands away from his face, forcing him to look at me. Every single cell in my body wants to take him in my arms and protect him from anything that would try to harm him. He wouldn't want that either, though.

What I can settle for is being here for him, being by his side as he navigates his uncertain future. I refuse to let him face this alone.

"Let's compromise." I brush the hair off his forehead, exposing his scrapes and bruises, and my heart clenches. I need to be careful not to show pity. Not only because I don't pity him but because that is the last thing Oliver would want. I know this about him already. "How about I learn what I can about Multiple Sclerosis, and then I get to decide whether or not it's something I can handle as a partner?"

He searches my eyes intently, probably looking for it being a trick or a ruse of some kind. He's not going to find anything like that in my gaze. The only things I'm feeling right now are sadness and determination. I can't get more honest with him than that.

After a minute, he nods.

"Okay." His emotions are still raw, and he seems unsure and vulnerable. The exhaustion on his face is evidence enough that this has wiped him out. Now I need to do whatever I can to let him know that I'm here for him.

I lean down, untie his right shoe, and gently slide it off his foot. I repeat the same with the left. He had indicated his right leg when talking about it being a problem, so I tentatively roll up his jeans to the knee and start gently massaging his leg and foot. When I glance at him briefly to ensure I'm not doing something wrong, I can't read him at all, so I continue. If he wanted me to stop, I think he would say something.

After a while, when I look up at him, his eyes are half-closed. He has been through the wringer and is done. I roll his pant leg down and climb into the middle of the bed. He shifts, lays back, and places his head on my chest, his arms wrapping my waist tightly.

We don't say a word, and I play with his hair and watch him drift off slowly to sleep. He fights it but eventually gives in with a deep sigh.

As I watch him sleep, I replay everything we both said to each other tonight. Every single word. I want to make sure I understand him completely before I go trying to swoop in and save the day. That isn't something he wants, and it's not something I would want to do either.

This is his issue. Absolutely. But if I'm in his life, it's my issue too. I really need to learn everything I can about it. It's the only way to make an informed decision.

Am I doing the right thing here? Or should I have left it alone? Left him alone like he said he wanted to be? Why didn't I believe him about that? So many questions rush at me as I watch him sleep. Too many to answer in one night.

When I awake the following morning, it's confusing for a second since this hotel room is still foreign to me. Also, it's just me in the bed with a blanket over me that I don't remember grabbing. I don't see Oliver anywhere, and I don't hear him either.

Panicking for a minute, I glance around to make sure his things are still here, and he didn't just get up and leave in the middle of the night. Luckily, I see his computer bag by the table, so I know he's still here somewhere.

I slide off the bed and go into the bathroom. The bright lights make plain the events of last night on my face, as my mascara has left dark shadows under my eyes. I look around for a washcloth to clean up and can't help but notice a clear bag full of pill bottles. I'm drawn to it by curiosity and pick it up gingerly, careful not to mess up the arrangement of the contents in case they're placed in some kind of order.

Counting them as I read their labels, I note there are eleven total, but not all are for every day. I put the bag back on the counter and stare at myself in the mirror. Last night was pretty heavy, and I'm not sure everything has completely sunk in yet.

Is this something I want to get involved with? It seems as though Oliver would give me an out if I wanted to take it. He's said he wants to face it alone, and whether I believe him or not, shouldn't I respect his wishes? Am I forcing myself into his life?

I take a deep breath. I haven't agreed to anything other than learning about the disease. I can't make an informed decision until I know more about it. So, how do I go about this? The internet? Oliver himself? Do I know any doctors? Does anyone I know have MS, or someone in their family?

I'm lost in thought when Oliver steps behind me in the mirror, scaring the shit out of me and making me jump. I didn't hear him come back into the room I was so lost in thought.

His brow furrows as he watches me. "Are you okay?"

Running the washcloth under the faucet and then wiping under my eyes as if nothing happened, I shrug. "Yeah, you just startled me. I'm not a hundred percent awake yet without coffee."

"Ah, well, I can remedy that. I've brought us breakfast."

"Great," I smile at his reflection. "I'll be right there."

Suddenly I'm nervous, and I don't know why. Nothing has changed since last night except the sun rising, so I shouldn't feel this way. I haven't changed my mind about anything either, so that's not it.

Maybe I'm concerned that Oliver has changed his mind and will stick to his guns about going it alone. That would be devastating. But then, would he bring us breakfast if he was going solo? I don't think so, but who knows where his head is? I sure don't.

Well then, find out.

Chapter 21

Ready For Something

Oliver

I did not anticipate any of this. Not telling Bianca about my MS, and certainly not her standing up to me the way she did last night. I still don't know what to make of it all. While I am somewhat relieved to have everything off my chest and out in the open, I feel like I'm waiting for the other penny to drop.

Bianca's reaction was above and beyond anything I could have hoped for, and I don't trust it because of that alone. Finding her in the bathroom a little while ago, completely lost in thought, only adds to my mistrust of the situation.

If she came to me now and told me she was done; she's decided that it's too much for her to handle, I would completely understand and wouldn't blame her for one second. It would hurt like a bastard, but it would make sense.

If I were in her shoes, I don't know that I wouldn't run for the hills at the earliest opportunity. Especially since it's such an unknown.

Her vow to learn about my disease to make an informed decision has only increased my respect for her tenfold. But my guard is still raised. I do not want pity of any sort, regardless of how it goes with her, and so far, thank God, she's not done that.

She's staring at the tray of breakfast items, debating within herself on what to eat.

"You know you can have whatever you want. You don't need to pick just one thing." I chuckle and stand next to her, debating my own choice.

All of the pastries look delicious, and my stomach grumbles loudly. She glances up at me, and we both burst into laughter. Leave it to my empty stomach to break the ice between us.

"Well, you better pick first, obviously." She gives me a smile that melts my insides. It's the smile from the airport. The one that told me in that first instant that I was a goner. "It sounds like we wouldn't want your stomach to get any angrier."

We take our time and eat our breakfast leisurely.

Neither of us has plans for the rest of the day, so it's nice to go at a slow pace for once instead of rushing from interview to interview like we typically have been doing. I do have to cram a lot into my schedule in one month. I'm lucky to have most of the weekends free like this.

"I should take you to Tahoe with me next weekend. I think you'd like it," she says to me over her coffee mug, a thoughtful expression in her eyes. It feels like a special invitation that isn't often handed out.

I arch a brow at her, curious. "Why do you think I would like it?"

She tilts her head, considering. "Well, it's peaceful, for one thing. And it's beautiful. These desert sunsets are great and all, but there's nothing like watching a sunset from a boat in the middle of a lake."

Her entire body relaxes as she pictures this in her mind, and I instantly want to be there with her to experience it. If it makes her react like this with a memory, I want to feel the real thing firsthand.

"Well, then, I would love to see that with you." I like that we're making plans, but it makes me wonder about my time left here. I will eventually need to go back home to write this book I'm diligently working on. I have a strict deadline with my publisher, and Darcie has warned me that there will be no further extensions of time. Almost two weeks have already passed, and I only have two left. I need to make the most of them. It hits me then what she said. "Wait. You have a boat too?" I'm starting to wonder if perhaps Bianca has money like the Carmichaels. It sure sounds like it.

She smirks at me as if she knows what I'm thinking. "It's an old power boat that my grandfather used to use for fishing, but yes, there is a boat."

This short jaunt sounds better and better. I guess I'm game for all kinds of new adventures now. So much has changed in the last 24 hours that it's hard to keep track of all the new possibilities.

"You should definitely see the Grand Canyon while you're here, too," she announces matter-of-factly as she rips off a piece of croissant and pops it into her mouth.

"Oh?" I kind of love that she's taken over my itinerary for me. All I had planned for my days off was going through my notes. These destination explorations sound a lot more fun than that. It begs the question, though, and I dare to broach the subject but keep it cheeky. "I can think of ways to spend time that doesn't involve any travel...."

That gets me a piece of croissant thrown directly at my face. She has good aim, perhaps from growing up with an older brother. I also got a laugh from her, so I didn't miss the mark by too much. Even I don't know how serious I was.

The week both flies by and drags at the same time. It's an anomaly of physics that would stump the most learned horologist. We agreed that Bianca would take this time to learn what she can about MS on her own and will bring any questions with her this weekend. So, I'm preparing myself for the onslaught waiting for me in Lake Tahoe. I am curious about what she's learned and where from. It should be an interesting weekend.

We take the short hour-and-a-half flight from Vegas to the Reno airport and then drive about another hour to reach the house on the north edge of the lake. It's dark when we arrive, and the place is secluded, so I'm unable to see much of the architecture as we pull up. It appears to be a normal-sized house with a modest two-car garage.

However, when we step inside, all comparisons to the word 'normal' go right out the window. The home is gorgeous. We enter through a small walkway into a large kitchen that opens to a dining area and a great room with tall cathedral ceilings and a wall of windows. There is a panoramic view of the lake beyond, but with the darkness outside, I can only see vague outlines of the horizon in the dim moonlight. A comfortable-looking sectional sofa faces the windows, and a wood stove is in the corner.

The minimalist décor here has a different feel than Bianca's near-empty flat. Here it's intentional and fits the large space, shifting the focus to its grand architecture and not the lack of furniture.

"Bianca, this is impressive. If I might ask, why don't you make this your permanent home?" I drop my overnight bag and turn in a circle in the middle of the great room.

"And do what, exactly?" She drops her own bag but watches me from the kitchen. "There's not really a lot for me to do here. Plus, I like my job."

"The writing I could do here...." I say, picturing myself tapping away at my laptop while enjoying the view, a steaming mug of tea at the ready, not a care in the world, and able to live in peace and solitude. It's a writer's dream retreat. "So, can I ask why you have this home if it's only for the weekends? Do you rent it out during the week or something?" The investigator in me is dying to know the answer to this. I've always been too curious for my own good. At least, that's what my mother always told me.

"It's actually a family home. It was our grandparent's first and then has been passed down to Enzo and me. My grandfather used to tell us that Frank Sinatra lived next door when he first built this house and would have huge parties with A-list Hollywood actors coming here for the weekend."

She kicks her shoes off and opens the fridge, pulling out a bottle of wine. I've noticed that she likes to be barefoot as much as possible, and it's one of those idiosyncrasies that makes her Bianca. I love that she is comfortable enough around me to let her hair down, both literally and figuratively.

"That sounds like a whole book in itself."

"Oh, the stories we would hear. My grandfather was a contractor and built a lot of the homes along the north shore during the first building boom in the late 1950s. That's how we got this house. My grandfather actually helped to build this with his own hands. It's been updated over the years, but the bones are his." She gets a dreamy, faraway look in her eyes as she talks about her family. They obviously mean a lot to her. "Do you want some wine?"

"No, thank you."

She eyes me curiously for a moment. "You don't drink, do you?"

"I do not." I shake my head, trying to hide my disappointment. I would love nothing more than to have a glass of wine with her right now.

"Is that an MS thing?"

"For me, it is, yes."

"Do you mind moving to the question portion of the weekend? I'd like to get it over with."

She pours me a glass of water, and a glass of wine for herself, and brings them to the great room, making herself comfortable on the sofa. I sit next to her but don't make myself as comfortable.

I feel the need to brace myself for the oncoming

questions. I'm still new to this whole 'being open' about everything wrong with me.

I exhale a deep breath. "Have at it."

Chapter 22

Gold

Bianca

I want to be careful with Oliver. I don't want this to become a third-degree interview. He's told me he has the relapsing-remitting type of MS and to research that this week. It turns out that my friend, who is the chef at The Library where we ate recently, also has that type of MS, so I was able to pick her brain throughout the week pretty extensively. That being said, she did warn me that everyone's experience with MS is different, and men especially can have more severe symptoms.

I grab Oliver's hand and squeeze it slightly

because I can tell he's nervous. I don't want to make this more challenging for him than it needs to be.

"Relax, Oliver," I say, trying to reassure him that everything will be fine no matter what happens.

"I'm relaxed," he mumbles. And I can't help but laugh because he is far from relaxed.

"Oh, ok then. Alright, I'm diving in. Prepare yourself." He makes to square his shoulders and straightens his back in response. "But first, give me a safe word."

He cocks his head at me. "A safe word? As in..."

"As in, the conversation has gone far enough, and you just don't want to talk about it anymore."

He stares at me for a minute, and I can't read him at all. Then, his mouth quirks into a smile. "You're amazing."

"Is that your safe word?" I smile back. It would be kind of cool if it is.

"Sure," he shrugs a shoulder, and the smile grows. I like how this is starting.

"Alright. First question, when were you diagnosed, and what were your initial symptoms?"

"A year ago, my right foot had pins and needles that weren't going away."

Okay. Good start. But now, it's going to get harder.

"You've said you can't or won't have children because of your MS, yet it's not hereditary, so why do you feel that way?"

He shifts a little, the question obviously hitting a sore nerve.

"It's not hereditary in a strict sense, but the risk increases quite a bit with a parent with it. Plus, there are other things that I think about, like holding a baby. You may have noticed that I didn't hold baby Grace last weekend. I couldn't take the chance that my arm wouldn't suddenly go numb, and I'd drop her. That would be disastrous. Who knows how this will progress and what participation I could safely have with a child? I don't want to take that risk. I wouldn't want to harm my own child."

My heart lurches as he talks, and I can see the pain it causes him to share these thoughts.

"Has that happened? Your arms suddenly going numb out of nowhere? Or are there signs beforehand?"

"No, it hasn't. But I don't want to risk it either." And the defensiveness has started.

Not what I wanted to happen.

I just nod my understanding. He's made choices for his life that, after my research, make sense but, at the same time, are very extreme. It's going to be difficult to express that idea to him without making him defensive.

I take a sip of my wine, giving us a second to recuperate. We have all night for this if we need it.

"I haven't come by these life choices easily, Bianca. Or quickly." He obviously read my thoughts, and runs his hands through his scruff, trying to calm himself. "You have to understand, I grieve every day for the person I was going to be without MS. I'm not suggesting it's healthy, but it's hard not to. When I say this is as good as it gets, I *literally* mean it. I will not be better than this."

His pain at this admission is undeniable, and I just want to hold him and never let go. That he's chosen to go through all of this alone is unfathomable. I'm surprised he's not in worse shape, actually.

"You doing okay?" I ask softly after a pause, wanting to make sure he's still willing to submit himself to my questioning.

He takes a deep breath, exhales it loudly, and nods. Bracing himself for whatever is next.

"Yes. I'm fine. Go on."

"So, extremely awkward question now." I can feel my blush spread on my cheeks, which gets him to arch a brow in interest. *Crap.* "I noticed you were able to get...excited. Is that a problem for you?"

The arched brow transforms briefly into a wicked grin that could set my underwear on fire, but then morphs into a scowl.

"It's not...yet. But it most likely will be...eventually." His face reddens, and his voice trails off. He looks away quickly, embarrassed.

I had thought that would be his answer since

that's what I'd read. Though everything is so individualized, I need to ask these things. These issues appear to be the most important ones to him and what he has based his whole life philosophy on since his diagnosis.

"So, what exactly was your plan? Just waste away by yourself and never know love?"

That question surprises him, and he studies me for a minute before answering.

"You make it sound awful, but yes. That is, was my plan. I don't know how past tense it is yet."

That surprises me now. Is he still unsure about me? Uncertain of how I'll respond to all of this?

"We've made it to my last question." There is enough information available to me or anyone else who wants to know it out there. I just wanted to know his experience and what is forming his thought processes now.

His shoulders relax slightly, and he nods. "Go for it."

"Do you still not want me in your life?"

His eyes close, and his head falls back to the top of the couch. This time he squeezes my fingers to the point that I might lose feeling in them shortly.

"It was never a matter of want, Bianca."

He turns his head to me, opening his eyes slowly. They are the saddest eyes I've ever seen. And it's not just sadness. It's regret.

I feel it, then. The weird tether between us that seems to stretch and pull at different times starts to hum, vibrating deep inside me. The regret in his gaze must be for the time we've wasted figuring this out.

Leaning over, I place my wine glass on the coffee table, then slide my leg over him, straddling him beneath me. It's not a sexual move, but I'm just putting myself front and center as close as possible.

I take both hands and capture his face under my fingers, feeling his warm skin against mine, savoring it. His steel gray eyes meet mine, and there's an unasked question lingering there.

"I'm in," I say, as sure as anyone can be in anything. "I'm in if you'll have me. You don't scare me, Oliver Bellamy." I brush my lips gently against his, sealing my vow.

I've given it a lot of thought during the week as I researched everything. I debated whether I wanted to get involved with someone with MS, and the answer is yes, I do. If that someone is Oliver, I absolutely do. Whatever hardship may come to us, I firmly believe that if we face it together, we can overcome any obstacles thrown at us. We have that kind of power together.

The corner of his mouth twitches up again, his smile crooked and perfect.

"But I tried so hard."

"Yeah, well, you'll have to try a lot...harder."

And that's precisely when it turns sexual, as I

grind myself against him, feeling his body respond underneath me. There are many more questions to be answered between us, but for now, we need to let our story play out however it will.

Memories of us together on the couch in my apartment flash in my head as we kiss. His hands were fire on me and inside me. It was beyond incredible, and I want to return that favor. I want to make him feel as sexy and wanted as he made me feel that night.

I scoot back on his lap and undo the button and zipper of his jeans. Then I slowly slide off, kneeling on the floor in front of him and taking his jeans and boxers with me as I go. I finally see the thick erection I've caused, and it's glorious. I glance up at him to make sure he's okay with what I'm doing, and his eyes are trained on me, lids heavy and full of desire.

As I take him in my hand, the skin silky beneath my fingers, I caress the tip of his shaft, teasing what's to come. His eyes close, and a rough groan escapes him, his back arching as I stroke him gently. The sound of his pleasure at this slight touch reverberates through me, down to my core.

I'm anxious to taste him, and as I take him in my mouth, his hands are instantly in my hair, not restraining or guiding, just feeling. The saltiness of his skin compliments the lingering taste of wine still on my tongue as I lick and swirl around him. I take him in as deep as I can, gliding into a long suck while my tongue flicks his most sensitive areas, and he grabs at my hair in fists.

"Fuuuuck, Bianca," he growls. I glance up, and he's watching me intently. I meet his eyes, never stopping my stroking and sucking while savoring the taste of him. He's having difficulty restraining himself, and I feel a low tremor start to roll through him, so I know he's close. "You're amazing," he pulls gently on my hair, lifting me off him. "But I want to be inside you."

"I can arrange that," I purr, keeping my hand on him, stroking deliberately.

"My bag. There are condoms in my bag." His voice is ragged, and his breath hitches as he speaks.

The smile that takes me over at the thought of him preparing for this weekend like this turns into a giggle as I grab his overnight bag and put it on the couch next to him. I slide my underwear off underneath my sundress and go back stroking him while he finds the condoms and pulls one out. To his surprise, I take it from him and roll it on his steel length smoothly.

His head falls back again as I climb into his lap and carefully lower myself onto him, taking a second to enjoy the fullness of him inside of me. His hands reach around and under my dress, grabbing my ass and squeezing me, lifting and releasing me steadily.

I arch my back and roll my hips as we move together, each movement building a tension low in my belly and rapidly increasing in intensity. If we keep this up, I will come very soon. I almost don't want to because this building anticipation feels so good.

We both open our eyes and gaze at each other, watching the other as the sensations between us steadily grow into bliss. It hits me first, and I can't help crying out as I come more intensely than I ever have before. My entire body shakes with the pleasure rushing through me, radiating from my center to every other nerve ending. The pulsating orgasm around him as he fills me completely is deepened as I see him watching me, enjoying my pleasure.

The aftershocks are still rolling through me as he reaches his peak, and I rock my hips harder, hungrily taking him in as far as he can go. His hips jerk to meet mine as he strains to contain himself. His hands slide up my back, and he pulls me to him, burying his face between my breasts, breathing deeply but unsteadily as he shudders inside me.

This position feels so natural, our arms wrapped around each other desperately, while he fits inside of me so perfectly. It's so good I don't want to move for fear of breaking the spell between us. Destroying the magic that seems to be elevating us to another level in our relationship.

It's almost too perfect if there is such a thing. Making this feel like a house of cards, delicate and fragile. I don't want to believe we're so precarious. I want to think that we're strong, building a solid foundation, and things like this only reinforce that.

That's what I want to think. Whether I do or not is another question.

Chapter 23

Never Wanna Leave

Oliver

In the light of day, everything is different between us. It's as though we've burnt a bridge, but not between us, behind us. Everything that was holding us back from being with each other is now dead and buried. Or so I thought.

As I watch Bianca sleep next to me, her face calm and peaceful, the sun streams through the sheer curtains behind her, causing a halo to appear around her if I squint my eyes just right. It suits her. I sit up carefully and rest on an elbow, looking down at her sleeping soundly, a small smile playing on her lips as she dreams. I'd like to think she's dreaming of me, but I'm sure that's wishful thinking.

We spent the night discovering each other, our sexual likes and dislikes, and otherwise. Between our explorations, we had some of the most profound conversations I think I've ever had with another human being. We discussed everything from A to Zed, including our mutual dislike of airports to our secret love of old zombie movies. Our philosophies on religion aren't too different to be a source of contention between us, and our taste in music overlaps enough to always find common ground. We also agree that goth and emo trends will most likely make a comeback sooner rather than later, whether we like it or not, as teenagers will always need an outlet for their angst.

I sweep her dark hair off her neck and shoulder, careful not to wake her. As inviting as her bare shoulder is, I don't want to wake her. She's earned her rest.

My body has been having difficulty adjusting to the new time zone, and I am still awake in London time whether I'm still tired or not. It's annoying most days, but today I'm enjoying having the time to study Bianca while she sleeps.

I have to push away my dire thoughts of my impending departure. My heart tells me to enjoy this time with her while I have it, and my head warns me that any time I enjoy, I'll equally regret when I leave. There is no getting out of this without pain.

We danced around it last night with our discussions, but there is a definite storm cloud hanging over us, ready to release the deluge of heartache that is inevitable when I return to London. There is no getting around it. This will have to end eventually, even though the two of us are pretending that's not going to happen for some reason.

It's as though we're both living in the same fantasy world, know full well that we are, and are too stubborn to admit what it is to each other, let alone ourselves. It's bordering ridiculous.

A noise downstairs grabs my attention. It sounded like a door shutting. I freeze and hold my breath, waiting for another sound, but I don't hear anything. I slide silently out of bed and into my sleep pants, looking for a weapon of any kind, but finding nothing. The minimalist décor now a clear disadvantage when there's a possible intruder downstairs.

I grab the only thing I can under the circumstances, one of my shoes, and pad quietly to the landing overlooking the great room below. I still don't see anyone, but I have that intangible feeling you get when you know someone is around but out of sight.

I know someone else is in the house. I just know it.

Descending the stairs slowly, I grip the shoe tightly, ready to wield it at a moment's notice at first sight of an intruder.

Crossing the foyer to the great room, I hear whistling coming from the direction of the kitchen. When I reach the sofa, I see a man in the kitchen, tall with dark hair, apparently whipping eggs in a mixing bowl.

"You know, sis, if you really want to sneak up on me, you'll need to work on your stealth skills. You've lost your edge." He turns and sees me, shoe raised in the air above my head, ready to throw, and he almost drops the bowl he's holding. "Jesus Christ, you scare me to death." He eyes the dangerous shoe warily. "Are you going to throw that at me? Or just threaten me with it?"

I lower the shoe, feeling foolish wielding such a poor weapon.

"You must be Enzo." I try to smile, but I'm still embarrassed about the shoe.

He's absolutely Bianca's brother. They look so much alike. Dark hair, dark eyes, high cheekbones, and a squared jaw. There's no way he could be anyone else. Plus, he called me "sis."

He tilts his head at me, curious. "You must be the brooding British writer. Oliver?"

That reddens my cheeks even more, and I remember him calling me Bianca's "British boyfriend" not long after we met.

"Yes, I'm Oliver Bellamy," I say, transferring my shoe to the other hand and extending the free one to him to shake.

He practically throws the bowl onto the counter and grabs my hand with a manly grip, shaking it fervently. It's more of an exuberant shake than a show of power. And while I appreciate the difference, it's still a bit much.

"It's nice to finally meet you," he says, nodding, holding my gaze, and still shaking my hand. "I've heard a lot about you."

"Oh, you have?" I can only imagine what he's heard. "Well, hopefully, you won't hold any of it against me." I laugh only slightly nervously and pull my hand carefully from his.

"Enzo! It's not your weekend to be here," Bianca calls from upstairs, looking down at us in surprise. Her hair is wild, and she's only got a sheet wrapped tightly around her, which she realizes as she catches my eye and jumps back out of view. "I'll be down in a sec. Enzo, that's Oliver. Oliver, that's my brother, Lorenzo. Talk amongst yourselves for a minute."

We turn back to each other, now awkward, as it is probably evident that Bianca and I spent the night together. I guess I should be grateful he's not the overly possessive type of brother that would beat up anyone who touched their sister. And that thought makes my face redden if it wasn't already.

I don't do 'people' very well, especially in one-on-one moments like this.

"So, this is a beautiful home that your grandfather built," I finally say. Somebody's got to break the ice, though I thought for sure it would be him.

He's still just studying me as if looking for some sort of flaw. It dawns on me then that Bianca has most likely told him of my diagnosis. Of course, she did. They are very close siblings.

His intense examination of me is unsettling now as it continues, and he hasn't responded to my comment about the loveliness of the house. And it's then that unsettling turns into annoyance. I'm not some sort of lab rat to be dissected and studied, and I don't appreciate him doing so.

"It's not something you can see," I snarl, irritated beyond belief. I wave my hand, indicating my body. "It's an auto-immune disease, where my body *internally* attacks itself. I don't have sores or rashes or even scars to prove it to you. But I assure you, it's there."

Now it's his turn to turn red with embarrassment. *Good.*

He takes a step toward me, his chin jutting out and his shoulders squaring. That is not the response I was expecting if he's embarrassed.

"Hey man, while I appreciate the lesson in MS that I didn't ask for or need, I was attempting to read your aura for your information. It was hard to see in this light. And what I did see appears to be spot on." He disappointedly shakes his head and goes back into the kitchen to whisk the eggs.

Well, I feel like an idiot now. Way to get off on the completely wrong foot with Bianca's family. While I'm not sure how much stock I put into aura readings, it couldn't hurt to find out. And maybe asking about it will bridge this gap I've wedged solidly between us. It was not my intention.

"I misread the situation. I apologize." He shrugs and nods as if it's no big deal, but it's not enough for me. I need to fix this. "So...did you see anything? With my aura, that is? Bianca didn't tell me you could do that."

He pours the eggs deftly into a frying pan and talks over his shoulder. "It was hard to see, to be honest. It's very close to your body, which isn't great. That denotes some negativity around you. I did see some yellow, which makes sense with you being a writer that does investigative stuff. It's more of a logical color than an emotional one. But..." He pauses, turning back to the eggs.

Now I'm invested. He can't leave it at that.

"But, what?" He can't stop in the middle of an analysis of my person.

He turns off the stove and spoons some scrambled eggs onto a plate.

"But it's not only contracted around you tightly,

it's also edged with like a gray smoke or haze or something, I don't know. I've never seen something like that." He scoops some of the food into his mouth. Apparently, he's not very concerned about this strange development in my aura.

"Is that a bad thing?" I'm thinking it's a bad thing. It doesn't sound very good, anyway.

"I don't really know, man. I don't do this very often, and I may not even be that good at it."

He sounds to me as though he's trying to cover something up. I've interviewed enough people to get a sense of when I'm not being told the entire truth. So, while it may be true that he doesn't do this very often, I have a feeling he knows what it means. He just doesn't want to say it for some reason.

"Well, if you had to take a guess, what would you say it means?"

I pull out an old interview trick and invite the subject to hazard an educated guess. Make it hypothetical, so they don't feel responsible for their response.

"If I had to guess..." he eyes me, measuring my stance. Perhaps rereading me. "I'd say you're under a lot of stress or have some kind of weight on your shoulders that is heavy for you. You might need a bit more rest as well."

I rub my chin thoughtfully and nod. He's not wrong there. But it's a bit like a carnival fortune teller, vague enough to apply to you, but it could also apply to just about the entire population.

"I see," I say, nodding in agreement with him.

He relaxes, and I think I may have smoothed things over between us.

"My brother isn't trying to force his party tricks on you, is he?" Bianca walks up next to me, reaching up to kiss my cheek. She's radiant and much more put together than a few minutes ago, though I did like her in just a sheet.

"Watch out for that one right there." Enzo points an accusatory finger at his sister as she enters the kitchen. "She's a full-blown red. Passion out the yin yang, this one."

"What's wrong with passion?"

Bianca is behind her brother, pouring a mug of coffee, and she winks at me conspiratorially.

I wholeheartedly agree that Bianca can be *very* passionate. I suppress my return smile to avoid getting her in trouble with her brother.

"Nothing is wrong with it per se, but it can be a lot. Passion about being happy, passion about being sad, passion about being bored, passion about being hungry, passion about a commercial you saw on tv that made you cry because it had a puppy in it. *Dio mio,* this one. *Pazza.*"

Enzo talks with his hands just as passionately as Bianca does, and the similarities between the two only intensify. It's a joy to watch them together.

They're so vibrant. There is obviously love between the two siblings, and I get a little pang of jealousy as they interact.

Having no siblings of my own, and even close cousins being few and far between, I didn't have that type of relationship with anyone. Sure, I had and have friends, what few I have left, but those relationships are nothing compared to the shared life experiences of siblings.

I've read something recently stating that no siblings have the same childhood. Everyone experiences things differently, especially family relationships. I don't think that's the case with these two. Even though they aren't twins, they definitely shared their childhood.

"Oliver?" Bianca is holding the coffee pot out to me in question. "Did you want some coffee?"

"What? Oh. Yes. Please. Apologies." I look down, trying to shake off my inner monologue about families and my jealousy surrounding them, and notice that I'm still shirtless and just in my sleep pants. "I'll be right back." I take the one shoe no longer needed to protect me and rush upstairs to make myself more presentable.

Chapter 24

Curious/Furious

Bianca

"Enzo, what the heck are you doing here?" I whisper, trying to keep my voice low so Oliver doesn't hear us upstairs. "I told you we were coming here this weekend."

"Exactly. That's why I came." He shrugs his shoulders and shoves more scrambled eggs into his mouth. "As your big brother, I needed to check this guy out for myself. I can't let just anybody date my baby sister."

I roll my eyes at him. He's incorrigible.

"Enzo, I am nearly thirty years old. I do not need my older brother checking up on me or my boyfriends. We're a little too old for that, don't you think?"

While I appreciate the sentiment, I don't like him inserting himself into our alone time like this. We don't have much time to spend together, and I don't want my brother to take any of it away from us.

"You'll never be too old for me to look out for you." He kisses the top of my head and then pushes on my shoulder playfully.

Damn it. I can't stay mad at him for any length of time.

"Well, you're not staying, are you?"

His eyes widen, pretending offense.

"Wow. You are so rude. Grandma and Grandpa Torino are rolling in their graves right now. Disparaging your big brother in their house. Tsk tsk."

"Oh, stop it. They are not." I push him back, maybe a little too hard. "And you're the rude one, showing up uninvited."

This back and forth continues until we're caught up in a full-blown slapping fight that only stops once we notice Oliver sitting on the couch in the great room, watching us with extreme amusement. I don't think I could be more embarrassed. Two adults slapping at each other like children.

"Don't stop on my account," Oliver laughs. At least he's entertained by our spontaneous immaturity.

"No, no," I say, straightening and tidying myself

up again after getting tousled by my brother. "Enzo isn't staying. He was just leaving, actually. *Isn't that right, Enzo?*" I glare at him pointedly, making sure he understands this is actually an instruction for him to leave.

"I was just about to leave. That's true. I'm meeting some buddies in Reno, but I wanted to stop by and meet you since I knew you'd be here." He glares back at me as he heads toward Oliver, who stands to shake his hand. "It was nice to finally meet you, Oliver. Don't hurt my sister, or I'll have to kill you. You know, as her big brother, I have to say shit like that."

Oliver looks panicked for a minute but then sees that it was just a joke and relaxes, taking my brother's hand.

"Of course. It was a pleasure to meet you as well."

"Man, that's a great accent," Enzo laughs, winking at me as he heads to the garage.

"Goodbye, brother!" I call after him as the door shuts.

I see Oliver standing at the windows along the back wall, facing the lake. He seems incredibly pensive, an abrupt change from how jovial he seemed with Enzo.

I walk over to him and slide my arms around his waist.

"Penny for your thoughts," I say, suddenly

unsure I want to hear them, and I don't know why. Maybe it's because the last time we stood like this in his hotel room, our lives exploded when he told me he had MS.

He takes his time to answer, which only increases my anxiety.

"Oh, nothing much. I just wanted to take in the view since I hadn't seen it. It was too dark last night. It's beautiful here."

"It is. It's why I love coming here so much. Enzo and I usually alternate weekends here."

"Your brother loves you very much." He sounds melancholy as he says this, and I wonder about his not having siblings. What a lonely childhood that would be. I can't imagine not having Enzo in my life.

"He does." I pull away, and, spotting my coffee mug on the kitchen counter, I move to retrieve it. "But sometimes he goes a little overboard with the whole big brother thing and turns into a real 'Big Brother,' if you get my meaning."

That gets a chuckle out of him. Good. I hope he's coming out of whatever funk he's fallen into. I'm still not quite sure how to deal with his mood swings. Just when I think I know how he's feeling, it changes, and I have to figure it out all over again.

We spend most of the rest of the day lazily on the couch. I promised I would give him time to review his work notes while we are here, so he does that, and I pull out my headphones and listen to my latest audiobook while resting my head on his lap. I keep my eyes closed but occasionally peek at him through lowered lids, admiring his features as he reads.

He's so expressive, scowling and squinting when he can't read his own writing, thoughtful when he's considering a specific item of interest, and what looks like sheer joy when he happens upon a particularly juicy train of thought.

Watching his brain at work is so attractive that I have to restrain myself from grabbing his notes and tossing them in the air just to make him look at me that way. A thoughtful Oliver is downright sexy as hell.

Toward the end of the afternoon, we pack a cooler and take the boat out to my favorite spot in the middle of the lake to watch the sunset like I promised. We're not the only ones with this idea, and we have to be careful not to get too close to anyone else.

Oliver is not an experienced boater but a quick learner who easily helps drop the anchor and position the boat. Watching him work the chains and rope while donning a baseball cap, aviator sunglasses, well-fitting t-shirt, jeans, and the oh-so-sexy scruff on his chin makes this adventure even more memorable.

He has never been more swoon-worthy than he is right now.

He catches me admiring him and smiles, turning up that hotness rating that much more.

"Are you enjoying yourself, Ms. Torino?"

"Why, yes. Actually, I am. Thank you very much."

When he finishes setting the anchor, he comes over to me, nudging himself between my thighs and pressing against me. There's a smirk on his lips, and his hands run along my bare shoulders and up my neck, sending shivers through my body.

As I look up at him, I see myself in the reflection of his sunglasses, and it makes me giggle.

"What is so funny?" He leans back and cocks his head at me, which makes me laugh more as my reflection warps further.

"Me," I chuckle, unable to stop now. "I'm making sexy eyes at myself in your glasses. It's a little awkward."

"Oh. Geez. I'm sorry about that." He quickly takes the offending sunglasses off and tosses them on the seat next to me.

"It's okay," I say, still laughing. "I just don't find myself that hot."

He moves back in, sliding his fingers through my hair and cupping the back of my head, he pulls me into a deep and languid kiss. It steals my breath, and I'm nearly gasping when we come up for air.

Nobody has had the effect on me that he does. Just a touch from him, and sometimes even just the *thought* of a touch from him, sends me into a tailspin of desire. If there weren't other boats within shouting distance, we would be doing something completely different right now.

"Well, rest assured that I do. What are you thinking?" he asks, playing with my hair. He still has that smirk, so I get the feeling he knows exactly what I was thinking.

Well, let's see what he does when I say it out loud.

"I was thinking that you look especially hot today, and I'd really love you to fuck me right now," I say matter-of-factly but low and breathy to get the full effect.

I see his Adam's apple bob as he swallows hard, and the smirk is gone. It's replaced with open-mouthed shock, and I can't help but smile wickedly at him. He was not expecting me to be so forward.

Well, here I am, in all of my full-blown red aura.

He turns away from me quickly, glancing around the boat, and I don't know what he's doing. Did I do something wrong? Maybe I shouldn't be so forward. It could be a turn-off for him.

Suddenly, he's in motion, grabbing the bench seat padding from the back and laying it on the boat floor. After checking on the other boats around us, he grabs me by the waist, lifts me off my captain's chair, and lowers me to the cushions. His mouth takes mine as he deftly undoes the button and fly of my shorts, and his hand slides down so his fingers can graze my center.

"Fuck, Bianca, you're already so wet," he whispers, his hot breath on my neck as he paints kisses across my collarbone. "Do you really want me to fuck you right now?"

I don't even think twice. My body blazes wherever our bodies meet, and my skin craves his where we don't.

"Yes. I do. I want you to fuck me."

"Christ on a bike," he mutters under his breath.

His fingers work me harder, pressing just the right angle of my clit to make me shudder beneath him, my breathing becoming ragged with desire. The scent of his cologne mixed with his sweat from being in the sun drives me crazy.

I need to feel him inside of me. *Now.*

Sliding my hands between us, I undo his jeans, frantic to reach him, to return this absolute bliss. I don't make it as Oliver slips a finger into me, curving it as he goes and hitting everything right on the way. Then a second finger repeats the movement and sends me into oblivion.

I can't help but cry out in pleasure, and he takes his other hand to cover my mouth, not wanting to draw attention, but it only drives me deeper into sensation. The idea that what we're doing is secret or clandestine makes it much more exciting.

As I come down, I finally reach him inside his boxers, and he is so hard for me that another wave of that familiar pressure starts to build inside me.

"Please tell me you brought a condom," I say, panting. I'm already so close again. I'm not sure how much more I can take.

He doesn't say anything but pulls out his wallet, and I see a flash of foil right before my shorts are yanked down, and he settles himself between my thighs, pushing into me.

He is so thick and deep. I don't think he can get any deeper. But he starts moving his hips, dragging in and out of me slowly, and I feel myself easing and making more room for him, which he takes completely. He's perched on his elbows, caging me securely beneath him, watching me react to his every move.

Again, our eyes meet, and the second they do, that strange tether between us electrifies, and I start to spasm intensely around him. My pelvis thrusts upward to meet his, taking him as deep inside me as possible, amplifying the pulsations rushing through me.

"Is this how you wanted me to fuck you, Bianca?" he growls into my ear and then bites my neck, careful not to hurt me. He thrusts again, harder, even deeper. "Is this how you want it?"

Somehow, my orgasm extends, or maybe it's a new one. I have no idea at this point. All I know is that I am in heaven right now. Sex has never been this intense or this good in my life. My body has never responded to someone like this.

"Yes. Yes." I can't think of words bigger than that as I dig my nails into his back, sure that I'm leaving marks, but not caring either.

This feels too good.

His breath quickens, his muscles tense, and he bites my shoulder as he comes, groaning low as his hips jerk and thrust hard into me. I again move to meet him, taking all of him deeply. I can feel him flex inside me as his body relaxes, pressing onto me as he traces kisses up my neck and along my jaw.

I also feel something else, something warm.

I freeze.

"Oliver." *He's got to feel it, too, doesn't he? Am I imagining it?*

"Hmm?" He's back at my ear, nibbling on my earlobe, but I can't move.

"Oliver, I think something's wrong."

He stops what he's doing and props himself up to look at me. His brow furrowed with concern.

"What is it? What's wrong?"

Good god. How do I say this?

"Um. I think the condom broke." I try not to

sound panicked, but I know I'm failing that miserably. "I can feel...well, your...you know...inside me."

He pulls out of me so fast I barely register what is happening. Then he's standing and swearing up a blue streak while readjusting his clothes, leaving me prone on the cushions, stunned.

"Oh, my Lord, Bianca, I am so sorry. Here." He finally notices me and moves to help me redress and sit up. "I can't believe that just happened, and then I just left you like that. I am so, so sorry." He's rambling, obviously upset.

My brain is trying to jump three steps ahead of me to figure out what to do now because I have to do something. Oliver has been more than clear that he doesn't want children, and I am not ready to be a single mother. I'm on the pill, but that might not be enough.

Tears are pricking the back of my throat, imagining Oliver's horror at my being pregnant. It is probably the worst thing that could happen to him.

"Are you clean?" I ask, my mind racing through every possible outcome of every likely nightmare scenario. As if getting pregnant wasn't devastating enough.

"I beg your pardon?" He looks at me as though I've grown a second head.

"Are you clean? I mean, do you have any—"

"Oh, no. I mean, yes. I'm clean. Sorry, I'm not

thinking straight at the moment."

"Okay, good. Not that you're not thinking straight." *Great. Now I'm rambling.* "I am on the pill, but we should get a Plan B just in case. There are drugstores back up in Reno..." my voice trails off as I look around at the sky, trying desperately to figure out what time it is and if we can get to a store before closing.

There are warm hands on my shoulders, and I glance up to see Oliver staring at me. His brow is still knotted with worry, but his eyes are now completely unreadable. Why can't I read him anymore?

I search for the tether between us that is always there, humming away in the background of our lives, and I almost don't sense it anymore. It's barely a ghost of an echo now.

"It'll be okay. Take a deep breath." He breathes in slowly to demonstrate, and I follow along, still half in a daze. "Okay, good. Let's pull up shop here and find that drugstore you mentioned. Everything will be fine."

I nod mechanically, still in disbelief at how quickly everything just changed between us because they most certainly did. Things went from the most beautiful dream to the darkest nightmare in an instant.

Abstractly I wonder what color our auras are now. They're probably as dark as the oncoming night.

Chapter 25

You'll Be Fine

Oliver

Nightmares really do come true. If you work hard enough and give it your all, you, too, can realize all of your worst nightmares. If my life ever needed a commercial, there's my tagline.

Bianca has completely changed. She's disconnected from me entirely. The whole ride into Reno, our brief time in the drugstore, and the way back was near total silence. It doesn't help that I, the wordsmith who gets paid to put words in a pleasing order for a living, am at a loss for what to say. I never envisioned being in a situation like this, and it's not exactly something you can prepare for.

The worst part was when Bianca took the Plan B, she made sure that I witnessed her take it, even sticking out her tongue to show the pill being swallowed. As if I wouldn't trust her to actually take it.

At that point, I had to walk away. Every attempt I've made to hold her, or even her hand, has been rebuked. I don't know what else I can do. I don't know how to make this better.

I've been in the bedroom, pretending to go through my notes again to give her the space she asked for until she wanted to come to bed. Glancing at my phone, I see that it's late. She should have come to bed by now. We can't keep this up. Well, I don't want to keep this up.

Making my way to the landing, I look down on the great room and see Bianca curled up on the sofa, a throw blanket over her. Did she fall asleep down there? As I approach her, it's obvious that she is sleeping, but I also notice a well-worked ball of tissue in her hand and a redness around her eyes that makes it clear she'd been crying.

My heart sinks at the thought of her down here, alone, crying about something I was responsible for, while I was upstairs pretending to work like nothing happened. I didn't hear a god-damned thing.

Was she that quiet? Or am I that good at ignoring what I don't want to hear?

My heart wants me to scoop her up, carry her upstairs, and hold her all night while she sleeps so I can chase away any bad dream that threatens her peace.

But, I'm afraid. I'm a fucking coward.

What if I lift her and halfway up the stairs, I drop her?

Jesus Christ, I'm pathetic.

I stand for another minute, watching her steady breathing with the rise and fall of her chest.

"Fuck this," I whisper to myself.

Bending down, I slide my arms carefully under her and lift, keeping her close to my chest for balance. After waiting a few seconds to gauge my ability, I carry her upstairs without incident and lay her on the bed.

It's only then that she stirs, squinting up at me, confused. I let out the breath I was holding the entire journey and crawl into bed next to her, pulling her close to me, and she doesn't resist.

"What...How did I get up here?" she asks, looking around, half asleep.

"I carried you. Go back to sleep." I brush back the hair that's fallen over her face.

Even with puffy eyes from crying, she's the most beautiful woman I've seen. I continue to rake my fingers through her hair lightly in an attempt to coax her back to sleep. I didn't mean for her to wake up.

Instead, her eyes fly open, and she pushes herself up to face me.

"You, what?"

"I brought you back to bed, so you could sleep more comfortably. So, please—"

"You carried...? Oliver, what if you dropped me?" She still looks more confused than anything else. At least it's not anger.

I stare at her, not sure if she's serious or being facetious. Could she be mocking me and my concerns about holding a child? I can't read her to tell.

"I didn't drop you," I say, keeping my relief at that point to myself.

She stares back at me, and I'm not sure what is happening right now. Are we arguing? Are we making up? Were we ever fighting?

"I'm so sorry," she whispers, shaking her head. Her words are choked as tears start to run down her cheeks. She's quick to wipe them away with the tissue in her hand before I can even think to move to do it.

I gape at her. Shocked.

"Bianca, you have nothing to be sorry about. It was an accident." I reach up and catch a few tears that are still falling. "Neither of us is at fault."

"Yeah, but you're so dead set against having

children. I didn't want you to think I would do that to you on purpose because I would never do such a thing. I wanted to make sure you saw me take it because you didn't see me take my regular birth control pill this—"

"Stop. Bianca. It's fine. It's over with. We've dealt with it, and it's done." Her words beat at my guilt, already down for the count. "And I would never think that of you. Get that straight out of your head."

"But—"

I grab her chin, forcing her to stop spiraling and look at me. She needs to stop beating herself up over this. I keep my tone clear and deliberate.

"It was an accident. Nothing more. Okay?"

She searches my eyes and must find the truth there because she nods and curls back into me, resting her head on my shoulder. I pull her close again, praying we can get through this.

I can't believe she thought I would be so cruel. Have I really been that cold? Or given her reason at all to think that of me?

I took a backseat to this entire thing to let her do whatever she wanted about the situation. I trusted her implicitly. I didn't realize that being so hands-off painted me as blaming her or not caring.

This may be another sign that I am not cut out for a relationship. If I can't handle something like this correctly, then I have no business being with someone. The pain on Bianca's face just now is all the proof anyone would need to make that decision. I have clearly failed her.

I have just over a week left in America. What the hell are we going to do once I leave? I don't believe that a long-distance relationship can work. Honestly, if neither of us is willing to go to be with the other person, there is no point. We can't stay an ocean apart from each other forever. And there is no in-between.

I've been doing everything in my power not to even think about what's next. To do so would acknowledge that there is an 'after' to the time I'm here. I don't want to face that yet. There's only now, and I've been screwing that up left and right.

I fall asleep with Bianca in my arms, and when I wake up with her still there, it's like a punch in the gut. That is not the ecstatic reaction that I expected of myself. Instead, I'm hit with the same thoughts that I fell asleep to, thoughts of being without her after this upcoming weekend. Thoughts of leaving her behind. Leaving forever. My jaw clenches as I grind my teeth, thinking about it. I don't want to face it yet.

I wrap my arms tighter around her, trying to

capture everything I can about her in my memory for good. The smell of her shampoo, the smoothness of her skin, the taste of her kisses, how she sneaks looks at me while listening to her dirty audiobooks when she thinks I don't notice, her soft little snore when she's deep in sleep, and how she grabs onto me while she's sleeping too, without even knowing she's doing it like she's doing right now.

All of these little things add up to a big thing. A big thing that can't happen. I think I knew it when I started this, but I didn't want to admit it to myself. I thought I could spend time with Bianca, and in the end, I could just walk away. I'm not sure I can do that now.

The following morning, we head back to Vegas without another word about what happened on the boat and afterward. It's been erased from our collective memory for the time being. However, thoughts of how incredible the sex was on the boat are never far from my thoughts. It feels shameful to even think it, but it's true.

Being with Bianca that evening went beyond a physical connection. I can't even put a name to it because I've never experienced it before. And it was so brief, if I'd blinked I would have missed it. But I didn't miss it, and it will haunt me.

I will be chasing that feeling for the rest of my life, like a drug addict chasing their high. For me, that was a once-in-a-lifetime feeling that won't ever come my way again.

In the middle of the week, we're invited to Normandy and Brandon's house again for dinner, and I'm surprised by another guest of theirs, Max Calnetta. He has been in hiding since testifying against his father and brother a couple of years ago and is only in town for a few hours to prevent being found. The more prominent Mamana crime family that used to own the Bliss Casino where I'm staying allegedly has a standing bounty out on his head.

He's agreed to speak with me for my book and arranged with the Carmichaels to be here secretly. I notice right away that the kids aren't here this evening. Probably a smart move, but if things are that bad, I would have been more comfortable not doing this in their home, either.

Seeing as I didn't have any say in this arrangement, I'll take what I can get. I just wish I had my notes with me. I'll have to wrestle with my faulty memory to get through this.

About half an hour into my conversation with Max, I find myself distracted, watching Bianca talk to Normandy in the kitchen. The window in the office we're in gives a perfect vantage point. I'm not bothered at all by all of the security currently circulating, but I would be mesmerized by that dark hair anywhere. She's wearing it pinned up today. She's been doing that the last several days, keeping her appearance strictly professional and begging off in the evening with a supposed list of errands or feigned exhaustion.

I can take a hint. She's avoiding me.

"Mr. Bellamy?" Max's inquiry pulls me back to this room, where I have completely lost track of our conversation.

I sit up, trying desperately to remember where we were and what we were talking about. For the life of me, I can't remember.

"I'm sorry. What were we discussing again?" I ask, embarrassed.

It's completely unprofessional of me to be this out of sorts during an interview. I've never been this discombobulated, and it would have to happen with my star character. I've got to salvage this somehow.

He examines me and must see that this situation will probably not get any better. For that, he is an intelligent man because I can guarantee that it's most likely going to go straight down the fucking hill from here.

"Oliver. I understand you've had a bit of a rough go of it since you've been here in America." He waves to the bruises, still coloring my forehead and cheek. "I think maybe we should do this by phone in a few weeks. Once you're back home and settled."

I sigh heavily. He's right. This is officially the worst interview I've ever participated in.

"Thank you. And yes, it's also not helping that I

don't have my notes in front of me. My apologies for making you go through whatever you did to be here."

He gets out of his chair and shakes my hand. "It's not a problem. I have your direct number now and Darcie's, so I will call in a few weeks."

Once he's out of the office, I drop my face in my hands. This also isn't the first interview I've fucked up this week because I've been too distracted with Bianca. I can't help but fixate on her when she's only a few yards away, or if she's outside in the sunshine by the car and unaware of my watching. I lose myself in her.

And I only have a few days left with her?

I'm fucked. I'm completely, without a doubt, indubitably, entirely fucked.

Chapter 26

Ordinary

Bianca

We're counting days and hours now. Not weeks. In two days, Oliver will be gone. Just gone. Not gone for a little while, or even a long while, just...gone. My eyes sting with tears every time I think of it. We've drifted so far apart this past week. Well, that's not entirely true. We've drifted apart since the boat incident. I don't think we ever recovered fully from that, or that we ever will.

Honestly, how could we come back from something like that? I think it's probably impossible, even though nobody was to blame. That might be the problem. If there were someone to blame, we could have closure of some sort, but this just feels open-ended and unresolved.

Oliver has said his goodbyes to everyone else since he'll be leaving straight from our trip to the Grand Canyon. He switched his ticket to fly out of Flagstaff instead of Las Vegas as originally planned. Poor little Ava was beside herself, saying goodbye, and I had a tough time watching. She kept asking for a set time that he would be back, for a specified time he would be gone, for a promise that he would return someday, any day.

All Oliver could say, or would say, is, "We'll see."

That wasn't good enough for her.

I can relate, and my heart broke for her as she tried to wrap her head around the inconceivable notion of possibly never seeing someone again. It can be hard to accept. I couldn't tell if Oliver was as affected by her sorrow as I was. He hasn't talked about it. He had on his aviators at the time and has been quiet all week, so the continued silence wasn't new.

Now it's Friday, the first day of our road trip, and as I pull up to the hotel to pick him up, he's ready to go. I automatically get out of the car to load his bags into the back of the SUV I brought, but he does it himself. A clear contrast to when he first arrived. I give him a tentative smile as I remember his first day here, but only receive a brief twitch of his lips in response.

If we don't talk, this could be a very long weekend.

About an hour into our four-and-a-half-hour drive, I can't take any more of the awkward silence between us. This has been building up all week, and I need to address it before we get to where we're staying. If I don't, I will explode into a million angry pieces.

"Oliver, we need to talk." I'm trying to work up my courage to talk openly with him about our relationship. I'm not usually so tentative about my feelings, but this is so delicate and fragile that I don't want to ruin anything.

"The most dreaded four words in the English language," he mutters, flashing a smirk at me. When I don't comment, he adds, "What would you like to talk about?"

"Us," I say plainly, and glance over at him to see if he reacts. He doesn't. In fact, he doesn't say anything but just kind of nods his head as if he expected this. "Things have been weird between us all week, and I just want to know where your head is at when it comes to us." I shrug a shoulder as if it's no big deal, and I don't know why. I do not mean to be nonchalant about this at all. This is important to me.

I can feel him study me as I drive, and I will myself to not flinch under his gaze. Whatever is going to happen, I need to be strong. I can't be a weeping willow every time things don't go my way. This is different and on a much grander scale than anything else in my life. But I tell myself that my reaction should be no different.

He doesn't answer for a long time, and I start to worry that he's not going to. I dare to glance at him again, and he's staring out the window. His face and body language are unreadable. I feel so disconnected from him lately. It just feels wrong, somehow.

"My head is a little muddled at the moment, unfortunately. I'm not sure what I think about anything, to be honest. Especially us." His words are stilted and far away, as if his foggy thoughts have clouded his voice too.

His answer does nothing to ease my mind, however. It was his typical 'dance around the topic without discussing the topic' deflection. That's not going to work this weekend. It resolves nothing.

"If you had to guess, what do you think you would say about us?"

I've seen him use this tactic to get answers from people during his interviews, and he even told me that it's what he does in situations like this.

He recognizes it, and I can see a genuine smile now out of the corner of my eye. I can't help the smug smile of my own.

"Well done," he beams with obvious admiration.

I take a slight bow but keep quiet, leaving room for him to answer.

He again takes a while to answer, and I worry at what verbal concoction he will come up with to not answer me directly again. If he tries, I may need to pull over, and I will not be responsible for my actions.

I grip the steering wheel a little tighter as I wait. My palms are sweating as my anxiety rises. I didn't realize how important this was to me until just this second.

His eventual answer comes slowly. "If I had to guess, I would say that we...are still up in the air. The jury is still out, as it were."

He seems pleased with his answer, but I'm not.

"Why?" I ask. I'm not going to let this go. It's too important. And I want it resolved before we get to our destination. "What more does this jury need to hear? What witnesses? What evidence? What questions could this jury still have?"

He seems surprised but doesn't hesitate to respond.

"What exactly are your expectations of me? Alright, Bianca. Logistically, how does this work since neither of us will budge on moving? And what about children? You still want them, I presume? Well, you know full well my opinion on that topic, as much as that horrifies you."

"Horrifies me? What on earth do you mean by that?"

I did not expect him to rattle off items so readily and so vehemently. It's as if he's been listing these things in his head for a long time, waiting for the right moment to spring them on me.

"You know exactly what I mean. When that condom broke on the boat, you were so afraid of my reaction that you didn't speak to me for hours afterward. I was vilified for a reaction I *wasn't having* while I was trying to be there for *you*, to support *you*. I was pushed away to give you space, and all it did was give you time to turn me into a monster in your mind." He takes a deep breath, trying to compose himself. "When you first woke up after I carried you upstairs, one of the first things you did was apologize to me. As if I was going to be irate with you for what happened. You were *afraid* of me, Bianca. I'll never forget that look on your face, and I never want to be looked at that way again."

That's it. I flick my turn indicator and move to the far right lane of the highway, then pull off onto the shoulder.

"What are you—" he starts, but I don't let him finish.

Throwing the car in park, I turn to face him. I reach over and gently pull off his sunglasses because I will not discuss this with a reflection of myself, and I want to see him while talking.

"I was never afraid of *you*, Oliver. *Ever*. Yes, I was afraid. You got that part right. But I was afraid of what you were thinking of *me*. I thought that you would think that I somehow made the condom break or was trying to trap you because I *do* want children someday. I don't know." I throw up my hands in exasperation, out of breath, and out of words.

"What would ever lead you to think I would blame you?" He grabs my hands, and it feels like the first time he's touched me in days because it is. "I was very careful to specifically tell you that I didn't blame you."

"I didn't say it made sense...."

He chuckles, lifts a hand to his lips, and kisses my knuckles, keeping eye contact with me. A jolt goes through me, and it feels like the tether between us that's been silent for days is singing again.

It pulls me forward, and must do the same for him since he leans in to meet me across the console, and his lips brush mine lightly, but then with more insistence.

The next thing I know, our hands are in each other's hair, and everything between us is just getting in our way.

A light rapping on the driver's side window startles us both, and we jump apart as if electrified. A highway patrol officer is standing outside the car with an amused smirk. He's older, with gray hair in a severe buzz cut. He's definitely seen some stuff in the line of duty.

Shit.

"Roll down your window," he orders, motioning as if I don't know what that would mean. I do so and paint on a quick smile.

"Hi. Officer. Sorry about that. We just stopped briefly to have a conversation. But we're done now, so we can get on our way and finish our drive to the Grand Canyon, where we're staying."

Shut up, Bianca.

He nods, hands still on his hips. "May I see your license and registration, please?"

Shit. Is he serious? Could we be cited for this? This is a Mischief Motors car. What if it gets towed? How will I explain that to Normandy?

"Ma'am? License and registration?"

"Oh, sorry." I have got to pull myself together. Why do people get so flustered around law enforcement? I open the console between Oliver and me and grab my documentation, handing it over to the officer.

"Hang tight," he drawls, heading back to his cruiser.

I notice then that his red and blue lights are flashing, too, so we're now a spectacle on top of everything else. I rack my brain, trying to remember if there's some sort of law we're breaking here on the side of the highway. I don't think there is.

Oliver stares at me suspiciously. "You don't have warrants for your arrest, do you?"

I stare back. "Only for that one murder."

"One?"

"Yeah, it was a passenger who actually looked a lot like you. Asked a lot of nosey questions about things that were none of his business. Get my drift?" I deadpan, turning this into instant improv.

We stare for a moment longer and then burst into laughter.

"Shhh. Shit. Act cool. He's coming back," Oliver says hurriedly, all the while laughing. Acting like we're about to be sent to detention or something.

I sit back straight, trying to suppress my laughter at the situation as the officer steps into view next to the car. He hands me back my license and registration.

"Right. Ms. Torino." He is acting all business, but he's still got that smirk of amusement. "You two are free to go, but next time you want to have a... conversation, you may want to exit the highway entirely. Do you get my meaning?"

I nod emphatically.

"I do. I absolutely do. It won't happen again." I'm about to cross my heart but somehow stop myself. At least I'm not laughing anymore.

"You two have a good rest of your afternoon. Safe travels." The officer tips his brimmed hat at us and heads back to his vehicle.

I start driving again and carefully merge back into the flow of cars. About a mile down the road, when it looks like the coast is clear of any further law enforcement, we glance at each other briefly and start laughing again.

Maybe this trip is salvageable after all.

Chapter 27

For the Love of God

Oliver

We're staying the weekend on a ranch owned by the Carmichaels just past the South Rim of the Grand Canyon. After a quick stop in a little town for dinner and to stock up on supplies, we arrive at the house. It's so remote, the driveway isn't really even a driveway, but a full-on road about a mile and a half long, so 'secluded' would be a good descriptor for where we're spending the weekend.

I was also warned that the wildlife in the area is

actually wild and not domesticated in any way, shape, or form. So that, too, has been duly noted.

After the make-out session on the side of the road was so rudely interrupted by law enforcement, the rest of our trip was much more comfortable than it was when we started. The air between Bianca and me seems to have been cleared for the most part.

We're still avoiding the central question and the gigantic elephant in the room, '*What happens to us once I leave?*' but I think that's a good thing for now. If we're going to enjoy our last days together, we need to stop any downward spiral before it starts.

My body's hyperawareness for Bianca's has only grown after being in such tight quarters in the car for so many hours. Every nerve in my body is charged with a yearning to touch her, taste her, and consume every part of her being.

These feelings are not going away as we settle into the house. We both leave our bags in the great room, not committing yet to a shared bedroom, I guess. I wonder if she's noticed that we've each done that or if I'm the only one paying attention to that sort of thing.

"So..." Bianca starts, suddenly awkward, shoving her hands into her jeans pockets. She's beautiful when she's bashful.

Who am I kidding? She's always beautiful.

"So..." I echo, being brave and making the first move. I don't have much time left, and I want to make the most of the time we do have. I want to experience Bianca while she's within my reach.

Stepping up to her, I frame her gorgeous face with my hands, stare into her dark eyes, trying to memorize their specific shades of brown and gold and the open expression in them right now, and brush her bottom lip softly with my thumb. Her mouth is so damned kissable, so I do. While I can, I am going to steal as many kisses from her as possible.

Something has changed about us now. Our kisses are more urgent, and our touches more desperate. We know the clock is ticking, and time is our enemy, so we're trying to cram as much sensation into what time is left.

As we kiss, we make our way to the nearest bedroom, leaving everything where we left it, including the groceries on the counter. They can wait. Our desire for each other can't.

As desperate as I am for her, I want to savor this. I want to remember every freckle, every curve, every sigh, and every groan of pleasure. I lay Bianca back on the bed and stand to take her in, her black hair fanned behind her on the pillow, her lips red from the friction against my own.

I feel a jolt of pride in that. I made her mouth look like that, and I'm making her body squirm under my gaze.

She's unbuttoning her blouse as I watch, her lids

heavy with want, and a knowing smile playing on her lips. She knows what she's doing to me too.

When she finishes with the buttons, she opens her blouse, exposing a delicate lace bra that was not worn for comfort, it was worn for me, and I love that I know that.

She keeps her gaze locked on me as she runs her fingers along her torso, trailing slowly from her belly button up to the clasp of the bra between her breasts. Her hand pauses, and the hesitation is almost too much.

I need that bra off of her right now.

"Hold that thought."

I rush out to rummage through my bag, where a brand-new box of condoms is waiting to be opened. My erection is starting to grow painful as it strains against my jeans, so I hurry back to the bedroom. I wave the box sheepishly and place it on the nightstand for now.

As I shed my t-shirt and jeans and slide onto the bed next to her, she starts to unhook her bra, but I grab her hand to stop her.

"Let me," I say, my voice low and full of air. Leaning down, I draw a trail of kisses across her stomach, savoring the salt of her skin with my tongue, and enjoying every inch as her back arches and goosebumps form under my breath.

I make quick work of unhooking the bra with my teeth, and as her breasts are fully exposed to the room's cool air, her nipples stiffen, inviting me to suck on them, so I do. Hungrily. Her hands rake through my hair as I make sure to give her breasts my undivided attention, teasing the nipples with my tongue and nipping on them with my teeth until she is grinding her pelvis against my thigh.

I gently push her hips down on the bed with my hands as I sit up to take her in again, this time at the beginning of her frenzy. I want to remember every moment of each stage of making love to her, the way her skin shimmers in the low light coming in from the kitchen, the way her breath hitches as I run a finger down her stomach to the top of her lace underwear.

Slowly, I hook my fingers into the waistband and pull them off, tossing them behind me and landing who knows where. The sight of Bianca completely naked, open for me, arching for me, reaching for me, is one that will have to last me probably the rest of my life.

I sear this heavenly vision into my memory and then gently push on her knees to spread open for me. She doesn't resist but makes a slight noise in her throat that tells me she's ready for me.

Running a line of kisses up her inner thigh, I reach under her and grab her ass, squeezing the flesh as my mouth finds her sweet center. She purrs and squirms under my greedy touch. As I firmly lick and glide my tongue against her sex, tantalizing with each sweep and swirl, I can sense a tremor begin to build inside her.

Knowing that my touch, actions, and movements are doing this to her, are giving her this pleasure, is the biggest turn-on there is. And watching it unfold before me, feeling it happen, only magnifies it.

I increase the pressure, stroking rhythmically on the exact spot she reacts to every time until she's begging me not to stop, and her hands are in my hair, grabbing and clawing at my shoulders. Then I suck hard on her clit, extending her orgasm and intensifying it, causing her entire body to shake and spasm beneath me.

She calls out my name, and I think swears in Italian, and as I ease up, she starts panting, her breathing unsteady. I work my way back up her body, her skin now heated. I savor one breast and then the other, holding myself up, careful not to press my body against her.

Not yet. I need to calm myself for a minute before I completely lose myself with one touch from her.

Once I'm sure I'm under control, I settle between her legs, cage her body carefully under me, and trace a languid line of kisses up her neck. When our skin meets, my hyperawareness of her goes into overdrive. The smell of her perfume mixing with our combined sweat, the salt and sweet taste of her skin, the little sounds of pleasure she makes in her throat, and the crinkling of the crisp sheets beneath us as we move only serve to enhance the visual of her body and soft curves as they respond to me. I've never had this type of connection with another person and never experienced something so profound.

I have a sudden urge to say something and tell her how I'm feeling, but I stop myself. We're in the middle of sex. Hormones and endorphins are raging, and emotions may not be clear. I don't want to say something I'll regret later.

But God damned if this isn't what I think love is supposed to feel like. I want nothing more than to make her feel this good all the time. Instead, I can just show her and throw myself into loving her the only way I can.

Our kisses have gentled and turned sweet. A slight respite from the feeding frenzy that just happened. I pull up and gaze into her eyes, trying to see if she's feeling what I'm feeling. I should say something if she is, but I can't quite read her expression. Not that she's guarded, but she's still lost in her ecstasy and not quite back down to earth yet.

She smiles slyly, tilting her head toward the side table.

"Shall we?"

I follow her gaze, landing on the box of condoms, and return the smile.

"I mean, I won't argue." I grind my pelvis against

her, my rock-hard erection leaving no doubt about just how ready I am for this to happen.

To my complete surprise, I'm suddenly tangled in a flurry of arms and legs and flipped onto my back, Bianca straddling me, her hair falling to curtain around us as she leans over me, laughing and more than a little proud of her move.

I'm impressed and a little confused at how she actually did it, but I don't overthink it. I like it. I like how in command she is of herself and, I guess, me.

I take the opportunity to grab her breasts in both hands, reveling in their fullness and rolling the nipples tightly between my fingers. This gets her moving again, and the box is quickly opened, and a fresh condom extracted. She expertly sheathes me in no time, neither of us mentioning or referencing the boat incident, thank God. Though I get the sense that we both thought about it simultaneously.

I wrap my hand behind her neck and pull her down into a kiss, chasing away any bad thoughts we might be having. Expressing to her, in the only way I can, the only way I know how, that we're okay. She's safe with me.

Her eyes are clear and unworried when she pulls away, and I love that we can communicate like that. I love everything about us, about her.

She leans forward again and rocks to guide me inside her slowly. The sensation of her so wet and tight around me is exquisite, and I can't help but draw in a sharp breath through my teeth. A hiss then escapes me as she settles more, taking me all the way in.

I open my eyes and watch her reaction, her head falling back, hair cascading down her back, and her long neck exposed as she swallows hard, her breath catching with mine.

She's simply beauty personified. Everything about her, even her flaws and her hot temper, not just her looks, is brilliant to me.

She meets my gaze and starts rotating her hips, stirring an intoxicating rush of sparks through my veins. The warmth of her splayed around me builds an aching within me that I've never felt before. A craving echoes through me that needs to be satiated and can only be satisfied by her.

Only ever *her*.

Sitting up to meet her, I pull a breast into my mouth to suck on a rigid nipple, then my hands slide under her to control our movements. I can tell she's close again, and I want to draw it out for her, build up to a euphoria that we will both remember.

She wants to go faster, to chase that quick high, but I slow us down and revel in teasing her. Pushing her to the edge, then pulling back until we're both feverish, and she's begging me to come.

Grabbing her hair, I pull her head back gently, tilting her face to mine, and kiss her slow and deep, rolling my hips and hitting where we both need it again and again. Her nails carve down my back as our pleasure builds exponentially together until we erupt, clinging to each other desperately, pulsating and shuddering in and around each other. Her teeth dig into my shoulder, stifling a cry, and I let out a breathless groan from somewhere deep in my soul.

It takes a minute for us each to catch our breath, and even then, it's unsteady. Our bodies stick together with sweat, and I brush Bianca's damp hair away from her face, trying to gauge her reaction to what just happened between us. I think it was as significant for her as it was for me.

Sex has never been like that for me. It's never been so intimate, so personal, so meaningful. But what did it mean, exactly?

I shake it off as quickly as the thoughts come. I can't be having these thoughts. Not now. Not ever.

Fuck. I hate this. But God damn this all to hell. I love her.

Chapter 28

Just Say When

Bianca

After a night that I never thought I would experience in my life, full of so much emotion never expressed in words, the next day seems rushed before it even starts. I barely have a minute to register anything. Time is going by way too quickly, and we barely slept because we don't want to miss a minute we have left together. At least, that's how I feel. I think Oliver feels the same way.

He did finally doze off, and I snuck out to grab a cup of coffee and watch the sunrise on the back deck of the house. I'm kept company by a small elk herd about fifty yards away. I'm used to the varied wildlife out here, and if I don't bother them, they won't bother me.

Hopefully.

I almost said it last night, that I love him, but it caught on something inside me before I could form the words. Fear. It snagged on my fear of rejection, of hurt, of abandonment. Oddly, in my head, if I don't create an attachment, it can't be ruined. If I don't trust, I can't be betrayed. If I don't expect anything, I won't be disappointed.

Since Colin hurt me, this is how I've operated with everyone. If I'm honest with myself, the difference now is that I actually feel more for Oliver in one month than I did for Colin with years together. So, maybe that's why I'm even more afraid. I know that this hurt is going to be devastating when it comes. And I know that it's coming. There's nothing I can do to stop it.

Today, we go to the Grand Canyon. I've probably been a hundred times after driving clients to various points along the park containing it, but this is different somehow. There's something about seeing it for the first time that changes a person's perspective, and I'm curious how it will affect Oliver, if at all.

Maybe he's too stoic and closed off for it to do anything to him. But maybe, just maybe, it will change his mindset about life, *his* life, and how precious it truly is.

I'm so lost in thought I don't hear when he comes outside to join me. When his arms slide around me and he starts kissing my neck, I just about jump out of my skin. Luckily, I don't spill my coffee or spook the elk, and only yelp to myself on the inside.

"Geez, you scared me," I whisper with a laugh, pointing at the animals not so far away. "Look. Look at how beautiful they are."

He ignores my directions and the elk, continues kissing my neck, then moves to my collarbone and shoulder. Fucking hell, this man knows exactly how to get my motor racing, even with as little sleep as I've had. We seem to be insatiable when it comes to each other.

"I'm already looking at the most beautiful thing out here." His scruff tickles my ear as he whispers. His voice is still gravelly with sleep.

"You know, you don't have to win me over anymore," I giggle, trying to get out of his reach before he drives me insane. "I already kind of like you."

"Just making sure you know. That's all." He stretches and moves in front of me, the morning light casting a glow around him that makes his dark blonde hair even more golden, giving him an aura of pure sunshine.

I take a mental snapshot of him like this,

gloriously happy and well-satisfied by the looks of his grin. I wish he could see himself like I see him.

"You're awfully smiley this morning." I can't help but smile, too, feeling equally satisfied after last night.

"Well, I wonder why...."

He leans toward me, placing his hands on each arm of my chair, and plants a solid kiss on my lips in one fell swoop, standing straight immediately. A hit and run. One that leaves me wanting more.

I know I can't act on it as tempting as it is. And, hell, it's tempting. I have a special day for us planned, and I don't want to mess any of it up. Our last full day together. I push the thought out of my mind and stand, gazing up at him. The bittersweet edge of the day is already creeping in, and I can't let myself get melancholy now. If I start, I won't stop, and it will ruin everything.

I know that I don't want this to be the end, so I need to do everything in my power to convince Oliver of the same. In my heart, I also know that words won't be enough, no matter what I could say to try to persuade him. I need to show him that we can work. Somehow. If we want it enough, and I *think* we both do, we can do this.

"C'mon. Let's go see one of the seven wonders of the world."

"Actually, it's not...."

"Okay, Mr. Smarty-pants. It's one of the seven

natural wonders of the world. Don't start with me," I admonish, suppressing a laugh. "You're so argumentative."

"No. I'm just usually right." He grins, and I roll my eyes, grabbing his hand to lead him back inside to get ready for the day.

It's mid-morning when we finally start to head out, and the sun is already beating down and baking everything in sight. I have to run the SUV for a while with the air conditioning on full blast before we can get in it so we don't burn ourselves on the leather seats.

As we're leaving, Oliver asks me, "So, are you going to tell me what this big surprise of the day is? Am I even dressed properly?"

I pretend to scrutinize him with narrowed eyes from top to bottom, when I'm actually taking the time to admire every inch of him. His well-fitting jeans and t-shirt are tight in all the right places.

"I mean, in my mind, pants are always optional, but you do you." I try to keep my face straight but fail miserably and crack up as his eyebrows shoot up in surprise.

He reaches for his belt and starts unbuckling it, "Well, if you insist...."

"No!" I laugh, rushing to seize his hands, but he grabs mine and pulls me to him, wrapping me tight in his arms, enveloping me in his scent and warmth. I have to force myself to pull away from him, or we'll never leave, and I don't want to be late.

It's about a half-hour drive to our first destination, and when we pass the Grand Canyon National Park Airport sign, Oliver glances at me curiously.

"An airport? Are we flying somewhere?" He's more than a little suspicious, and I start to get worried.

Maybe this was a horrible idea.

"You're not afraid of flying, are you?" If he is, then I reserved a helicopter tour for nothing. I grip the steering wheel tightly.

He scoffs. "Pfft. No. I'm not. I'd not be here if I was."

I sigh with relief. Thank God.

"Ok. Good. Because you're about the see the Grand Canyon for the first time from the air."

We check in and meet our pilot before taking off on our nearly hour-long tour. After we leave the area surrounding the airport, the topography changes, and we see what looks like a plain old forest for a while.

That changes when the ground seems to disappear, and a sheer drop off the canyon proper opens up to us, revealing the stunning multicolored tiers surrounding the twisting and turning Colorado River.

Oliver grips my hand tightly as he first takes in the canyon's vastness. It's hard to see his reaction with those damned sunglasses on again, but he looks a little pale for a minute. As we approach the North Rim, with its green rolling hills, it's a sharp contrast to the reds and oranges of the rock walls.

It's hot in the helicopter, which I didn't consider, and the sun raging through the little glass bubble we're traveling in only seems to turn up the temperature that much more. By the time we land at the airport, I have that too much sun feeling, like I've spent the entire day soaking up rays on the beach.

Oliver seems to be affected the same way as me and is a little dizzy when he steps out of the helicopter. I grab his arm to hold him steady, and we laugh it off as him being so impressed he's stupefied. And that's fine. If he wants to joke about things, I am happy to do so today.

We drive a little north into a business district with hotels and a park visitor center and grab dinner at a local steakhouse. We're able to cool off while going shop to shop in the area before and after we eat, looking at the overpriced souvenirs.

"I think this is the one," I hear from behind me as I peruse the snow globes. When I turn around, I see Oliver holding up a t-shirt under his chin that reads, *'A Hole. A Big, Big, Hole.'*

I burst into laughter, trying to imagine him ever wearing something so novel and kitschy.

"I think you're right. It's perfect."

After one more hour of playing tourist, it's time to drive to the park's last stop of the day, Navajo Point, near the East entrance. It's my favorite spot in the canyon to watch a sunset. It's basically a parking lot with an overlook, but the great thing, and the scariest thing about the Grand Canyon, is that you can pretty much walk up to the edge just about everywhere.

The drive takes under an hour, but Oliver falls asleep not long into the journey. He looked exhausted right before we left, and I was worried he was overdoing it.

I don't know what his limits are with his MS, and he sure as hell has made it clear he isn't going to tell me. So, I need to be extra diligent and observant to watch for changes in him.

Another thing I noticed was that he was also covering up a very slight limp toward the end. He's very good at hiding it, stopping every other step to look at something, but putting his weight on his left leg while standing still.

I'm not fooled.

With all of that, I don't mind that he fell asleep. And he can fall asleep on the way home too, but he has to see a Grand Canyon sunset.

I pull into the parking lot and am glad there

aren't too many other tourists with the same idea. During the summer, these spots can get overcrowded with buses full of people, but at this time of day, most touring jaunts are over. It's perfect timing as the sun is low but not too far gone yet. The color show has just started.

After shutting off the car, I lean over the middle console and kiss Oliver's forehead lightly.

"Hey, sleepy head. We're here."

A smile spreads on his lips, but he keeps his eyes closed.

"But I don't wanna go to school today..." he whines, then chuckles, returning the forehead kiss to me. He looks around and notices where we are, eyes wide. "Is it starting?"

"Just about," I say, opening my door and jumping out. "C'mon, let's go find a good spot." I reach into the back seat and grab the blanket I brought for us to sit on.

He takes a minute, but steps out of the SUV, balancing himself against the car briefly. I pretend again not to notice and busy myself folding and refolding the blanket.

I wish I knew what he wanted me to do in these situations. If I acknowledge it, I feel like I'm somehow undermining or babying him, which I know he doesn't want. I'll need to be stealthy.

"C'mon, slowpoke," I chide with a laugh.

Walking back for him, I slide my arm through his

on his right side, slowly helping him along by leaning against him but holding him up at the same time. It's a balancing act, but I think it's working.

I usually would sit a little way out, but I see a spot not too far away that will be fine for us. Away from other people, but still with a great view.

Once we get to the edge area I'd set my sights on, I let go of him to spread the blanket.

"Do you want to dangle your feet into the canyon? Or play it safe from the edge?"

He frowns, stepping toward the edge briefly to check it out, but then sways on his feet slightly.

"Whoa," he mumbles, rubbing his forehead, obviously dizzy.

I panic and nearly tackle him as I push him away from the edge. My heart is in my throat as my mind flashes visions of him falling over and into the canyon.

For a second, I can't breathe.

"Oh my god. Oh my god, Oliver. That just scared the shit out of me. Are you okay?"

When I glance up at him, he's staring at me in horror, and he suddenly sits down where he stands.

"I... I just..." His head is shaking from side to side, and his voice sounds like he's dazed. "A little vertigo, that's all. Like in the helicopter...."

"You had vertigo in the helicopter?" I ask, kneeling in front of him and grabbing his hands. I can't tell which of us is trembling. Maybe we both are. "You didn't say anything about it."

I don't like that he needed to keep that to himself. I should know these things. At least, I think I should. Maybe I have no business knowing anything.

"I, I grabbed your hand, real tight, when the ground fell away. You didn't notice?" He still seems confused, and I don't like it.

I think about the helicopter ride and remember him grabbing my hand, but I thought it was because he was moved by the sight of everything. It's an incredible view to take in the first time.

"I did. But I didn't know that was why."

I'm talking to myself again in his sunglasses, and it's starting to irritate me to not be able to see his expressions. I need to see his eyes. They truly are the windows to his soul, and I hate when they're hidden from me like this.

However, the reflection of the beginning sunset in the mirrored lenses is fascinating. I hold up a finger, letting him know this is just a pause, and grab my phone out of my bag.

"What are you doing?" he asks, now thoroughly confused.

"I'm being artsy. One second." I pull up my camera app and angle my phone at him from the side to get the canyon's reflection, not mine. "Keep looking straight. Don't look at me." I instruct.

He sighs but does as he's told. His jaw is set, and he's so serious. Not a happy line on his face. Then again, if I almost just fell into the Grand Canyon, I'd be pretty upset too. Hell, I am upset. But I'm trying to do anything and everything not to have to talk about it.

I take several pictures and then show them to him. They came out pretty amazing. I don't think I've taken any pictures of him, or us for that matter. I reach over, push his sunglasses to the top of his head, and do the same with my own. Then I lean in, put my head on his shoulder, and hold the phone up for a selfie.

"Here, give me that. I have longer arms than you." He's grumpy about it but appeases me by at least trying to smile for the picture. We both look questionably happy, and I suppose it's the best we'll get tonight.

"Thank you," I say, kissing his cheek and arranging the blanket I dropped a little while ago. I make sure it's safely far enough from the edge of the canyon that it's unlikely either of us will fall in. Oliver again just watches me, and when I take a seat in the middle of the blanket, it takes him a minute to move my way.

I splay my legs into a 'V' and pat the blanket in front of me, directing him to sit. He raises an eyebrow but sits, and I pull him back against my chest, forcing him to lean against me. He finally relaxes, stretching his long legs out carefully and crossing them at the ankle. I run my fingers lazily through his silky hair, taking care not to shake or tremble.

We sit silently for a long while, both of us taking in the light show as it starts, first with a dusky purple haze that seems to color everything, including us. That turns into pinks, then catches fire with red and oranges. And not just on the horizon, but on the entire sky. What few clouds there are reflect lighter shades of colors and then darker ones. Finally, navy and teal take over, with a slight bit of yellow edging the horizon, making it look like the far-away ground is burning.

When navy blue takes over everything, it's done. The whole thing started slow and then sped up exponentially like a fireworks show with a grand finale.

Next, the stars make their appearance, and with no electric light for quite a distance, the constellations start their own show.

The sunsets are always breathtaking to watch, and I'm glad that Oliver witnessed it.

I finally break the silence. "So, what did you think?" I slide my hands down the front of his chest and rest my cheek on top of his head, breathing in his shampoo.

"That. Was *the most* amazing sunset I have ever witnessed." He tilts his head back to look at me upside down from my lap, and I can't help but lean down and give him a quick kiss. "Thank you."

"No, thank *you*," I say, kissing him again. Getting them while I can. "I haven't been out here in a while, so it was nice to experience it with you." I smile down at him, and I think he's smiling at me, but since we're upside down from each other, it looks more like a frown.

I want so badly to tell him how I feel right now. I'm biting my tongue so hard that I think I might be drawing blood. I swear I feel a hesitation in him too, or an anticipation, like he wants to say something but is holding himself back like I am.

That makes me want to say it even more, be the one that breaks this stalemate between us, but I can't. I know what he'll say if I do, and I can't face that now. Maybe once he leaves, I'll be able to handle the rejection of it all, but right now, I'm in self-protection mode.

"We should get going, it's a bit of a drive back to the house, and it's getting late."

My heart pangs as I mention the time. Time we don't have. Time that's running out so damned quickly.

Chapter 29

Is It Really You?

Oliver

We drive back to the house in relative silence, and I can tell we both feel the end approaching rapidly. The trip allows me to consider what happened while we were at the Grand Canyon today. First, the effect of the extreme heat on my body is kind of scary. Not only was I dizzy in the helicopter on several occasions, but it also worsened my leg's numbness. I think I hid my resulting limp successfully from Bianca, but who knows. She's too observant for her own good sometimes.

And the pièce de résistance, my nearly falling ass over tea kettle to my certain death into the canyon itself when suddenly hit by a wave of vertigo. I should have known that the heat would affect me this way and prepared for it. I also should have known that my balance isn't the greatest shortly after waking, so the nap in the car wasn't the best idea either.

I can blame the heat for everything all I want, but it's me. I'm the one putting myself in these stupid positions to begin with. I definitely know better. I just wanted to appear normal to Bianca for one fucking day. Just one. And I failed that in magnificent style.

It's no wonder things have been strangely quiet between us today. She's probably counting down the minutes to be rid of me. I would be. And me? I'm counting the minutes until my heart gets ripped out of me. A dark sense of dread is washing over me already, and I imagine it will stay with me for a very long time, if not forever, however long that might be.

When we reach the house, we dance around each other uneasily for a bit before agreeing on sitting by a fire in the firepit out back. Bianca grabs a glass of wine, and I make a mug of hot chocolate.

Once a decent fire is going, I sit next to her and place an arm around her shoulders. I need to take in as much Bianca as I can tonight because it needs to last.

Instead of looking into the fire, I look up at the vast roof of constellations above us. The moon's brightness washes out most of the starlight, but it's still better than anything I can view at home.

Bianca leans against me, turning her attention to the sky as well.

"There's supposed to be meteor showers now, but I don't think we'll see anything this early or with the moon out like that." As soon as she says this, a bright blue streak quickly shoots across a small section of the sky and disappears. That makes her giggle and take a sip of wine. "Nevermind."

We sit silently for a long while, alternating our attention to the fire and the sky. I'm soaking in her presence beside me because I know that this is what I will miss the most when I leave.

I am typically good company for myself and don't mind living alone, unlike a lot of people who need to be with someone at all times. I think that's now changed for me. It's not that I've gotten used to being with Bianca. It's more that I *want* to be with her.

"So, you go back home tomorrow...."

Shit. Here we go.

"I do."

I don't want to do this. I have to do this. But how?

"Have you thought about what happens with us after tomorrow?"

I can hear the hopefulness in her voice, and that

shroud of dread covering me earlier starts to suffocate me. I really don't want to hurt her, but we don't have good options.

"Have you considered moving to London?" I ask softly. I don't want to sound like this is all on her. It isn't.

"I have, actually."

This surprises the shit out of me. Could this be a possibility after all?

"Oh? And what are you thinking?" I don't even try to cover my own hopefulness.

"I'm thinking I still need to think about it some more. That would be a big step."

"I see," I say quickly, my hope disappearing as fast as that meteor we saw.

"And what about you? Have you considered moving here?"

"Unfortunately, the dreadful heat of Nevada and I are neither mates nor friendly acquaintances. So, no. A move here is not in my future."

I feel her nod against my shoulder, and we both fall quiet again. This is absolute torture, and the pain that's been growing inside me as my departure approaches is now all-consuming. A few more hours and I'll be entirely empty.

"So, what are we going to do in the meantime? Any ideas?"

That hope is back in her words, stabbing at me like knives. Maybe becoming empty and numb is for the better since I won't have to feel this anymore.

"I think we should end things here rather than trying to carry on once I leave and things petering out slowly and painfully. That way, if it becomes unbearable to be apart, we'll know we must act." I've considered this more than I should, and this is the only way that makes sense.

She sits up and faces me, her face half in shadows from the fire, so I can't read her expression.

"That's kind of a reverse way to do things."

I nod. "It is. But that's kind of our thing, isn't it?" I smile a little bit, trying to lighten this heavy emotion pushing down on us.

Her brow furrows as she considers my proposal.

"How would it work? How much time do we wait to see if we need to act? What if we can't wait?"

These are all excellent questions, and at this point, I'm making it up as I go.

"Six months. We go back to living our regular lives again. We give it six months without any contact. No emails, no texts, no phone calls. And if it's ultimately going to work between us, six months will be nothing in the long run. Right?"

Her sad eyes study me closely. Surely six months will be enough for her to move on and forget me. She'll realize how horrible the idea of a relationship with me is and thank her lucky stars that we did things this way. She'll be unburdened by and unobligated to me in any way, shape, or form, able to have a normal and happy life with someone else.

The thought of Bianca with somebody else almost makes me take it all back, but what would I expect? She's too special to go long without someone discovering that like I have. I swallow hard, pushing down my instinct to fight for her.

"But..." she whispers, lowering her head and staring at our entwined fingers.

"But, what?"

She hesitates, then meets my eyes, the pain behind them now bare to me, though she's withholding her tears bravely.

"The thing is, I love you, Oliver."

I shut my eyes and breathe in sharply.

No. No. No.

"Don't. Bianca. Don't do this."

My heart is kicking me in the head, telling me to say it back to her because it's true, isn't it? I do love her as well? Then why not fucking tell her that? Because there are too many damned reasons to list, not to mention the worst of them, that I don't deserve her.

She pulls her hands out of mine and frames my face with them.

"Look at me, Oliver, and tell me you don't feel the same because I know you do." The pleading in her voice will haunt me for the rest of my life.

My god, this is fucking killing me.

I return the action and grab her face, her soft skin warm and dry, but those unshed tears she was holding back now threaten.

"Love has nothing to do with this. Whether or not you or I love each other isn't the main issue between us, and you know it. There are fundamental differences between us, Bianca." She breathes in as if to argue, but I put a finger over her lips, silencing her. "Just because you think you don't need everything on your life's wish list, and to be honest, maybe you don't, that doesn't mean you don't deserve to have them. You *do* deserve them. *All of them.* Every single thing your heart desires should be yours. And I can't be the one to give those to you."

That does it. The tears fall, streaking her cheeks, catching and reflecting the dying firelight. Each one that falls fills me with disdain and drowns me in self-hatred.

This is cruel. And I know it. I can see what it's doing to her. It's breaking her heart. I know this is the right thing to do, though. It has to be.

I meant every word I said. She does deserve so much better than me. She should have a full life, with as many children as she wants and as little worry as possible. I need to believe that she'll find that, even though I die inside at the thought.

She inhales a little sniffle and takes a deep breath, looking up at the night sky.

"Okay, six months, let's see. This is August, so

September, October..." Her voice trails off as she counts the months in her head and on her fingers.

It's adorable and heartbreaking at the same time. I just want to pull her to me and never let go. Fuck counting months or hours. I could stay here. With her.

I turn my eyes to the sky, too, wishing for inner strength to do the right thing. To leave her be and let her have the life she really wants.

"Okay. February 21st. That's six months from tomorrow." She is so determined, her shoulders set and squared to me, her voice more confident. "That's when you'll be hearing from me again. Okay?" She pulls on my shirt, yanking me to tear my gaze from the stars and face her. We've ignored the fire while talking, and it's down to embers now. The pale moonlight shines off her dark hair that now looks like ink blending into the night shadows behind her. "Okay, Oliver? February 21st."

I nod, not only not as confident as her but resigned to the fact that the day in question will come and go without incident or fanfare. It will be a regular day for both of us. One full of sunshine and happiness for her, and, well, not the same for me.

"Okay," I finally give in, if only to appease her. I don't want to argue on our last night together.

The day's exhaustion has caught up to me, and I am weary. Besides my heart being broken and dying inside me, I am beyond tired and worried I'm not thinking straight. I know I've done the right thing so far, but I still need to be cautious.

In my current state, I could give in to just about anything Bianca asks. I stand up carefully and hold a hand out to her, not wanting this night to end but resigned to my fate.

"Let's go to bed."

Chapter 30

Just Pretend

Bianca

We lay in bed, holding each other all night. I doze occasionally but mostly stay up, memorizing everything about this night. The feel of his arms wrapped around me tightly while he sleeps, the sound of his deep breaths as his chest rises and falls beneath my head, resting on top.

Every sensory input I have hungrily absorbs everything about him. And in the back of my mind is a ticking clock, counting down to when he leaves, and I will have to say goodbye to him.

In my mind, it's only temporary, just for six months, but I'm scared to death that in that time he will forget me. Any feelings he might have for me now will only weaken with that much time apart. My worry chases its tail in circles until I eventually fall asleep, holding onto Oliver for dear life.

I wake up with the sun slanting sideways through the bedroom window. I stretch lazily, feeling more refreshed than I thought I would with such little sleep. The sheets are cold as my arm hits the bed.

My eyes shoot open, glancing next to me for Oliver, then around the room for any sign of him. My ears perk up like antennae, listening for any sign of him, and it's deathly silent in the house.

A deep chill snakes through me, making me shiver, and my hair stands on end.

Where the hell is Oliver?

Maybe he's outside drinking his coffee. I jump out of bed and run into the great room, no sign of him. I look out of the windows onto the back deck, and again, no Oliver. I quickly check every other room in the house. There's no sign of him anywhere.

No suitcases. No laptop bag. No toiletries in the bathroom.

He's gone.

The sinking feeling that was spreading in my chest turns into a gut-wrenching sob, and the tears are a flood. I lean against the refrigerator and slide to the floor as it all pours out of me.

I am full of so many emotions right now. The deepest sadness I've ever felt, but also probably the deepest anger. Enzo is right. Everything is passionate with me, both good and bad. And now, I'm feeling everything all at once.

How could he just leave without saying goodbye? Without a single word? I must have scared him away when I told him I loved him.

My first instinct is to call or text to see if he's okay. Check that he made it to the airport in time for his flight. It's such a long trip for him to get home. I hope he's getting through it alright. I know sitting for an extended time isn't great for him.

And I need to stop that shit right now. He left. He left *me*. He left me here without a fucking word. Six months? How about six seconds? Decision made.

You don't just up and leave someone that you know you're not going to talk to for that long without saying goodbye. It's just not right. It's downright rude.

My eye catches on something sticking out of one of my bags by the door. It looks like a thin tube mailing container. I pick myself up and off the floor, approaching the bag tentatively. That tube isn't mine. I didn't get any souvenirs in a container like that.

It has to be from Oliver.

Carefully, I remove the plastic cap on the end and peek inside. Still unable to tell what it is, I upend the tube's contents onto the kitchen counter. It's a roll that appears to be a poster, and there's a note attached to it, secured by a rubber band.

What the heck? I work the message free and unroll the poster. It's a photo of the cutest little kitten hanging on a branch with the words "Hang In There!" in large type underneath.

The sound that escapes me is both cry and laugh, and it's appropriate, too, since I feel both. It's perfect. Memories of us at my apartment discussing my possible décor run like a movie in my mind. Then it shifts to other things we did there, and I have to shake it off.

I roll the poster back up and tap it into the container again. I'll have to think later if I really want to hang it up or not. I may not want the reminder.

Next, I turn to the note, picking it up gingerly as if it might bite me if I'm not careful. I know that whatever is in it will hurt me regardless, so I'm sure I'm not that far off. I have to work my anger back to the level he deserves.

This note in my hand is all he's left me with instead of facing me like a human being.

Drawing in and exhaling a super deep breath, I open the note with shaking hands.

Bianca,

I know this is not how you envisioned things ending between us, but I think this is for the best. As I told you last night, even if you require less, that doesn't mean you don't deserve more. And you do. You have no idea how much I wish I could deserve you. Maybe in another life, and under better circumstances, I will.

Until that happens, in this life, know that you were right last night. I do feel the same. But, as we both know all too well, sometimes love just isn't enough. As much as that hurts, it's equally important.

I made a hundred wishes for you on the stars last night, but you don't need them. I'm positive you will find the life you want to live without any celestial intervention.

Yours,
-Oliver

I sit on one of the barstools at the kitchen island, rereading the note several times until I can probably recite it verbatim if I want to.

I don't want to.

I don't want to think about his words and how final they are. He couldn't even tell me directly that he loved me, just that I was right. He has given up.

What a coward.

I am so tempted to draft a response text, email, or something to tell him off, but glancing at the clock on the stove, I can see he wouldn't get it for hours yet. By that time, I might have changed my mind and would regret it.

But would I really?

My phone starts ringing in the bedroom, and I leap off the barstool and grab it. It's Enzo. Of course, it is. I debate sending it to voicemail, but I know he'll just keep calling. I clear my throat and try to sound as normal as possible.

"Hey, Enzo, what's up?" I hold my breath and close my eyes tightly.

Please don't be intuitive right now.

"You tell me." That's it. That's all he says. God damn him. I try to think of what to tell him, but I must not answer quickly enough because he adds, "Do I need to jump on a plane to jolly old England to keep my promise to kill a certain someone if they hurt you? Because say the word sis, I've got air miles burning a hole in my pocket and a severe dislike of tea."

"Enzo..." I know he's trying to cheer me up, but it's making it worse.

"I'm serious." There is an edge to his voice that tells me he isn't playing. That I wasn't expecting. "I warned him."

"It's fine. I swear," I lie. "I'll be okay."

"I mean, I knew he was leaving today, but I wasn't sure how you guys would leave it. I take it things didn't go as you planned, huh?"

I sigh. I'm going to have to have this conversation sooner or later. May as well get it out of the way.

"He left early this morning without saying goodbye. He just left me a note."

"What?? Are you fucking kidding me?" I haven't heard Enzo this angry in a long time. "I swear, I'm hanging up and calling the airline now."

"Stop it, Enzo. It'll be alright."

I toss Oliver's note that I carried with me for some reason on the bed and plop down beside it. This downward spiral is pointless right now. I just want to go home. Begging off the call, I tell my brother not to do anything stupid and that I'll call him when I'm back in Vegas.

Once we hang up, I look around, my memory flashing to every moment in this house with Oliver. Like the house in Tahoe, it was like our little getaway, tinged with good and bad.

Suddenly it becomes too much again, and I throw myself onto my pillow, crying like I haven't in years. Letting my emotions overcome me for once and allowing myself to feel this pain. I know that when I leave here, I will need to cover it up, push it aside, ignore it, and pretend it doesn't exist. That's just how I do things.

While inside, I'll be dying a slow death by a thousand cuts, on the outside, I'll be *Bianca Torino, unruffled by life's curveballs* and ready to take on the world. Only I'll know better.

For now, I need to let it hurt, and it takes my breath away how much it does. Even when I caught Colin in his betrayal, it didn't hurt this deeply. This is new and fresh, and overwhelming. If I'm not careful, it could paralyze me. It could break me. Honestly, I think that's already happened.

I'm completely broken.

Chapter 31

Special

Oliver

Three Weeks After the Grand Canyon

A few weeks have passed since I arrived home, and little has changed. Actually, nothing has. I'm still miserable and miss Bianca every single day. I can't seem to avoid reminders of her, even being an ocean away. When I work on my book and review my notes, I remember exactly where we were and what she was doing while I was writing. She was always in my periphery, and I was always aware of her.

That's what makes this so hard, she's nowhere

near me, just *not there*. A hollow feeling starts to spread in my chest whenever I think of it, which seems to be all the time now, too.

I'm a mess.

I'm waiting to have lunch with Darcie at the most bougie Covent Garden hotel in a three-story glass atriumed restaurant that would otherwise impress me, but not today. I'm already bristling at the barrage of questions that are about to be hurled at me.

I've avoided Darcie since my return, limiting our communications to email and text, though she has left me many voicemails that I simply ignore. I only agreed to this lunch under heavy duress because she promised to have another lead reconnecting with elusive Max Calnetta.

Flipping through my phone to pass the time while I wait, I go through the pictures I took in Las Vegas. I find myself doing this more and more just to keep my memories fresh because some days, it feels like I'm forgetting everything. I go into full-blown panic at the idea.

The MS brain fog that hits out of nowhere can make me question my entire existence and every experience I've ever had. When it clears, I realize how crazy that is. Still, it plants an unsettling worry in my head that someday I'll completely forget everything about Vegas and Bianca. I know that's not how it works but try telling that to an already anxious brain when you're in the middle of it.

I come across a particular favorite picture of mine that I took of Bianca when she didn't even know I was looking. It was the morning of our trip to the Grand Canyon, after a very memorable night before, she was singing and dancing in the kitchen while she cooked us breakfast. Her hair is a sexy tousled mess, and she's wearing my t-shirt and nothing else. While *I* know there's nothing else, the picture isn't graphic. I like that I keep that little secret nobody else could see if they looked at it. It's mine and mine alone.

Her eyes are closed as she belts out a Billie Holiday song, just a little off-key but with full passion as always, swaying her hips smoothly to the beat. She was so comfortable with me, so open, so vulnerable, and I chose to turn my back on that only hours later. Not even a full rotation of the sun, and I was gone, leaving only a note.

Fucking coward.

I swipe quickly, going backward in time to Tahoe and the boat, which brings up even more memories of me being a complete twat. I keep going and come across a picture of Bianca and Ava at the Carmichael's house during the family barbeque. The two are in the large kitchen, scooping ice cream for everyone. They each have fingers in their mouths and sly grins at each other after "testing" the ice cream to make sure it was still cold enough.

The tether between us that I push down constantly, pangs. When I can't push it away, like now, I ignore it. There isn't anything else for it.

"There he is," I hear Darcie's cheerful voice cut through my reverie. I quickly shut off my phone and stand to greet her. At least I haven't completely lost my manners. She air kisses each cheek before holding me at arm's length with a judgmental eye. "Oh, Oliver. You look absolutely horrid."

I glance around briefly, seeing if her voice carries like I think it does. Luckily there isn't anyone in earshot.

"Thanks so much, Darcie. You're looking lovely as well." The sarcasm in my tone cuts the air between us sharply as I pull away from her.

I ignore her pained reaction as best I can and retake my seat. Just because I ignore it doesn't mean it doesn't affect me. I internalize every barb of pain I inflict on someone else. It just adds to my internal wounds.

She sits across from me and waives down the server, a bleach blonde emo girl with charcoal eyes and a nose ring that somehow both feels out of place and right at home.

"I'll have a Negroni Sbagliato, please."

I roll my eyes, knowing this is an idiotic trend she's trying to follow.

The server also knows this and seems to contain her angst about the entire thing.

"Would you like that with Prosecco?" The deadpan on this girl is remarkable and impressive. Though, working here, I'm sure she's seen a lot of pretension at play.

"Of course," Darcie replies, like there would be any other way to make a Negroni. It was Bianca that told me that *'sbagliato'* meant *'broken,'* so I have to bite my tongue not to correct Darcie about the whole thing. It's not worth it.

"So, why am I here, Darcie?" I ask, glancing around at the posh crowd, feeling highly inadequate in my jeans and jacket.

"Well, I wanted to check on you, for one thing," she snaps, getting just as irritated with me.

Fair play.

"As you can see, I am indeed alive and well." I force the smile that covers all of my press materials, the fake one.

She sees right through it.

"Alive? Yes. Well? To be decided." Frowning at me intensely, the concern in her eyes is edging on that line I don't want her to cross. "You don't look so well, Oli. What happened in Vegas? I know what happens there stays there or whatever, but something happened, didn't it?"

God damn it.

I guess three weeks is more time than I could

have hoped for to keep my pain to myself. I had to know that eventually, Darcie would get me in this position, where I would need to open up about Bianca.

And I do. I tell her everything. Well, almost everything. Some details wouldn't be gentlemanly of me to divulge, even to a friend. That includes the boat incident. I also skip the six-month break and the February 21st deadline. I don't want to have to explain it if it doesn't pan out like I want it to.

It takes Darcie two broken Negronis for me to finish. All the while, I watch her emotions as they unfold for her, and it's as if I'm watching someone demonstrate what every emotion looks like.

She stares at me long and hard when I finish, choosing her words carefully. I don't like it. When Darcie is quiet or careful, I never like what follows. Never.

"You're an idiot, you know that, Oli?"

I laugh, but she's not smiling as she says this, so this isn't a joke.

"Right. Thanks. Never said I wasn't. Brilliant, Darcie."

Sometimes she can be super unhelpful, like now. I don't know what I expected. Actually, I didn't expect to be talking about this today. I thought we were here to talk about my book.

"I have someone I want you to meet."

That came out of nowhere.

"Oh? Who?" I arch a brow, my gut telling me that I'm not going to like this sudden change of subject.

"His name is Oscar Goodwin. He's an old friend of my father's. I've told him about you, and he wants to meet you." She avoids looking at me or even in my general direction, checking her watch anxiously. That's never a good sign.

This gets even more dubious the more she talks.

"What exactly did you tell this Oscar person about me?"

She waves a hand. "Oh, you know. This and that."

"Darcie."

At that moment, she must notice someone she recognizes because her expression turns into relief, and she waves at someone across the restaurant.

Quickly, she leans over and whispers. "Please don't kill me, but Normandy already told me a couple of weeks ago all about what happened with you and Bianca while you were in Vegas. Also, Oscar is here. I invited him to join us so he could meet you."

The sensation of being blindsided slams into me at her words. But I don't have time to register it in time to react. I'm stunned.

She stands, holding a hand out to someone behind me. "Oscar, so good to see you. Here, take my seat." She picks up her bag, making room for Oscar to sit across from me. "Oscar, this is Oliver Bellamy that I talked to you about. Oliver, this is Oscar Goodwin, whom I just told you about a second ago. Please don't hate me." She kisses the top of my head as she passes to leave. "Okay, you two. Have a good talk. Bye now."

And she's gone.

I don't know where to look or what to say. I'm paralyzed by the whirlwind that just blew through here in the form of my best friend, who, I'm thinking, may no longer be my friend. It will depend on the impending conversation with this stranger.

Finally, focusing on him, I see he's an older gentleman, probably about my father's age too, with neat greying hair and bright blue eyes. He's on the thin side and uses a cane that he hooks the silver handle of to the top of the table. As I glance down at it curiously, I note that the handle is in the shape of a fox's head.

He holds a hand out to me over the table. "I'm Oscar," he declares sharply.

I hesitate only for a second, shaking his hand with a nod. "I'm Oliver."

His grip is firm, and his gaze is steady, but it's dawning on me what this is all about. The cane is a dead giveaway.

I'm going to kill Darcie.

"So, I hear you have MS," he snaps.

I knew it.

"That's correct." No point in denying it. It's why he's here, after all.

"Well, boo hoo." His tone is snide, like a boy in school. It throws me.

"Excuse me?"

"You have MS. Big deal. Supposedly you think it's the end of the world." He shrugs tightly. "I'm here to tell you it's not."

"Listen, I don't know you, but—"

"No, *you* listen. I just took two trains to come to talk to you as a favor to Darcie. You have people that care about you that you are shutting out for no *good* reason whatsoever." He waves down the emo girl and orders a tea. "Look. The truly insidious thing about MS, especially for us men, is that it strikes us right in our prime. We think we've got the world by the bollocks, you know what I'm saying? And, boom, game over. Well, here's a little secret. It's not over."

I stare at him. Part of me wants to listen to this, but a bigger part of me is still rebelling at being tricked into this conversation to begin with.

He sighs heavily. "Okay, so tough love doesn't work with you. Let me try this." Pulling his phone out of his jacket pocket, he scrolls for a bit, then holds it out to me, swiping at the pictures as he talks. "That there is my wife, Nan. We've been together for almost forty years now. She stood by me during my whole diagnosis. Never treated me differently a day in her life. She's the one that kicked me in the arse to go and start talking to other fellas about it. Got me to get a group going every other Thursday at the pub on the corner of my street. It made it easier for us to get together. It wasn't a support group as much as it was a bunch of mates getting together for a pint. But we'll talk more about that in a tick."

I simply nod, at a complete loss for words.

Swiping again, he pulls up a picture of a happy family. It looks like a mother, father, and three small kids in a back garden.

"This here is my daughter Elizabeth who's 33, and her family. Husband Jerry, and kids Georgia, Jack, and May." Another swipe, and another family. "That's my son Daniel, 37, with his wife Tracey, and their two boys, Jordan and Jacob." He pulls his phone back, studying the pictures with a small smile playing on his lips. Remembering himself, he puts the phone away and looks at me, growing serious once again. "None of them have MS."

I nod. "That's brilliant." Of course, it doesn't mean anything.

"Out of the twenty or so gents that meet in my group that are my age, eighteen of us have adult children. Out of those children, *none* of them have MS, either. Now that's not to say that it couldn't happen to you because it sure as hell could, but it's not likely. Is it *more* likely for you than someone else? Absofuckinglutely. Should that stop you from having your own kids someday? Hell no. Why would it?"

"That's great and all, but—" I again don't get to finish my thought.

"But do you know what *has* happened?" I shrug because, of course, I don't know where this is going. "Mike's daughter Lucy died two years ago from uterine cancer, leaving his son-in-law with two little kids to raise on his own. Joseph's son Cary had an incurable lymphoma that took him at ten years old. Marvin's daughter Margaret was killed in a car crash the night she graduated uni by a drunk driver."

I can see him getting a little choked up by these stories, which makes my stomach clench. I understand what he's trying to say, but I'm still not sure I buy into it.

"Do you think you're a unicorn or something? So damned special? You're the only one with this worry?"

"I see we're back to the tough love portion of the lecture." I can't help the smirk, and I suddenly feel very immature. I don't like it.

Is he right about all of this? Have I been too stubborn and fixated on the bad possibilities?

"It's kind of my thing. Royal Navy still in my blood." He snaps his palm to his forehead in a quick salute with a chuckle.

I don't salute back because I don't think I'm supposed to, being a civilian.

"Tell me, who else in your family has MS? Your father or mother? Grandparent? Uncle or Aunt?"

"Nobody." I shrug.

He raises an eyebrow at me but stays silent.

I raise my hands. "I get it, okay? I get it. But it doesn't change my mind about things. It's still a choice I can make for myself."

Oscar stands and grabs his cane, reaching into his jacket. He pulls out a card and hands it to me. "See you Thursday. As the newbie, the first round is on you." Patting my shoulder, he leaves.

I stare at the card, considering everything Oscar said. I feel like a hit-and-run victim, still trying to figure out what the fuck just happened.

Then, I get an idea.

Chapter 32

I Am the Fire

Bianca

Three **Weeks** **After** **the** **Grand** **Canyon**

"You don't have to wait around, Bianca. I can wait for Terry to get back from his run." I glance up from my desk and see Normandy leaning in the doorway, a look of concern on her creased brow.

"It's no problem," I say, shrugging. "I'm not going to Tahoe this weekend, so I don't mind staying late."

I haven't been back to the house on the lake since I was there with Oliver. I don't know if I'll ever be able to go back there. I'd hate for it to be ruined for me forever. What I need to do is let it go.

She walks into my office, sits in a chair across from me, and unconsciously splays a hand over her belly. I note it in my head but don't say anything.

"So, how are you doing, really? We haven't had a chance to really talk since... a few weeks ago, now." Her cheeks redden as she alters her words to avoid saying Oliver's name.

"You can say his name, Normandy. Since Oliver left." While internally, I scream, on the outside, I shrug again. "I'm not going to fall to pieces at the sound of his name."

"Okay, fine. How are you doing since Oliver left?"

"Not the greatest, but I'll be alright. Eventually."

I check my computer screen for the time. One of our drivers, Terry, was supposed to be back from the last job of the day by now, and I'm starting to get worried.

"Well, you don't look alright. You look like you're running yourself ragged. Have you eaten today?" She's getting that maternal tone in her voice that she uses with Ava.

I study her closer.

"Yes. I ate earlier."

"What did you eat? And when?"

"Gosh, mom. I had a Pop-Tart at lunch. Geez." I glare at her.

While she's my boss, I know I can get away with stuff like that since we're also good friends.

She glances at her watch and frowns. "Bianca, it's almost nine o'clock at night. Lunch was forever ago. You need to eat."

"I'll eat. Don't worry. I'm not going to wither away to nothing over a late dinner. It's all good."

"Well, it doesn't seem very good." Now she takes her splayed hand and rubs her belly without thinking.

That's it.

"Are you pregnant?" I ask, my tone accusatory because if she is, she should have told me by now.

Her hand freezes. "What? Why on earth would you ask that out of the blue?"

I pointedly glance down at her hand on her belly, then back up to her with an arched brow. She has to know I notice stuff like that.

She lets out a long sigh. "Fine. Yes. We're pregnant. Little Ava will finally get her wish of a younger sibling, and Jett can finally have some peace. Well, until Grace starts walking and talking. Poor kid."

"Oh my god, I'm going to be an aunt again!" I jump up from my chair and round my desk to hug her. "How far along are you? Do you have names picked out? How much baby stuff did you save? If any?"

The flurry of questions pours out of me without

thought. I am so happy for them since I know they've been trying for a while now. My smile is so big it almost hurts.

"I'm about three months along, I guess. The doctor put the due date at February 21st, so a late winter baby this time."

The smile on my face freezes as I hear that date. The day is supposed to be when Oliver and I either find each other again and live happily ever after or move on from each other.

I'm careful not to flinch. Normandy has no idea about the date or its significance to me. While she knows most, she doesn't know all of what happened between us.

"Well, I tell you what, Ava will be beside herself when she learns about this. That girl was built to be a big sister to somebody." I lean back on my desk and fold my arms, more as a hug of myself, but to hide my shaking hands too.

Normandy is right. I really should have eaten dinner by now. I just haven't been hungry lately. When Oliver first left, I ate everything in sight, then everything just switched off, including my appetite.

"You've got that right. We're telling her tomorrow at breakfast."

"Oh, I wish I could see her face. You better take a picture of her reaction. Or better yet, a video." I can feel my smile get weaker as our conversation goes on.

Even though I am beyond excited for Normandy

and Brandon, the self-pity for myself is starting to creep in too. I hate it. I should be able to be happy for my friend without being jealous of something I'll never have. It's not how true friends act. A wave of guilt washes over me.

Just then, Terry finally returns and hands the keys to the limo used for the job. It's perfect timing, as I'm able to wrap up work and get out of talking any more about Normandy's good news.

I really am a horrible person.

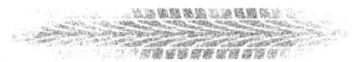

A few weeks later, I'm hit with another blow straight to the feels. Enzo and I each receive invitations to our cousin Gina's wedding. In Italy. On February 18th. It's not the 21st, but it's close enough to make me not want to go.

If Gina and I weren't as close as we are, I'd almost consider staying home. But we are tight, and she's even asked me to be one of her bridesmaids, so there's no way I could miss it.

Enzo knows it's close to our deadline, so he calls as soon as he receives his invitation.

"You gonna make it, sis?" he asks, a little distracted. That's not like him. Usually, when he calls, his full attention is on the conversation.

"Yeah, I'm a freaking bridesmaid, so no choice.

Hey...what's the matter? You don't sound like yourself." If I didn't know better, I'd swear I heard a female voice in the background. "Are you with someone?" I gasp dramatically. "Oh my god, are you on a date?"

I can almost hear him roll his eyes over the phone. "Yes, I am, actually. Not all of us are celibate like you seem to be now."

Ouch. That one smarts. Out of everyone, I didn't expect snark like that from him. He's usually the protector, not the antagonist.

I have not gone on dates since Oliver left, nor do I intend to. That doesn't necessarily make me celibate, just off the market.

He realizes his offense right away and apologizes. "I'm sorry, Bianca. I didn't mean that. You know I didn't. It was just something stupid to say while trying to be funny, I missed the mark. I'm sorry."

"It's okay. Jerk." I withhold the threatening sniffle. "Tell me about your date." I hope I sound nonchalant because I am genuinely interested, but like with Normandy's pregnancy, good things are happening to everyone else. That's not a group you want to be on the outside looking in at because that means good things aren't happening to you. And again, I feel like shit for even thinking such things.

"Well, her name is Theresa, and that's all you get today."

"Oh, man. No fair," I whine.

"I don't want to be rude with her here. I just wanted to make sure you got your invite to Gina's wedding."

"Okay. But I expect a full report the next time we talk."

We hang up, and I smile to myself. Enzo hasn't had a steady girlfriend in a while. He is very picky, and for good reason. He's a great guy. I don't think that just because he's my brother, either. He truly is incredible. Any girl would be lucky to have him. I hope this Theresa person, whoever she is, knows this.

Maybe I should work on my *'hurt my brother, and I'll kill you'* threat like Enzo gave Oliver. Nah. That's not me. Or maybe it is? Well, I guess if she hurts my brother, we'll find out.

Chapter 33

Sans Soleil

Oliver

Three Months After the Grand Canyon

The final draft of my manuscript for my book about the history of the mob in Las Vegas has been turned in and is even early. I went on a writing spree after finally being able to talk to Max Calnetta in earnest. And the book only needed a little polishing after that, much to my editor's delight.

Editing can sometimes take longer than writing the damn book, so I'm glad this one flew through the process. Darcie is ecstatic and is meeting me for lunch to celebrate.

It's a dreary London day, with rain forecast daily for just about the entire near future until spring. We meet at a local fish and chips place near my flat and grab a table by the front window.

It's a Saturday morning, and a group of guys here is watching a football match. I have no clue who's playing, but it's red kits versus blue, and apparently, red is preferred.

I never got into football, much to my father's chagrin. Now, if reading was a sport, I'd have been an Olympic gold medalist. Since becoming a writer, I don't read as much as I used to, but it still beats sports.

Unlike me, Darcie *is* a football fan and is splitting her attention between me and the TV hanging in the corner. According to her, this is a London derby, which is very important. As I've not heard it was happening today, I highly doubt that to be the case.

"You picked this place because it has a telly, didn't you?" I ask, masking my smile by popping a chip into my mouth. "Go on, admit it."

She glances at me, back to the screen, then at me again. "Sorry? Did you say something?"

I grin. This is going to be pointless until halftime of the game.

"I'm shaving my head and moving to Tibet," I say, barely above the crowd noise.

She nods at me briefly. "Uh-huh. That's nice, Oli." Then back to the telly.

I shake my head and sigh but have to laugh. Only Darcie would be this interested in a football match when I've told her I have an important book idea to discuss.

"Apparently, Martians are invading next Friday, so you should stock up on loo rolls and bread." I keep my face stone serious.

This time I only get a side eye and partial nod. "Oh, that's cool."

Something exciting happens on the screen, and everyone in the room amps up for a second and then lets out a simultaneous groan.

"There is no way he was offside. These refs are idiots, as usual," Darcie yells at nobody in particular.

I just keep shaking my head but turn my attention out the window. I wonder what the weather is like in Las Vegas today. I'm sure it's not as depressing as it is here. I also wonder what Bianca is doing right now. Probably still sleeping, or maybe just waking up...

"So, are you becoming a monk *because* of the Martians? Or are the two subjects not related?" Darcie asks, her head tilted. Of course. She doesn't miss a trick. "It's too bad, though. You do have nice hair. It's one of the few things I like about you lately."

That gets her a glare from me. "No need to be persnickety. I was just messing with you."

She raises her hands. "Fine. Fine. So, what did you want to talk about? We have fifteen minutes until the game is back."

I resist rolling my eyes and focus, realizing I have a short window for her attention span.

"Right. Well, I have a fantastic idea for my next book."

"Ooh, are you finally going to do that complete book on Dillinger? Or the one you've been talking about with your theory on where Matteo Denaro is?"

"Nope. My next book isn't going to have anything to do with organized crime."

Squinting at me suspiciously, she asks, "Oh? What's it about then?"

"Men with MS."

Her brows shoot up in surprise.

"Whoa. Did you just say your next book is going to be about men with MS? Are you really going to go public?"

I can feel heat rising in my cheeks since I'm the last person who likes to talk about themselves. In this instance, though, it might be helpful.

"Yeah. I think it's time I did." I square my shoulders a bit, trying to give myself the confidence that isn't quite there yet. "I've met a great group of guys, thanks to your introduction to Oscar, who meet every other week and sometimes talk to each other about their MS. Sometimes they don't, which makes it so great. They've really become friends."

Darcie grins, but her eyes tear up slightly. *Great. I did not want to face waterworks today.*

She reaches over and squeezes my arm. "That's amazing. So, what exactly is your book going to be about?"

"Everyone's stories. I've asked, and most have agreed to document their experiences from diagnosis to today. I think I'll add some experts to weigh in on things too, so I'm not giving out any misinformation. I think it might be helpful to someone like me, who gets MS and then gives up on life. I want to show that life goes on. Or, well, it should."

My eyes drop to my fidgeting hands on the table. Thoughts of how much I fucked things up with Bianca roll through me. I can't even fathom that she would forgive me after how much I hurt her. But something in me still believes that maybe by February 21st, I'll be mentally in a position where I can be the man she deserves. I need to believe it. I'm kind of hinging everything on it, which might not be the healthiest thing, either.

"Oli?" Darcie is leaning forward, trying to get my attention.

"Huh?" I laugh. "Sorry, my turn to space out."

"Have you talked to the publisher yet? What's going on there?"

"Yes, but I'll still need you to do your agent

thing. They said they'll forward contracts to you in the next week or so."

"How are you going to find time to write this other book? Your book tour for this current release starts in a couple of months?"

Her concern is appreciated but unwarranted.

"Don't worry, Darcie. I'll manage. I can take my time with the MS book. I don't think there's a deadline since we're not doing an advance on this one."

Darcie's eyes widen in shock. "No advance? Why not? Do they not know who you are?" She's chuckling, but I get the feeling she's only half kidding.

"No advance. And the proceeds, minus your fees, of course, are going to charity."

"Charity?" She puts the back of her hand on my forehead. "Are you sure you're well? What charity?"

I swat her hand away lightly. "I'm not sure yet. There's a social network for people with MS that I'm looking into called *Shift.ms*, and I might look into starting my own foundation to help support groups like the one Oscar started. Maybe both? I don't know quite yet." I shrug because I'm *not* sure. There are a lot of different charities in the world, and a lot are aimed at MS. Most are both worthy and need financial help.

Out of nowhere, Darcie grabs my hands with both of hers, her eyes shining with tears.

"Damn you, Oli." She wipes her eyes with the back of her hands. "Take my fee too. Just don't tell Pamela, okay?"

I chuckle. "My lips are sealed."

The crowd behind us cheers as if on cue, and Darcie glances up and joins in the celebration. Apparently, the guys in the red kits are now doing well.

So am I, boys. So am I. I just hope it's enough.

Chapter 34

Heartache Melody

Bianca

Three Months After the Grand Canyon

This has been the longest three months of my life. It doesn't help that I look at the calendar every day and count the days since I last saw Oliver, and the days still to go to February 21st. To be honest, I thought if he really did love me, he wouldn't be able to wait until February. Obviously, I was wrong. Either he doesn't really love me, or he's got a hell of a lot of willpower. Or, he's just damned stubborn. It could be any one of those.

We're halfway through our self-imposed cooling-off period. Why haven't I broken down and reached out to him? I have to tell myself these reasons daily so I don't forget.

First, I already told him I loved him, and well, he didn't. He specifically didn't say it, which isn't something that can go unnoticed. I think I was already too sad when that happened, and it blended in with all the other pain hitting me that night. The more I think about it, the more profound it is. If he felt it, he could have said it. Even if he didn't want to stay with me at that moment, he could have been honest. *If* he honestly felt that. He must not have.

With that fact in the back of my mind, the second reason I don't reach out is absurdly clear: there's no point. If he couldn't say it back to me, then he's not suddenly going to be able to say it after not seeing me for six months. It's ludicrous to think anyone could.

I'm not going to put myself in the position of exposing my vulnerability and subject myself to that embarrassment. I've made a fool of myself around Oliver enough for a lifetime. I always showed and said how I felt, never getting anything in return.

The problem with all of this is, and it's a big one, I *do* still love him. I can't help it. A couple of weeks after he left, I bought every single one of his books just so I could read his words. It's the closest I could get to his thoughts and voice. I could almost hear him reading to me from the text. He writes as he speaks, effortlessly and with a dry humor. I found his books fascinating, too, which was a bonus. They're something to decorate my fireplace now, and they offset the kitten poster hanging above it nicely.

It's Thanksgiving and my least favorite holiday. I don't know why, but I've never enjoyed it. I like having the family together, but that's it. Maybe because there aren't any presents involved. I like presents.

This year will be extra lonely since Enzo is staying in Los Angeles to spend it with his new girlfriend, Theresa. I can't begrudge him that, though. It's a new relationship. They're still getting to know each other and impressing family. I don't need to be impressed. If my brother is happy, I'm happy. It's pretty straightforward where we're concerned.

Normandy and Brandon invited me to their house, probably out of pity that I'd be alone, but I didn't care. I said yes. I get to see the kids and don't have to cook, so I'm in. Plus, the Carmichaels have the most fantastic wine cellar. With all that going for it, why would I refuse?

I arrive a little early so I can get some extra Ava time. Ever since Normandy started showing in earnest, Ava's been a little withdrawn. I thought she would be climbing the walls with excitement at having a new sibling. I guess I don't know as much about kids as I thought. Or at least as much about Ava as I thought I did.

All of the thoughts about Ava being withdrawn go out the window when I walk in because she practically knocks me over as she runs to give me a hug.

"Aunt B!" She screams, coming at me at top speed.

I crouch down to catch her, and she barrels into me, wrapping her arms around my neck and squeezing tightly. I pick her up and swing her around, making her giggle.

When I stop, I see Normandy and Chelsie staring at me, horror-stricken. My heart stops.

"What? What's wrong?" I ask, pulling back to look at Ava to see if something is wrong with her, but I don't see any injuries.

What I do see are her hands. One has red paint on it, and the other has yellow. All over the palms of her hands. Little hands and fingers that were just in my hair, around my neck, and on my back.

Shit.

"Oh no, Bianca. I am so sorry about that," Normandy says, coming up and peeling Ava off me, who looks scared to death that she did something wrong. "We were finger painting turkeys for place settings, and well, you know the rest."

Seeing Ava so worried breaks my heart, so I roll with it as best as I can.

"Well, I need to see these amazing turkeys immediately." I give her a wink and a smile. "I do have their feathers in my hair now, after all."

That gets her to smile, and it's when I notice Jett standing next to Chelsie, paint on his own hands that is now smeared all over her jeans around her knee. I can't help but point at her leg and start laughing. Chelsie looks at what I'm pointing at, rolls her eyes with a sigh, and laughs too. At least I'm not the only one playing the part of an art canvas today.

There's a special kind of energy that kids emit on holidays when there are a lot of people around. A buzz in the air is full of their excitement at all the extra attention they get. It's not that they're deprived otherwise, but it's a day for excess. Excess food, excess attention, excess everything.

All day I soak it in, reveling in their spirit and imaginations. Jett is turning out to be quite the storyteller, availing us with some amazing make-believe tales. And every time I held Grace, I got a running report about what she can and can't do now. It's all very exciting.

By the time evening rolls around and the turkey coma is starting to hit everyone, especially the kids, I make my excuses and leave for home. I'm not tired. Quite the opposite. I'm overloaded.

While I'm used to a lot of daily activity at the depot, it's nothing compared to today's onslaught. I thought I was ready for it and even craved it, but I was wrong. It was too much.

When I enter my apartment and switch on the track lights by the fireplace, something inside me cracks when I see that poster of the kitten hanging on that dumb branch. *Hang in there.*

I can't anymore.

It starts with a sob, and I wrap my arms around myself as if they could hold me together, and the tears don't stop. I haven't cried since the day he left, and I don't know why today is so different from any other.

I think today it felt officially over because it's a holiday. Loved ones spend holidays together, or at the very fucking least, they call or text. I don't receive either, nor do I expect them. I know now that it's truly over.

I need to give up the idea that happily ever afters happen for everyone. They don't. Some people end up cold and alone, pining for someone who doesn't care.

It's me. I'm some people.

Straightening myself, I wipe my tears, not caring what it's doing to my makeup. With the paint still in my hair, runny mascara is the least of my worries. I walk over to the fireplace and rip the poster off the wall, my heart tearing with it. I crumple it into a ball as I take it to the kitchen and throw it into the trash can, but I'm not done.

I return to the fireplace, grab Oliver's books off the mantle, and then return to the kitchen. I'm about to drop them into the trash, but I can't bring myself to do that. Something makes me hesitate, hovering the books above the opening for a minute. I stare at Oliver's picture on the back of the cover of the bottom book, and I suddenly can't breathe.

Laying the books on the counter, I try to gather myself. I can't throw them out. Finally, I put them in a box, write the word "FREE" on it, and take them out into the hallway, leaving the box by the elevator. Out of sight, out of mind.

The theory works until I go back into the apartment, where the bare mantle and wall above the fireplace now remind me of what used to be there.

They look empty. *Like me.*

Chapter 35

Traveling On

Oliver

Five Months After the Grand Canyon

Two weeks into the publicity tour for my book, *Open City Las Vegas: The Modern Wild West*, and I'm already starting to feel burnt out. Darcie did her best to space out the appearances as much as possible, to give me time to rest, but there's just something soul-draining about having to be 'on' for hours at a time.

Add to this crazy pace the fact that I'm traveling through the Northeast and Midwest of the US during January, and it's a perfect recipe for being absolutely miserable. I appreciate that it's not unrelenting heat because that's like kryptonite to MS, but this is a little ridiculous.

At least we'll be heading south and west in a few more weeks. That's how I instructed Darcie to schedule the agenda to ensure I'm where I need to be on February 21st.

The holidays were a blur, and I spent Boxing Day with Darcie and Pamela, who were kind enough to invite me to their home. However, they insisted on watching football matches all day, so I bowed out relatively early. I should have known better on that one. And I was in bed early on New Year's Eve, so my party days are apparently over.

It's incredible what a difference five months can make when you concentrate on improving yourself. Rather than playing the stagnant hermit like I did the first year after my diagnosis, I've broken out of that shell and made some significant changes.

I've completely altered my diet to battle the inflammation associated with MS, and I've started various fitness activities, from yoga to cycling, to keep my strength and balance issues at bay. I've even started regular acupuncture and massage therapy.

The final and most significant change has been engaging a therapist. The Thursday group with Oscar is still helpful, but even with that, there are things you don't want to talk about with your mates.

Peeling back the onion that is the human

experience layer by layer has been enlightening. Recognizing that I was letting my fear rule every aspect of my life was a start. Now the task becomes letting go of that fear, which I'm finding is more difficult than anything else thus far.

I'm perfectly okay having someone stick me with a bunch of tiny needles on the auspice of feeling better, but tell someone how I'm genuinely feeling about anything? *Pfft*. No thanks.

I am working on it.

Sitting in an airport in Cleveland, waiting for our flight to Chicago, Darcie has decided that this is a great time to talk about the break I insisted on in February.

"I mean, I think it's brilliant that you've baked in a little bit of a respite into the itinerary, but why can't you tell me what you have planned? And why I'm not invited. It's rude." She chuckles, but the thought of that time revives my anxiety.

I try to think of a way to explain it without explaining it while trying to get comfortable in the airport seating.

"It's just a break from everything. Including you. So, I couldn't very well invite you along, could I?" I flash her a smile, letting her know I'm joking. But she still examines me closely.

"Fine. Keep your secrets." She goes back to her phone, scrolling with a shrug.

My therapist is the only other person besides

Bianca who knows about that time's significance. Honestly, he's not a fan of the agreement at all, but I'm committed to seeing it through regardless. I needed the time to work on myself. It didn't start out that way but evolved unexpectedly.

I thought for sure this long time apart would extinguish the fire that had ignited in me for Bianca, but it hasn't. If anything, it's fanned those flames by making me think a real relationship might be possible between us now that I'm in a better place mentally and physically. The transformation that needed to happen for me was immense, and something that big can't change overnight. It needs time.

While I can't and, for the most part, don't live based on my fear anymore, one huge worry keeps me up at night, that Bianca has moved on. I have no right to think that she would do anything other than forget me and find someone else. To be honest, she should. I won't blame her one bit if she has. I was an idiot, and she does deserve better than who I was back then.

When I arrive in Las Vegas next month, with my heart in my hand to offer to her, I can only pray that my deepest fears won't become a reality.

Besides my scheduled signings at various bookstores in Chicago, Darcie has arranged press interviews with both television and print outlets. I would much rather meet with readers and discuss my books than meet the press and discuss my life.

While readers come from a place of honesty and interest, it always feels like the media comes with ulterior motives. They want to get exclusive information or salacious details that they can twist and warp to their own purpose. Whatever gets them the internet clicks they want.

What I didn't expect, and I have mixed emotions about, is that the media want to discuss my new book project more than the book I'm touring on. Darcie isn't sure how to feel about it either, so I'm left to fend for myself on what I can or should say about it.

"So, are you going to include your personal experience about living with MS in this new book?" a young and eager reporter asks. He's the third interview of the day, and the first to directly or indirectly ask if I have MS. This is a clever way to ask the question, and I respect the care that went into it.

"I am, actually. I was diagnosed about eighteen months ago, and the journey from then until now has been quite enlightening."

He arches a curious brow. "Enlightening? How so?"

Well shit. I guess I need to follow up on that, don't I?

"When I was first diagnosed. No, actually, the entire first *year* was dreadful. A nightmare, really." I shift a little in my seat. It's suddenly hot in this studio, and the lights are too bright. "I was a bit of a monster at first. I didn't understand my limits and found myself pushing them too far quite often. That would, of course, only feed the monster, and other people would get hurt in the process. I became extraordinarily good at that, unfortunately. Hurting other people."

He stares at me a moment, maybe surprised at my candor or stumped on how to follow that up.

"Have you made amends? To those you hurt?"

It's my turn to be surprised, and I'm not sure if the question is intended to pursue the train of thought, or if it's proffered to expose some sort of drama. In the end, it's a legitimate question. My thoughts instantly snap to Bianca. The biggest apology not yet given. The amends I'm dying to make.

"Not everyone. But soon. I hope to very soon."

Behind the reporter, I see Darcie nod to herself as if my answer just confirmed something for her. She gives me a knowing look, and I think she now understands my intentions during the tour break. And who I'm referring to when I say '*soon.*' I guess I wasn't going to be able to keep it a secret for very long anyway, so it ultimately doesn't matter that she knows.

"I also understand that you'll not be taking royalties for this project. Is that true? What's the story there?"

"It is indeed true. Not only do I want to share real-life stories about living with MS, but I want to help fund organizations that maintain a person's independence as long as possible, because not everyone has the support they need."

"Do you have any particular charities in mind?"

My research into charities has settled me on a particular focus. "Yes, actually. Service dogs have become a real source of support for people with MS. They can help with balance issues, household tasks, and even pulling wheelchairs if necessary. They are frightfully expensive to train, and rightly so since they do such an important job. So, I will be focusing on those sorts of programs."

Part of me doesn't like talking about the royalty issue because I don't want to appear pretentious. The last thing I want to do is try to sound like a better person than I am. I was perfectly happy not discussing it at all. However, Darcie convinced me that letting it be known might increase interest in the book and subsequent sales, so I conceded the point. I hope it does both.

As the tour continues to drag on, my anticipation of the reconciliation I referred to in the interview grows to the point of distraction.

For me, '*soon*' isn't soon enough.

Chapter 36

Need You Now

Bianca

arly February

The rest of the holiday season is full of activity. I join my brother in Los Angeles for Christmas and finally meet his girlfriend. She is beautiful and lovely, and I've never seen my brother so smitten with another human being. Theresa definitely received my sisterly seal of approval.

New Year's was spent again at the Carmichael's for their annual party. It's a much more formal affair than Thanksgiving was, and I got the feeling that Normandy and Brandon were trying to hook me up with Brandon's brother Jon. While he was charming and not too harsh on the eyes, neither of us was interested. It was nice to have someone to speak to most of the evening, but that was about it. I ended up heading home not long after midnight.

Each holiday was bittersweet for me. I enjoyed my friends and family, but I also felt incredibly alone. Probably more alone than I've ever felt. I used to be able to do things solo, but ever since Oliver left, the sense of something missing from my life has only grown. To this day, I'm still haunted by his absence.

The rest of January dragged on, each day feeling longer than the last. And now, February is here, and it's impossible not to focus on what's *not* going to happen in a few weeks. Not just because I'll be in Italy for Gina's wedding, but because Oliver won't be here anyway.

As much as I want to think that he meant anything he said, I also read between the lines, between his words, and know that it's a lost cause. I don't get the happily ever after.

A week before I leave for Italy, I step into the break room at work for a coffee refill when I hear Oliver's voice. I freeze in place, unable to breathe.

What the hell?

"That would, of course, only feed the monster, and other people got hurt in the process. I became extraordinarily good at that unfortunately. Hurting other people."

"Sorry about that. I forgot I left the TV on when I was in here for lunch earlier." The sound of Oliver's voice is gone and replaced by that of Noah, our head mechanic. I turn and see his face reddening as he stands next to the TV. It's either an odd coincidence, or he must have recognized Oliver on the television and wanted to shield me from it.

"Thanks, Noah. I appreciate it." I force a small smile since that's the best I can do now and go back to retrieve my coffee.

Everyone has been doing their best to try to cheer me up and distract me, but sometimes you just want to feel sad. So, this is extending for an abnormally long time. It's going to be okay.

Eventually.

Once February is in the rearview mirror, I'll be able to start healing. Right now, I'm still being hurt every day and will be until the 21st passes. I just have to endure until then.

There are moments where I let myself believe that he'll be here on the 21st. I dream he'll apologize and profess his undying love for me, but then my alarm usually wakes me up and brings me back to reality. I also need to remember that I won't even be here on that date. I'll still be in Italy.

That evening, when I'm eating my takeout dinner on my couch, it dawns on me that Oliver was being interviewed on TV. He was also talking about being a monster? Is that right? My memory is sketchy since I was so surprised to hear his voice.

I've sworn that I wouldn't look him up on the internet. It will only make things worse for me. I compromise with myself. I won't do a full-blown search because that is the most bottomless rabbit hole in the world, and I don't want to jump into it if I want to maintain what shreds of sanity I have left.

Grabbing my phone, I find his author website. Seeing the picture of him on the home page wearing what he calls his "publicity smile" makes me long to see his genuine smile in person something fierce.

I have to admit, though, he does look damn good. He seems more vibrant or something. I can't put my finger on it, but it yanks at me, twisting me up inside. I'm so happy to see it, and tears sting my eyes as I think of him feeling well, rested, and relaxed. I don't think I ever saw him like that, and I feel a strange comfort in knowing he's taking good care of himself.

Maybe he met someone else, and it's done him a world of good. As much as that would hurt me even more, I would be so relieved to know that he would be okay.

Clicking through his site, I see that his book about Las Vegas organized crime was released. That was quick. More good news for him.

There's also a link to his book tour dates, so of course, I have to check that out. Maybe that's why he was being interviewed.

Scanning the dates and locations of his tour, my heart skips and then sinks. He's not coming to Las Vegas. He's going straight from Colorado to Arizona. That doesn't make any sense. The book he's promoting is about Vegas. How could he not stop here?

Wow. He wants to avoid me so much that he completely skips over the city the book is about. What the hell? I can't believe his agent or publicist would let that happen. Maybe they have other events that aren't listed here? I don't know. I know nothing about the book world.

If my heart wasn't already broken, it shatters completely when I see that not only is he skipping Las Vegas, he's cutting everything in the middle of February. Of course. He would want to make sure that I couldn't find him on the 21st. How better to do that than not being findable at all on that date?

The tears that nearly appeared when I was happy to see him healthy and well, now shift their attention to my utter destruction. I can handle this. I can be devastated and happy for him simultaneously, right? I'm a complex enough individual for that kind of thing?

That could be, but right this second, I want to be the selfish bitch that feels sorry for herself for once. I want to let myself feel that despair and dwell in it for a minute. Just a minute. I don't want to stay this way.

My phone rings, and I have to start laughing, but

it sounds like choking to my ears. I glance at the screen that has switched from the usual photo of Oliver at the Grand Canyon to my brother being goofy, but I'd know who it is without looking.

Of course, Enzo would be calling right this second. This universe we're all traversing on this spinning globe sure can be downright scary.

I pull myself together. Or, at least, try to.

"Hey, brother. I'll be fine." I try to cut him off at the pass to keep this as short as possible. I don't want to drag him down with me. Not when he's got such a great thing with Theresa going.

"Of course, you will be. You're a Torino. In the meantime, I will drag every little thing that makes you doubt that out of you."

I sigh deeply and loudly. "Really, I mean it. I will be fine. You know we'll have to get to a point where you don't do this all the time, right?"

He gasps, and I can't tell if he's joking. "Why wouldn't I use my superpower? It was given to me for a reason."

I still can't tell if he's playing around, but we do need to address this.

"Enzo. We have been adults for a while now, and you have your own life. You don't need to be fixing me all the time."

"But if I don't, who will?" He asks this honestly, but the words cut through me, making me feel even more alone than before he called.

I clear my throat and make sure my voice is steady when I answer. "I will. I'll see you in Italy," I say, and I hang up.

Chapter 37

It's Not Over

Oliver

February 14th

I thought that surprising Bianca on Valentine's Day would be a romantic way to end our separation early. What I did not count on was being stranded in Boulder, Colorado, during the worst winter storm they've had in decades, if not centuries. I begin to think that the entire world is conspiring against me when I also discover that every hotel room in the nearby vicinity is taken.

To top everything off with a neat little cherry, outside my computer bag and carry-on, I haven't the slightest idea where the rest of my luggage is. Oddly, I don't care.

My main concern is getting to Las Vegas, and from the sounds of it from other travelers and airline employees, this could be delayed for days, not just hours. I guess I should be glad that I started the journey early, so I have a few buffer days until the 21st. If things in Colorado continue to go straight to hell in a handbasket, I have a little flexibility in my timeline.

I've found a reasonably secluded corner near an outlet where I can charge my phone and laptop, and I sit on the floor to close my eyes for a few minutes, enlisting the meditation techniques that I've learned recently to destress. It's much easier to do when there isn't constant noise, like in a crowded airport.

"Excuse me. Aren't you Oliver Bellamy?" A female voice pulls me fully awake and alert.

I glance up to find a woman in her mid-20s, with dark hair, dark eyes, sweet smile, and I instantly think of Bianca. While this woman is undoubtedly attractive, she doesn't hold a candle to her, though she does look vaguely familiar for some reason, but I can't figure out why. Maybe it's just the Bianca likeness.

I blink a few times to clear my head. "Yes, I'm Oliver Bellamy. Is there a problem?"

"What? Oh, no. No problem." She smiles again, and her cheeks redden slightly. She holds up a copy of my latest book and taps on my photo on the back cover. "I was just at your book signing yesterday." She flips the book open and points to my illegible signature, which worsens daily.

"Ah, I see." I nod and give a smile. I'm still not used to ever being recognized. Historians aren't exactly well-known public figures. And it's awkward as hell.

"Do you mind if I...?" She indicates the ground on the other side of the outlet in the wall.

"No, not at all. By all means." I unplug my laptop, the most charged of my two devices. "Here. I'll even share my power with you." And that sounded just *wrong* on *so* many levels.

Jesus Christ.

I quickly turn my attention to my computer, open it, and start it up.

"Oh, thank you." She nods at me and holds out a hand to shake, so I politely do. "I'm Valerie, by the way."

"Nice to meet you, Valerie. I hope you enjoy the book."

Now, as you can see, I'm busy, so kindly leave me alone.

"Are you stuck here too?" She asks, not reading body language very well. "I'm going from Los Angeles to New Jersey to visit my parents. I saw you were scheduled to sign here and planned a little side trip. And well, *that* was a bad idea, huh?"

"Indeed. And yes, I'm delayed as well." I glance around, seeing if there's any way I can escape this person without being extremely rude.

"You know, I've been reading some internet forums and threads about your theory on the location of Matteo Denaro. I think you might be on to something."

This catches my interest. The man currently most wanted for his organized crime dealings in Vegas and other cities around the world has been a subject of research by me and others for years. He's thus far evaded authorities but still has a stranglehold on his mafia "family."

"Do you? I'd be interested in hearing why you think so."

What the hell. Who knows how long I'm going to be stuck here. I may as well make the most of it and discuss one of the biggest fugitives currently running from the law.

It turns out that befriending a stranger is beneficial for both of us. Not only do we have interesting conversations, but we can alternate sleep schedules to watch the other's things, and do the same for walking and relief breaks. So, even though it started awkwardly, it was good that I didn't completely shut myself off from Valerie when we first met.

Thirty-six hours later, on the afternoon of the 16th, I finally say my goodbyes to Valerie, agree to a quick selfie though I'm sure I look as haggard as I feel, and board a plane to Las Vegas.

The weather is remarkably better. Still chilly, but I can deal with that. There is at least sunshine, and the Vitamin D is most welcome after days couped up in an airport gate lobby.

I don't try to find a hotel, I don't stop at a restaurant, and I don't even attempt to clean myself up very much. I just grab a taxi and go straight to Mischief Motors. I am on a mission and won't stop until that mission is complete.

When I arrive, I tell the taxi to wait on the off chance that she's at her apartment and I'll need to go there next. I ring the gate buzzer and wait to be let in.

And wait.

Ringing again, I wait some more.

Surely, somebody has to be here. It's not the end of the workday, even if they had regular hours, which they don't. According to Bianca, someone is almost always on the premises.

After an extraordinary amount of time, the tall gate opens, and a very pregnant Normandy appears, not looking pleased to see me at all. I guess that's to be expected, but it pulls me up short. I'm not sure what to say to her now.

She stares at me long and hard, then unleashes. "Really, Oliver? It's been what, six months now since you disappeared? Since you broke Bianca's heart? And you have the nerve to show up here after this was just posted a couple of hours ago?" She holds her phone out to me, and I take it from her to look at the screen, shading it from the sun.

My stomach craters. It's the selfie I took with Valerie at the airport. The one where I was ecstatic to finally be called to board a plane to come here. It also appears that we are very cozy, and the caption that reads, *"Spent the night with this handsome devil. #bejealous #handsoff #oliverbellamy #dreamy"* does not help whatsoever. I think I'm going to be sick.

"What? How?" I can't get words out. I'm stunned.

"We have an excellent security company that monitors a lot of...things."

"Normandy, please. I have been traveling for nearly three days to get here, and I can actually explain this." I hand her back her phone, careful not to drop it with my now shaky hands.

She eyes me warily but doesn't budge.

"Oliver, to be honest, I don't want to hear what you have to say. Also, it doesn't matter. Bianca isn't here, or even in the country." She rubs her lower back, obviously uncomfortable, and I wonder what she's even doing here. She must be due any minute.

It hits me what she's just said. "Not in the country? Where did she go?" My mind flips through hundreds of scenarios for why she would leave the country, and most of them include a new love interest.

There must be something in my expression that softens Normandy just a little bit.

She sighs. "She's in Italy for her cousin Gina's wedding. She'll be gone for a couple of weeks."

My heart sinks. She wasn't even planning to be here for the 21st. We can't very well keep to our agreement or reconcile if she's not even in the country. Didn't she know that I would be back for her? Of course not. I didn't give her any reason to think I would.

"The wedding is this Saturday. In Milan. Her cousin's last name is Morello. That's all I know." A shoulder rises in what I think is a sympathetic shrug. "Sorry."

I take a deep breath and look Normandy straight in the eyes. "Will I be a total fool if I show up there? Please be honest."

After about another full minute of scrutiny, she replies, "I don't know the answer to that, Oliver. All I do know is that she hasn't been the same since you left."

I dare to ask, "Is there someone else?"

She doesn't hesitate this time. "No. Nobody else."

There it is again, only this time, it's welcome.

Hope. I have hope.

The final and most insidious and brutal of Pandora's gifts. The siren that tempts you down dark paths that lead to ruin. I will take that hope, however, and run with it. Straight back to the bloody airport.

Chapter 38

Ave Maria

Bianca

February 18th

Leave it to my cousin Gina to have the most extra wedding ever. She couldn't have it near home in Turin. She had to go big in Milan. Mind you, her soon-to-be husband is super rich and isn't letting her parents spend a dime on it, but still. Restraint has never been a word in her vocabulary, so she's lucky she found such a generous husband.

She's also got a heart of gold and aims that extra toward the kids she teaches in elementary school. They absolutely adore their "Miss Morello." If the ceremony were in Turin, I'd bet most of her class would be in the wedding party.

As it is, I'm surprised she's not having her wedding at the cathedral in the main square in Milan, but instead at another equally beautiful church, Santa Maria del Carmine. It's not the easiest for the wedding party to get to as it's hidden away and attached to a small courtyard with only alley access.

Of course, the weather doesn't cooperate either, and it's raining off and on, but we do our best to run through with long plastic rain cloaks covering us, dodging raindrops and giggling like schoolgirls as we go.

The entire week here has been busy with wedding preparations, dress fittings, and last night's rehearsal dinner. It's been a nice distraction and has also kept my mind occupied. I've needed that with the outrageous jet lag I'm currently dealing with.

I've been able to throw myself into making this wedding perfect for Gina too, which has been kind of healing for me. I even worked with her wedding planner without breaking out in hives, despite my self-imposed allergy to those. It's kept my mind off of Oliver and the upcoming date of total destruction.

And there he is. Right in my head where he always is. I keep doing that. I tell myself that something is distracting me from Oliver when just the act of thinking that brings him up in my mind.

And it, of course, starts the downward spiral of wondering where he is, what he's doing, and if he's genuinely as happy now as he looks on his website.

"Bianca, come on!" Gina pulls on my arm to put me in line. There are five of us regular bridesmaids apart from her Maid of Honor in the procession. I hadn't noticed that the music for *Ave Maria* had started already, so I jump into place and pull myself together and follow the flower girl as she heads to the top of the aisle.

When we practiced yesterday, she basically ran down the carpet, but thankfully she's a little more sedate today and has promised to try to walk slowly. That leaves me to set the pace for the rest of us, which feels like a super important job.

Gina is supposed to get to the altar at a specific part of the song, so I can't be too fast or too slow. I didn't realize I was signing up for this responsibility when I volunteered to be first behind the flower girl, but here we are.

I straighten the gorgeous deep red, empire-waisted gown, pat my hair to make sure it's not fallen too much with the rain, and grip my bouquet tightly. I turn, give Gina a quick smile, nod, and start down the aisle.

The smile I'm wearing is genuine. It's been amazing seeing family this past week that I never get to see in person. And seeing Enzo and Theresa has been great too. I think I'll be doing this again in their wedding sometime soon, from the looks of things.

About halfway up the aisle, I look for Enzo. He's pretty tall, so he should be easy to spot. Plus, Theresa is wearing a bright yellow dress that will be hard to miss. When I find him in the crowd on the left side, the bride's side, he's not looking at me or the procession at all. He's looking at something further up across the aisle, and his posture is so tense something in my stomach clenches. Something must be terribly wrong. Theresa seems worried about him too.

No. Not on Gina's big day.

Enzo catches me staring at him in confusion, still walking at my stilted procession pace, and flashes the fakest smile I've ever seen on him. If I could read auras, I'd say his was black.

Keeping my placid smile plastered on my face, I start to look in the direction he was focused on. I don't see what he's so concerned about, until I do.

Oliver.

The blonde hair and perfect scruff immediately draw my attention to him. And those steel gray eyes that seem to see through me. I'd know him anywhere.

Almost tripping, I freeze, and I think I even yelp, but I can't be sure. Goosebumps rise all over my body, not just my arms. I glance down at a non-existent watch on my wrist and then around in confusion.

I could swear I just saw Oliver. Here. In Italy. In Milan. At my cousin's wedding. Is today the 21st? Am I dreaming right now? Still asleep?

Suddenly there's an insistent voice behind me, "Vai avanti." *Move on.*

Shit. I'm holding up the line. I'm fucking this all up. I'm ruining Gina's wedding with my crazy imagination.

I try to shake it off and start walking again. How long is this stupid aisle? I look back at Enzo quickly to make sure he's still upset because then maybe I'm not hallucinating. He's now looking at me with concern, so I don't know what to think about that.

Then I glance back to where I imagined Oliver to be, and holy shit, he's still there. Maybe I'm not hallucinating. Maybe he's really there. Here. He's really here. He looks concerned at me too. Why does *he* look concerned?

It's then that I notice other people giving me the same look, and some even have sad frowns on their faces. Why would they look at me like that?

The beauty of the song strikes me at that moment, and I realize why people are looking at me strangely. I'm crying.

I'm fucking crying. No. No. I will not cry in front of Oliver. He will not see me weak.

I hurry and wipe my eyes with the convenient handkerchief I've tucked around my bouquet. Weddings, in general, make me cry, but being a bridesmaid crying as she leads the procession is just not right.

I finish my part and take my place at the end of the bridal party line at the altar. When I get situated, I search again for Oliver, and he's still there, watching me, but not as concerned as he was the last time I looked at him, so that's good. Hopefully, he sees that I'm strong and not as affected by seeing him as originally thought.

The ceremony is a beautiful blur, and I do my best to keep focused and stay in the moment, but it's impossible. Oliver sits only yards away, and I can't keep my eyes off him. The shock of him being here has not worn off in the slightest, and I think my brain might actually be broken because of it.

I have forgotten everything that is supposed to happen in the ceremony that we practiced last night. I don't like this feeling, but at the same time, something deep in me is so happy to see him. I want to jump up, run over to him, and fly into his arms.

Unless he's here to tell me it's actually over. We never said what we'd do if that were the case. Would he track me down like he obviously has if it was to say he's moved on? I can imagine that being something Oliver would think would be the proper thing to do. The polite thing. Do it in person.

Let me down easy.

I search again for Enzo, and his concern has only deepened since the beginning of the ceremony. I'm worried about the so-called innocent threat he made to Oliver in Lake Tahoe about what he'd do if I got hurt. Enzo is not one for violence, but the look on his face has me thinking he might actually be considering it. I try to glare at him without being obvious about it. Hopefully, our connection is strong enough for him to know what I'm trying to say without words.

The ceremony ends. I wasn't paying attention enough to know that it was coming to an end, and have to scramble to my position in line. As the procession reverses back down the aisle, I find myself glaring at everyone. Family. Friends. Brother. Oliver. Even Theresa gets caught in the crossfire.

I guess nobody escapes a wedding unscathed.

Chapter 39

Whatever It Takes

Oliver

February 18th

I made it. I don't know how, but I made it. And not only that, I found the right church, and the right wedding. Thanks to one of my mates from the Thursday support group who has an Italian wife, I was able to figure out where to go. However, even knowing where to go, getting here wasn't easy. It still took four flights to get me here, and finding the church was challenging since I don't speak any Italian outside of menu items.

While I make it, it's only with a few minutes to spare. I sit when the bridal party comes in, giggling from their apparent run in the rain. When I see Bianca for the first time in six months, laughing and utterly unaware that I'm here, I just want to run up to her and grab her into the most passionate kiss we've ever shared. Somehow, I restrain myself from ruining the entire wedding by doing that and let the ceremony unfold.

Glancing over to the other side of the aisle, I notice Enzo. He sees me at the same time, and if looks could kill, I'd be at least critically wounded. I understand the protective brother instinct he has. The connection he shares with Bianca is a sibling relationship I've been jealous of since we met. I suppose if I were him, I'd probably like to do me harm as well.

Turning my attention back to Bianca once the music starts, I am so captivated by her, I lose time. The next thing I know, she's staring at me in confusion, holding up the procession.

Maybe coming to the wedding was a bad idea. I've obviously surprised Bianca, and not in the best way, apparently, because she's now crying. *Bloody hell*. I can't seem to do anything right when it comes to her.

The ceremony goes by in a blur as I only pay attention to Bianca during the entire thing. She is even more beautiful than I remembered, as if that's somehow possible. It shouldn't be possible, but here we are, with her beauty outshining everyone in the room, even the bride, if I may be so bold.

We watch each other the entire time, and I can't tell what she's thinking about my presence here. I want to believe that she's happy, or at least pleased to see me, but I can't tell what she's thinking. She might just be happy about her cousin's nuptials and not about me.

When it's over, and they make their way down the aisle again, all I get from Bianca is a glare. Actually, she glares at everyone she passes. Even her family. And it's not just passing glares. She pointedly looks at people with disdain, as if she's cursing every person in attendance. It's a bit startling.

The next thing I know, I'm being almost body-slammed into the section next to me behind a column. It's Enzo. Of course. He's careful not to manhandle me too much, at least.

"What the heck are you doing here?" he snarls in my ear. "I'd swear, but I'd go straight to hell without passing *Go* if I swore in a church, and my Nan would be disappointed in me."

"Hello to you too, Enzo," I say, trying to gather my bearings after being transported so swiftly to this new location.

"I'm being serious, Oliver. What are you doing here?" He glances around to make sure we're not being overheard.

"Actually, I'm here for Bianca." I look him

straight in the eyes. "Remember how you read my aura in Tahoe? Can you do that here and now?"

Curiosity has me in its clutches, and I need to know if he sees the change in me or not. That might tell me if Bianca will see it too.

He backs up, examining me carefully. I try not to wither under the scrutiny and prove the changes I've been through the past six months. I have no idea if that can be done through my 'aura' since I'm not even sure I believe in them, but Enzo does. So, I put it all in his hands, trusting it's the right thing to do.

Something shifts behind his eyes. I think he sees it. He can see that I've changed. At least, I hope that is what's happening.

"Well, I'll be damned. You've turned your gray skies into blue." He's nodding, primarily to himself because I have no clue what a blue aura means, but apparently, it's positive.

I arch a brow at him, hoping that he'll elaborate on his pronouncement.

"It means that you're finally living your truth. Whatever that means for you is up to you." His expression still doesn't give me the warm fuzzies, but his words do.

I sigh internally in relief. He's not wrong. I am finally living in my truth. But a part of that, a *crucial* part of that, needs to include Bianca.

My jet lag, exhaustion, and excitement at finding

Bianca after searching for days are catching up to me.

"Can I go find your sister now? I kind of need to tell her that I love her and can't live without her. If you don't mind, of course."

His eyes widen briefly, and I don't know if it's at what I asked or how I asked it.

"Are you asking me for permission to—"

"Ask her to spend the rest of her life with me. Yes."

It's so close that I can taste it, and I want to get there as soon as possible. Words are getting in the way and holding me back. I want to be moving.

His eyes narrow for only a heartbeat, but then he grabs my hand and shakes it heartily, leading me back to the vestibule, a massive smile on his face that lights up his entire being.

"Go. Go find her. Tell her I gave you my blessing."

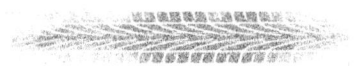

It takes me quite a while to find Bianca again. The rain has stopped, and everyone is gathering in the square outside the church so weaving my way through the sea of people is extremely difficult.

Once I find her, part of why it took so long is she's crouched down and talking to the flower girl, who is fidgeting as though she's frightened. Bianca is soothing her and trying to calm her down. I approach and crouch down next to her.

"Hi," I say, smiling.

Both the little girl and Bianca are surprised by my sudden appearance, but that was the point. Distract. Give something new to worry about, even if it's something benign.

"I'm Oliver." I smile, holding out a hand. "What's your name?"

The girl takes my hand and shakes it but doesn't say anything.

"This is Bridget, the amazing flower girl from the wedding," Bianca fills in for her. "She's still working on her English, but she's pretty good at it, isn't that right, Bridget?"

The girl nods shyly, a small smile peeking through, but still stays silent.

From behind me, a flurry of Italian is sent in our direction, and I turn to see who I assume is the girl's parents, relieved at finding her in the crowd. She was apparently missed.

Bianca and I stand, and she conveys that Bridget was safe and okay the entire time, just a little scared. At least, I think that's what is said. The parents offer their thanks and lead the shy girl into the crowd.

That leaves me alone with Bianca. Alone in a crowd of people.

It's not awkward. It's perfect. At least, I think it is.

"What are you doing here, Oliver?" she asks, but I can't read if she's upset in a bad way or a good one. "How did you find me? This place?" She waves around, indicating the square we're standing in. Using her hands with such passion when she speaks is something that I've missed seeing terribly. "And why?" This last question comes with fear attached to it.

"Why? Bianca, it's six months. I'm actually early. And I tried to be even earlier on Valentine's Day in an attempt to be even more romantic, but I got stuck in Colorado for days. Then once I got to Vegas, Normandy told me you were here. It took some sleuthing of friends back home, but we eventually figured it out because it's important. *You* are important. To me."

She takes a small step toward me, and I close the distance, grabbing her waist, and it feels so damned good to touch her again.

Her dark eyes search mine. "But I thought for sure if that were true, you would have done this earlier. You would have bypassed the six-month rule."

I see now where all of this trepidation is coming from.

"You probably don't see it now, in my current state, but I had a lot of growing to do in these six months. Even I didn't know how much I needed that time to be able to stand here in front of you, so sure about how I feel about you." I dare to pull her closer, and she doesn't resist, letting me wrap my arms around her. "There is so much to tell you about what's happened, but just know this, I love you, Bianca. I have loved you since baggage claim in Vegas, and I think you know it. You felt it too."

Her cheeks catch fire, probably remembering our first interaction at the airport when she first picked me up. How we knew the minute we saw each other that this was special.

"I did." She pushes on my chest lightly. "But you made it so damned difficult."

"It's kind of what I do," I laugh. "I am constantly the Devil's advocate in all things. Sometimes that's a good thing, but in our case, it made me get in my own way. And I'm sorry about that. You have no idea how sorry I am."

She turns serious and shivers a little. The sun peeks through the threatening rain clouds but does little against the day's chill. I shrug out of my jacket and wrap it around her shoulders, rubbing her upper arms for good measure to warm her up.

"Oliver, you left. You just left. You left me with a fucking cat poster and a note." Her disappointment claws at me, and I take it. I've prepared myself to take whatever she throws at me because she has earned the right to hurl every hurt at me that she has.

That doesn't mean it doesn't affect me. It does. It solidifies my need to make amends. To make this right. To fix this. "What the hell was I supposed to do with a cat poster and a note? And you couldn't even tell me in your note that you loved me. Just like you couldn't say it the night before. I bared my soul to you, and you just left."

Tears are starting to well in her eyes, and I need to act. The problem is that I wrapped my jacket around Bianca's shoulders.

I need what is in the pocket.

"This is going to sound a bit odd, but could you reach into the inner pocket there...?" I point to the left side of the jacket.

She gives me a curious look as she wipes at her tears before they fall. I'm hopeful that what she'll find will chase away further tears.

Reaching into the inside pocket, she pulls out a small velvet box and then stares at me, expressionless.

Well, shit, that's not helpful.

"Bianca. I have fucked this up since day one. And here we are seven months later, and I'm still fucking it all up. I have fought against 'love at first sight,' 'destiny,' 'soulmates,' and even the entire universe at times, trying to deny that this could be real. That *you* could be real." I take the box from her hands and open it, holding it out to her. "I hope you'll forgive my not getting on a knee, but I'm afraid

I won't be able to get back up after all the traveling I've done."

A hand flies to her mouth and the tears are back, but she turns her eyes to me, and I think I see the same love I feel for her, so I go on.

"The last six months have shown me exactly how much you have affected me. I was lost. Adrift. Determined to stay in the in-between. Not alive. Not dead. Just barely existing. You brought me back from that oblivion. You showed me that things can be different. My life isn't over. It's just beginning. But I want to spend the rest of it with you because now I can't imagine it without you."

Suddenly, there is a commotion around us, and Bianca and I both notice a crowd has formed to watch the spectacle that is my current proposal. This is entirely unexpected, and I hope it doesn't put undue pressure on her to say yes.

"You can say no, Bianca," I whisper. Making sure she knows that the crowd around us should hold no sway on her decision.

"What about children?" she whispers, and when she leans away, I see the concern and hope that is holding her back, and I am so glad I can answer her how she wants me to, honestly.

I pull her closer, positioning my mouth next to her ear so she hears me clearly. "As many as you can handle. And I'm more than ready to start on that endeavor as soon as possible."

Her eyes meet mine, and I see it. All of my dreams are about to come true. She nods so emphatically that I think she might hurt herself. I take the ring out of the box and am suddenly nervous, but I've never been more sure about anything in my life. I need to do this before the crowd turns on us.

"Will you make me the happiest man in Italy, except for maybe your cousin's new husband, of course, and marry me, Bianca?"

There is no hesitation from her at all, and my heart overflows as she answers.

"Yes."

Epilogue

(There Is) No Greater Love

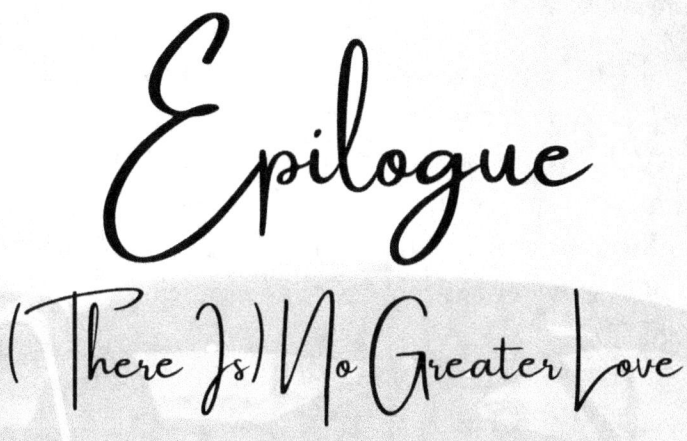

Bianca

June

"I bet Oli told you that summers here would be better, huh?" Oscar asks me, a glint in his eye. It is very warm here, in this pub where Oliver's support mates, for lack of a better word, meet every other Thursday night. Okay, that's an understatement. It's freaking *hot* here.

Just because the Celsius number is lower here doesn't make it cooler by any means. I still don't understand what the British have against air conditioning, to be honest. It's not in every home like it is in America.

I have to laugh, though, because Oscar is right. We agreed to spend summers in the U.K. on Oliver's word that it was better for him here. Oscar has been so great to us and has welcomed me into their fold with no reserve. His humor has been a real bright light in some serious conversations between everyone here.

"He did, actually. I'm feeling a little bit taken advantage of right now."

Oliver swiftly pulls his phone out, ready to stand his ground, and swipes to the weather app, holding it up for all of us to see.

"It happens to be one hundred degrees Fahrenheit in Las Vegas right now, I'll have you all know. I think we're doing okay."

"Yeah, but how hot is it in here right now?" I ask, fanning myself with the pub menu and giving him a facetious grin.

We're in the process of applying for dual citizenship so that we can travel between countries easier. Neither country makes it easy, that's for sure. We are at least legally married in both places since we had ceremonies in both countries. That only helps slightly to cut through all of the red tape.

Normandy had a baby boy they named Emerson just before we returned to Vegas after my cousin's wedding. So, I spent the few weeks after arriving home babysitting a lot of kids while Oliver went on to finish his book tour. I didn't mind one bit. Aunt B was in heaven.

Oliver even replaced the kitten poster with the neon sign he envisioned with *'Aunt B'* now hanging above the fireplace.

Enzo is planning his own wedding. Well, Theresa is. He's just an innocent bystander, and I love it. They both are going to be deliriously happy. Maybe just as happy as Oliver and I are. Not quite, but a close second.

My brother has forgiven Oliver, and the two have become good friends. That's something I worried about for a long time. Things were contentious between them for a while, each vying for their spot in my life as my protector, but eventually, Enzo gave way. Since then, the two have been inseparable when we get together.

I've quit my job at Mischief Motors to dedicate my time to the foundation that Oliver and Darcie have created to fund service animal training for people with MS. We both wanted to get it going even before his book about MS comes out, and with the help of a very generous donation from the Carmichael's, we're already well underway in both the U.S. and the U.K.

As for our own children, we've stopped all barriers to the possibility and will let nature do its thing if it wants to. If we need to move things along in the future, we'll cross that bridge when we get to it. For now, we are enjoying each other, our friends and family, and seeing the world together while we can.

Every day with Oliver is a gift that I never thought I would be able to experience. He shows me daily what it means to be brave, what it means to love, and the true capabilities of anyone with enough willingness to try to achieve their dreams. He really makes me think that anything is possible.

Neither of us is adrift anymore. Oblivion is behind us. We've been found and grounded. And it turns out I was wrong. Happy endings do happen to people like me. It just takes a little patience.

Okay, a *lot* of patience. But I can honestly say that it's worth the wait.

--THE END--

Afterword

While Multiple Sclerosis affects women more than men, that carries with it a stigma that men with MS need to overcome. This is particularly true since MS is such an individualized disease, impacting everyone differently. Many of the symptoms are "hidden," making diagnosis, acceptance, and treatment that much more difficult.

I hope I've done justice to men dealing with MS with Oliver's portrayal of the disease. Everyone deals with their symptoms, diagnosis, and treatments differently. My goal is that awareness and sensitivity to its prevalence and the ability to cope with it are expanded with this story.

My mother and aunt had MS when it wasn't as well understood as it is now, and I know firsthand how it can alter the person and the family dynamic. It's not easy for anyone.

Like I've heard several times, and I hope you have too – you never know what someone else is going through, and with MS, you may not see it outwardly, so be compassionate to everyone you can. It costs you nothing to be kind.

Many local service animal charities work with people with MS, so I won't list them here. But I will encourage you to seek them out and support them if you can.

For broader MS-focused charities, try the following:

National Multiple Sclerosis Society (US)

MS Society (UK)

Ms. Lead Playlist

https://open.spotify.com/playlist/
3FJ2LoqJH6dZLT3lrS6s2Q?si=
dc4ec63f41e54b83

1. Man-Made Sunshine, *Life's Gonna Kill You (If You Let It)*
2. Mokita, Charlotte Sands, *Crash*
3. French Cassettes, *Santa Cruz Tomorrow*
4. Music Travel Love, *I Knew I Loved You*
5. Waterstrider, *End of Sequence*
6. One OK Rock, *Save Yourself*
7. Måneskin, *The Loneliest*
8. The Hunna, *Can't Break What's Broken*
9. Imminence, *Ghost*
10. Bea Miller, *I Can't Breathe*
11. Imagine Dragons, *Dull Knives*
12. Electric Enemy, *Save Me (I'm Not Crazy)*
13. Shinedown, *How Did You Love?*
14. Sky Ferreira, *Everything Is Embarrassing*
15. The Maine, *Black Butterflies and Déjà vu*
16. Alexisonfire, *World Stops Turning*
17. Taur, *Cowards*
18. Wolf Alice, *The Last Man on Earth*
19. Brkn Love, *Like A Drug*

20. Wax/Wane, *The Way Down*
21. The Amazons, *Ready for Something*
22. Fyfe, Iskra Strings, *Gold*
23. Hate Drugs, *Never Wanna Leave*
24. Willow, *Curious/Furious*
25. Palaye Royale, *You'll Be Fine*
26. Yonaka, *Ordinary*
27. Steve Vai, *For the Love of God*
28. Nothing More, *Just Say When*
29. Sleep Token, Loathe, *Is It Really You?*
30. Bad Omens, *Just Pretend*
31. Shinedown, *Special*
32. Ghost Monroe, *I Am the Fire*
33. Alexisonfire, *Sans Soleil*
34. Electric Enemy, *Heartache Melody*
35. Kongos, *Traveling On*
36. Lady A, *Need You Now*
37. Daughtry, *It's Not Over*
38. Céline Dion, *Ave Maria*
39. Lifehouse, *Whatever It Takes*
40. Amy Winehouse, *(There Is) No Greater Love*

Contact

My website: http://www.amybookerauthor.com
Facebook: www.facebook.com/amybookerauthor
Instagram: www.instagram.com/
amy_booker_author/
TikTok: www.TikTok.com/@amybookerauthor
Email: amybookerauthor@gmail.com

Add my books to your Goodreads: www.goodreads.
com/author/show/22225202.Amy_Booker

Sign up for my VIP mailing list: You'll be the first to learn about new releases, sales, available preorders, and freebies. Note: Be sure to add admin@ amybookerauthor.com to your contacts before signing up to ensure the emails go straight into your inbox.